MURDER IN PARIS

BOOK 4 OF THE MAGGIE NEWBERRY MYSTERIES

SUSAN KIERNAN-LEWIS

SAN MARCO PRESS

Murder in Paris takes Maggie back to Paris for a very personal sojourn. This time it's all on the line for our intrepid ex-pat—with a murder that happens close to her—and for a reason that not even the deceased's nearest and dearest would ever suspect.

For a woman who loves fashion, there is no place on earth more exciting than Paris where the clothes are to die for and everyone you meet is dressed to kill.

Maggie's visit to the City of Light in the midst of Paris Fashion Week turns into a nightmare when she witnesses a murder within her own family. Determined to find out who the killer is—before her husband's patience and her marriage expires—Maggie steps into the glittering world of fashion as cutthroat and vicious as any drug cartel. It could be Maggie's grandest hour–if she can survive it.

Books by Susan Kiernan-Lewis

The Maggie Newberry Mysteries

Murder in the South of France

Murder à la Carte

Murder in Provence

Murder in Paris

Murder in Aix

Murder in Nice

Murder in the Latin Quarter

Murder in the Abbey

Murder in the Bistro

Murder in Cannes

Murder in Grenoble

Murder in the Vineyard

Murder in Arles

Murder in Marseille

Murder in St-Rémy
Murder à la Mode
Murder in Avignon
Murder in the Lavender
Murder in Mont St-Michel
Murder in the Village
Murder in St-Tropez
Murder in Grasse
Murder in Monaco
Murder in Montmartre
Murder in the Villa
A Provençal Christmas: A Short Story
A Thanksgiving in Provence
Laurent's Kitchen

The Claire Baskerville Mysteries
Déjà Dead
Death by Cliché
Dying to be French
Ménage à Murder
Killing it in Paris
Murder Flambé
Deadly Faux Pas
Toujours Dead
Murder in the Christmas Market
Deadly Adieu
Murdering Madeleine
Murder Carte Blanche
Death à la Drumstick
Murder Mon Amour

The Savannah Time Travel Mysteries
Killing Time in Georgia
Scarlett Must Die

The Stranded in Provence Mysteries

Parlez-Vous Murder?

Crime and Croissants

Accent on Murder

A Bad Éclair Day

Croak, Monsieur!

Death du Jour

Murder Très Gauche

Wined and Died

Murder, Voila!

A French Country Christmas

Fromage to Eternity

The Irish End Games

Free Falling

Going Gone

Heading Home

Blind Sided

Rising Tides

Cold Comfort

Never Never

Wit's End

Dead On

White Out

Black Out

End Game

The Mia Kazmaroff Mysteries

Reckless

Shameless

Breathless

Heartless

Clueless

Ruthless

Ella Out of Time

Swept Away

Carried Away

Stolen Away

1

Maggie brushed the leaves from the table and squinted into the setting of the early October sun. The long wooden farm table had been set for an elegant dinner: crystal goblets, silverware, matching china dishware on a stark white linen tablecloth. She flicked another leaf from the table.

"You are dressed?"

She turned to look at her husband who had materialized in the frame of the double doors leading into the house. Like everything he did, he did it silently. If she didn't know about his long and mysterious history which sometimes involved being on the wrong side of the law, Maggie might have found his stealth a little more disconcerting.

"No," she admitted, turning away from the outdoor scene. "I'm running a little late."

She watched him inspect the table. He would never say if anything were not as he preferred or expected. She would never know if he found it wonderful, either, unless she asked him. And she had stopped doing that a while ago. He always said yes and always in a way she found less than convincing.

"And yourself?" she said, moving past him to enter the house. She could smell the fragrances of their dinner cooking, especially the garlic. She knew Laurent was dressed and ready. He always was.

"*Bien sûr*," he said, turning away from the terrace. "Hurry, Maggie. Our guests will be soon here."

That made her smile. After four years of living with her, he was fluent in English but she still found his phrasing awkwardly charming. In fact, his occasionally mangled English was the only thing awkward about him. She realized that that was partly why she enjoyed it so much. It was the one thing he didn't appear to do perfectly and effortlessly.

"There's no rush," Maggie said. "Two of them are our neighbors and one is my uncle. It's not like we've got the Sarkozys coming. They've seen me in my jeans before."

"*Incroyable*!" Laurent said, frowning. "Why bother to set the table at all? Why not serve them *dans la cuisine*, eh?"

She could see his frustration with her and it surprised her. Up to now, she thought *she* was the only one not adapting particularly well to married country life.

"It might shock you to know that I have had many a happy, exceedingly memorable meal with good friends in the kitchen," she said.

"That does not shock me at all," Laurent growled. "If it happened in Atlanta, of course it is superior in all ways."

Before Maggie could think of a retort, Laurent turned on his heel and left her where she stood in the hallway.

THE DINNER PARTY WAS, as usual, perfect. Maggie enjoyed the smell of the night air full of wood smoke and the snap of fall and coming winter. She had worried it would be too cold to eat outdoors—something they did nearly every meal during the summer—but when Laurent got the braziers going at two corners of the terrace, it was perfectly comfortable. She and Laurent had silently acknowledged a détente from their earlier spat as they donned their roles as hostess and host. Laurent was the cook and Maggie led the way in banter and amusing stories. It was an arrangement that had worked for them since the day they met.

Their neighbors, Jean-Luc and Danielle Alexandre were the first to arrive. The Alexandres had become a steady and pleasant part of Maggie and Laurent's daily round in St-Buvard. Maggie watched Jean-Luc, a farmer in his late sixties and, until Danielle said "yes" to him six months ago, a confirmed bachelor. Now, he was the picture of a man in love: a man who could not spend enough time with his beloved. Danielle was probably the sweetest human being Maggie had ever met. Endlessly patient and accepting, she had been brutally used in her first marriage. The way she returned Jean-Luc's mooneyes made it clear she felt the same way about him.

Their other guest had been a surprise. A phone call from her father earlier in the week had revealed that her uncle Stan—a family member she only vaguely remembered meeting—was staying in Paris for business and had asked if he might visit Maggie and Laurent in Provence.

As the meal was ending, Maggie leaned back in her chair and surveyed the table—a pleasant tableau of glasses in varying depths of wine or water, ashtrays and used stacked plates. She looked at her husband at the end of the table. He looked relaxed and amiable although she, of all people, knew how deceptive his expressions could be. When she met him, he made his living conning people.

"You look tired, my dear." Her uncle spoke to her softly from where he sat at her side.

Maggie turned her attention to him. Stan was tall and tan with a touch of gray at the temples and a dimpled grin that was permanently on display because he was always grinning. He was a handsome man and strongly resembled her father in appearance.

"I'm fine," she said. "I'm still amazed that you're here, though. How long has it been since we last saw each other?"

"You were ten, I believe."

"Wow. Way to stay in touch, Uncle Stan," Maggie said.

Stan laughed. "It wasn't intentional," he said. "Living in California...Your father and I do call from time to time." He glanced at Laurent who had lit a cigarette and was now speaking French in a low voice to Jean-Luc and Danielle. "Your father mention me much?"

Maggie frowned. "Why? Is there some family scandal I don't know about?"

Stan lifted his wine glass to his lips. "Very probably," he said. "Is this one of Laurent's?"

"To tell you the truth, I don't know," Maggie said sheepishly. "I'm not really involved with the whole wine-growing thing."

"In any event, I'm here now," Stan said. "And delighted to get to know my niece all over again."

A few moments later, Jean-Luc and Danielle said their goodbyes and Laurent walked them to the front drive. When Maggie and Stan reseated themselves. Maggie found herself feeling more relaxed than the wine and fragrant night air could take credit for. She watched her uncle pour himself another glass of the table wine and realized that her feeling of ease was because of the connection—the surprising, warm and immediate connection—that she felt with this man.

When Laurent returned, he gathered up a stack of plates and when Maggie started to stand, he waved her back.

"*Non, non,*" he said. "Continue talking. I will bring the coffee and dessert."

"Thanks, Laurent," Maggie said.

When he disappeared into the house, she turned to see her uncle watching her.

"Are you happy, Maggie?" he asked. "I only ask," he said hurriedly, "because I hear through the family grapevine that it's kind of an inside joke back home about how you're living in paradise yet somehow are still homesick."

"What can I say?" Maggie picked up her wine glass. "I guess I'm just a grass-is-greener kinda girl."

"At least you have self-knowledge. That's a good sign."

"You aren't the first wave of my intervention from Atlanta, are you? Because I gotta tell you, my memories of a better time back home run pretty deep."

Stan laughed. "No, but if you'd let your old uncle give you some advice..."

"You have the floor, oh wise one."

"I've noticed when you talk about home, you always refer to Atlanta."

"That's right. Where all my friends are and my family."

"Well, at least I'm sure where all your friends *used* to be. Haven't a lot of them moved on?"

Maggie frowned.

"Anyway, it's always been my belief," Stan continued, "and you can absolutely take this with a grain of salt because I've travelled very little up until now—that home is really not so much a place as it is a time. Do you know what I mean?"

Maggie said nothing. Her glance fell on the steep pitch of Domaine St-Buvard. A few leaves scuttled across the tiles and floated to the ground. The house that Laurent had inherited four years earlier, their home, was a very old stone *mas* situated deep in the heart of Provence. It was connected to fifteen acres of prime vineyard that Laurent cultivated for the *vin de pays* he produced and called *Vin de Domaine St-Buvard*. The original plan had been to live in Provence for three months to get the property ready to sell. That was four years ago. Never one to enjoy travel, Maggie had struggled with her status as an expat ever since.

"And for you, if I may be so bold as to suggest it," her uncle said, "that time is here and now, not..." he reached out and took her hand. "...where your *memories* are."

"Wow, Stan," she said. "Very deep."

"Yes, well, we wise ones are nothing if not deep," he said, almost sadly.

THE NEXT MORNING, Maggie slept late. When she finally came down the broad smooth stone steps of the staircase to the cavernous kitchen that Laurent had claimed as his own, she went in search of the breakfast she knew he would have set aside for her. She settled herself on a stool at the kitchen counter and poured a coffee out of the carafe. From where she sat, she could just barely see her husband and her uncle—both tall men—walking the perimeter of Laurent's vineyard. She had a silly moment of trying to imagine what Laurent could possibly be saying during the tour. Was he introducing her uncle to a "naughty little vine over here" and a "robust fat fellow of a grape *la bas*?" *What in the world was there to say? It's a vineyard. There's a bunch of grapes. We make wine out of them.* Knowing Laurent, he could not only talk about and walk about his vineyard for hours, he could happily believe that most normal people would like to do so too. She ate her croissant and observed the men through the French doors. She watched Laurent pointing to some feature and Stan turning and looking in that direction as if it was all very interesting.

Such a polite man, Maggie thought. *Try living with it twenty four seven, Uncle Stan. Little harder to drum up enthusiasm for a bunch of vines strung along wires when it's day in and day out*. As she watched the men, she recognized that she was taking particular pleasure in watching Laurent as he moved and pointed and gestured. He was a big man, not just tall. His chest was full, his shoulders were broad, but his hips were slim. He may look like a linebacker, Maggie thought with amazement, but he moves like a cat. As she finished her breakfast, she found herself watching him and thinking: *The problem isn't that I don't love him. I probably love him too much.*

When she could tell they were heading back toward the *mas*, she put her dish and cup in the sink and went upstairs to dress for the day.

STAN EASED his shoes off and massaged his feet. He wasn't used to this much walking and between Laurent's tour of the property and a day in the village of St-Buvard with Maggie, he'd quickly hit his limit. He hated to beg off from dinner this evening—especially with it being his last night before he returned to Paris—but he knew when he was done in. Besides, having guests was stressful and he figured Maggie and Laurent could both use a breather from the pressure of having to be on their best behavior.

A chime from his cellphone on the dresser made him turn his head to see if he could see who it was without getting up. Groaning, he padded over and squinted at the screen.

Jeremy. *Again*.

He turned the phone to vibrate and tossed it down on the bed. He was well aware that if tonight was anything like this morning, it would take all his energy and mental faculties just to get the ancient showerhead to function properly.

LAURENT DRAGGED the chaise lounge over to the brazier and set two wine glasses down on the stone side table. He tossed one of the heavy cotton knit throws he'd taken from the living room onto the lounge and then looked to see if he could see his wife. Through the French doors, he saw her silhouette standing in the door of the kitchen. She balanced a plate of cheese and, under her arm, what was left of the baguette from lunch. Just watching her like this when she was unaware of him, gave him pleasure that never ceased to surprise him. She was slim and graceful, moving like a dancer. Every gesture she made was unselfconscious and fluid. He loved her body. Loved to watch it, loved to run his rough, callused hands down the length of it. He grinned at his thoughts and shook himself out of them.

She stood in the doorway of the French doors.

"Is it too cold, do you think?" she asked, hesitating.

"I will keep you warm," he said and then gestured to the blanket and the brazier.

She moved toward him and set the plate down. "A long day," she said. She looked at him, he thought, as if asking a question. As usual, he had no idea what she was really asking.

"*Oui*," he said. "I have enjoyed meeting your uncle."

"I'm glad."

"Never have you mentioned him to me before."

"I guess that's weird. But I haven't seen him, myself, since I was a kid."

"Your father and he fought?"

"No, I don't think so." Maggie reached for her wine glass and settled onto the chaise lounge. Laurent draped the throw across her knees and pulled up a large outdoor armchair next to her.

"Perhaps it is as he says," Laurent said. "California is a long way from Atlanta."

Maggie looked at Laurent and frowned. "You think it might *not* be as he says," she asked.

"Of course," he said shrugging. "Always it is possible with whatever one says."

"And whoever is saying it."

"Now I am losing the meaning of what *we* are saying."

"Never mind. The point is, you're right. He's a bit of a mystery."

"Why is he living in Paris, has he said this to you?"

"Just that he always wanted to. What sounds weird about that to you?"

Laurent shrugged. "*Rien*," he said. "People love Paris."

"You don't, do you? And you born there."

Laurent's eyes glittered as he thought of the Paris of his youth. Filthy, painful, hungry, ugly Paris.

"Stan spent forty years as a buyer for Gumps, one of the biggest department stores in San Francisco," Maggie said, tearing off a piece of bread and tucking a wedge of cheese in it. "He told me that every year he went to Paris to the fashion shows and eventually, he got to thinking that that was where he'd go when he retired." She shrugged and popped the piece of bread in her mouth.

"So that is where he went," Laurent said, reaching over and tucking a long strand of loose hair behind her ear. "*Evidemment*."

"Yeah, *évidemment*," Maggie said, sipping her wine. "And you're sure you're okay with me going up there next week to stay with him and see the shows?"

"Of course. It will be good for you."

Laurent watched her catch her breath as if she were about to say something, then think better of it. Unusual for her, he thought. It was a new sensation, watching her guard her words. He found it unsettling, as if she'd given up on something. A chill breeze came down through the dogwoods, their leaves long since gone, and flapped the cotton throw. Laurent had an image of the *mistral* darting through Provence, stopping just long enough to rattle his cage before moving on.

"We should go in," Maggie said, gathering the throw in one hand and her wine glass in the other. "Summer's long over, Laurent." She hurried into the house.

Wearily, Laurent got up and turned off the fire in the brazier and picked up the cheese plate. He looked at the light coming from inside the house and felt strangely lonely.

Unfortunately, tonight he would have to agree with her.

2

It had been awhile since Maggie had worn heels quite this high.

In fact, she had *never* worn heels this high. Or this expensive.

Sitting with Stan at a bistro across from the *Musée d'Orsay*, she kept glancing down at her new shoes.

Had Laurent really said "Go for it?" Had he heard correctly when she told him the price?

"Darling, they make your legs look miles long." Stan patted her hand as he sat next to her in the booth. "You can't possibly regret getting them."

Maggie had to admit they were beautiful. Black velvet platform pumps. Six inches high. She had literally tottered to her seat.

"I live in the country, Stan," she said.

"So of course you need a pair of special-occasions pumps."

"They cost seven hundred euros."

"Just proving what a good thrifty girl you are. You turned down the fifteen hundred Blahniks. I, for one, marveled at your restraint."

"They are stupendously gorgeous," Maggie said, wagging her foot. "And I haven't worn anything but Keds or hiking boots in three years."

"I can already hear your husband calling to thank me."

"Really, Stan, these three days have been amazing. They were exactly what I needed."

"I could tell that, darling," Stan said, pulling out a cigarette and offering it to her. She shook her head. "Since you've been in town, you've positively radiated relaxation and *bonhomie*."

"How did you get tickets to the Gaultier show again? I was agog just being there. I'd heard of Paris Fashion Week all my life."

"I go every year," Stan said, shrugging. "And what with my blog, they practically throw the tickets at me." He lighted his cigarette. "So often it's a disappointment, or just cliché. But even those years, it's always fun. Great fun. Especially the parties. Tonight you'll meet my whole crowd. I hope you're ready for them."

After two days of nonstop shopping and attending the fashion shows, Maggie felt nearly ready to write Stan's fashion blog herself. She had never given much thought to her clothes before.

"It is amazing to me how you could get to be thirty and never own a single piece of couture clothing," Stan said shaking his head. "I mean, you didn't always live in the backwater of France."

"I worked when I lived in Atlanta," Maggie said. "And working girls don't tend to prance about in Dolce and Gabbana and six inch heels. It's not practical."

"Plus you weren't interested."

"I admit it," Maggie said. "I didn't really care."

"What *do* you care about, darling? I mean, everyone has something that floats their boats, as it were. Laurent and his vineyard. Me, fashion. Your father, golf."

Maggie laughed. "I know, I know. My problem is I really loved what I did. I was in advertising. I didn't have a hobby or anything. I had my work. Without it..." She shrugged.

"Have you thought about having kids?"

"Not you, too!"

"Why? Is Laurent pressuring you?"

Maggie shook her head. "He's never said a word," she said. "Laurent's the strong silent type."

"Too silent?"

"Maybe."

"Communication is pretty important in a relationship."

"He's French. He's a guy. He doesn't talk. I'm supposed to just intuit what's going on with him."

"Do you have any girlfriends you can talk to?"

"I did. My best friend went back to the States."

"And nobody since then?"

"Not really."

"My darling, I have to say, while I haven't known you as an adult very long, you really do strike me as the kind of woman who needs girlfriends."

"I talk to Grace pretty often," Maggie said. "We Skype."

"Not really the same as putting your heads together over a good Pinot, is it?"

Maggie shook her head and felt very close to tears. "I'm ready to have a baby," she admitted. "And I'm pretty sure Laurent wouldn't mind."

"Wow. Rousing recommendation."

"But if I did, it would just be a case of: Maggie has her baby and Laurent has his damn vineyard."

"Are you sure?"

"Well, you've seen him, Stan. His vineyard is his obsession."

"That's not really what I saw."

"Are you serious?"

"I saw a man lucky enough to love what he does for a living. It didn't look out of proportion to me."

Maggie stared at him with her mouth open. Then she looked

away. "Is it me, then?" she said. "Grace said I depend too much on Laurent to make me happy."

"I don't believe another person can make you happy."

"You're just a font of unexpected, bizarre adages today, aren't you?" But they both laughed. "What if I had the kid and I was still unhappy?"

"Oh, wait, I know the answer to that one! Don't have a kid to try to fill up the thing inside you that you think you're missing."

"Yeah, I guess I already knew the answer to that one, myself."

"Maggie, dearest girl! You are so bright and so talented. And we must all have a life's work that engages and enriches us. Even those of us who are retired."

"Okay, so how does that work?" Maggie frowned. "You're going to be living in Paris without a job and filling up your days with shopping and opera and your fashion blog and dinners out with friends?"

Stan laughed. "Pretty much. But I'm also registering for classes at the Cordon Bleu."

"Really? What in the world for?"

"Spoken like someone who does not like to cook. For no other reason than to master my omelet flipping skills, my knife chopping abilities." He shrugged. "To learn something new."

"So not to open a restaurant or anything."

"In Paris?" Stan laughed. "Haven't you ever done something just for the fun of doing it?"

"Wow," Maggie said. "I wonder what that would be like? Doing something for no reason..."

Stan turned in his seat and waved to a man just entering the restaurant. He was blond and handsome, his teeth very straight and white, his smile broad.

He must be American, Maggie found herself thinking.

"Maggie, darling, I want you to meet a friend of mine." Stan stood up as the man approached. It was cold outside and the man, easily Stan's age, brought a whiff of fresh air and chilliness to the table. He wore a dark pea coat, unbuttoned, and a cashmere muffler loose at his throat.

"Jeremy," Stan said as he exchanged brief cheek kisses with the man. "I want you to meet my niece, Maggie Dernier."

Maggie shook his hand and smiled.

"Stan's told me so much about you," he said. "I'm glad to finally put a face to the name. And a beautiful face it is, too. May I?" He pointed to the extra chair at the table.

"Please do," Maggie said.

Stan signaled the waiter to bring another coffee.

"So you're American," Maggie said. "In town for the shows?"

"Yes, yes," Jeremy said, slipping out of his coat and draping it on the chair next to him. "It's why we're all here except for Stan, lucky bastard."

"Did y'all used to work together in California?"

"We did," Stan said quickly. "We are ex-colleagues." It seemed to Maggie that Stan was giving Jeremy a meaningful look of some kind.

"Why, Stan," Jeremy said, smiling at the waiter when he set the coffee cup down in front of him, "that's exactly what we are. Ex-colleagues. Nicely put."

"Did you see Gaultier?"

"You know I did, darling, since you saw me there."

"I guess I was really asking what you thought of it."

"And step on your toes for your blog post for tomorrow? Not on your life." Jeremy turned to Maggie. "If I say I loved it, and Stan goes easy on them, he'll think *I'll* think I influenced him..."

"I never would."

"...and if I say it was an embarrassment and derivative like we've seen for the last two seasons, and he says as much in his post, well!" He took a dramatic sip of his coffee. "You see the problem."

"Best to just keep your opinion to yourself," Stan said, his customary grin missing.

"Exactly what I thought. So, Maggie, how long are you in town for?"

"I take the train back to Arles tomorrow," she said.

"Stan has definitely kept you all to himself, hasn't he?"

"She'll be at Bijou's party tonight," Stan said.

"Oh, very nice! You'll meet the whole gang then. Meanwhile, I must toddle. Did I mention I got tickets to Yiqing Yin?"

"Awesome," Stan said.

"It's at least that." He turned to Maggie. "So nice to meet you, Maggie. See you tonight then."

"Great," Maggie said. "Nice to meet you, too."

Jeremy gave Stan what could only be described as his own kind of meaningful look before pulling on his coat and departing.

"Interesting guy," Maggie said. "You guys have kind of a weird friendship, though, I have to say."

"Oh, you have no idea," Stan said, taking a long drag on his cigarette and smiling at Maggie.

THE PARTY WAS every bit as loud at two a.m. as it had been at midnight and showed no signs of ending. Maggie sat in the center of what could only be called a maelstrom of noise and gorgeous bodies wearing spectacular outfits. The laughter and the music, the talking—and more than occasional shrieking—and the sounds of clinking (and breaking) champagne glasses swirled around Maggie in a constant vortex of color and sound. Stan had been dragged away as soon as they arrived by a long, leggy creature in the shortest miniskirt that Maggie had ever seen. Assuming the bare requirements for a skirt involved covering one's bottom, Maggie was shocked and amused to see that this skirt felt no such compunction. Instead of feeling abandoned by her uncle, Maggie felt electric with the attention and the stimulation of so many beautiful people swarming around her.

Are fashion people all this friendly? she couldn't help but wonder as yet another handsome male model brought her a drink and jockeyed for position on the couch with her. At five foot three and wearing her best black sheath and brand new pumps, Maggie was surprised to realize she didn't feel inadequate or plain in this crowd. She felt welcomed and feted.

"Sorry to be stealing your uncle away," a voice purred in her ear from behind the couch where she was sitting. Maggie twisted around to smile at the super model grinning down at her.

"Bijou, right?" Maggie said. The woman had long blonde hair, flaxen and straight which accentuated her strong cheekbones. Her clear blue eyes made Maggie wonder if her hostess was drinking anything beyond seltzer. "Great party." She nearly had to shout to be heard over the din.

"You should have been here last night," Bijou said. "Now *that* was a party." She tapped the shoulder of the man sitting next to Maggie and he got up, allowing Bijou to swing her legs over the couch and slide into place next to Maggie.

"Sorry I missed it," Maggie said. "Stan and I were catching up."

"He told me," Bijou said. "So what do you think of Paris Fashion week? Is stupendous, *non*?"

"Yeah, definitely," Maggie said. "I can't believe Stan does it every year. Has to make the other fifty-one weeks of the year seem bleak."

Bijou narrowed her eyes and frowned as if trying to understand what Maggie was saying.

"Did I see you on the catwalk this week?" Maggie asked.

Bijou smiled and affected an insouciant shrug.

"*Peut-être*," she said. "If you were at the Armani show?"

"We were! Which one were you?"

"I was many people in that show," Bijou laughed. "I wore the big satin dress tight here, yes?" She grabbed her small breasts, loose under her silk tee. "And then flowing to the floor. You remember?"

She had just described every dress Maggie had seen at that particular show.

"Oh, yeah, I remember," Maggie said. "That was you? Wow. You were beautiful."

"Oh, it is for the clothes to be beautiful," Bijou said. "Me, I must disappear, yes? Become a clothes hanger upon which Giorgio's creations must shine."

"How long have you been doing Fashion Week?"

"Years," Bijou said. "Oh! There is Stella. You will excuse me, yes? If I see Stan I will shoo him back to you. But you are okay?"

Maggie nodded, craning her head to catch a glimpse of *Stella*.

In a flash, one of the ever present, non-English-speaking hunks had taken Bijou's place next to Maggie on the couch.

"*Boisson*?"

Maggie took the champagne flute from the young man—he had to be at least ten years her junior—and smiled. He put his hand on her stockinged thigh and she wagged a finger at him. "No, no," she said and held up her hand with her wedding band on it.

"*Quelle dommage*," the young man said sadly, but didn't move his hand.

She spotted Jeremy from across the room and waved to him. He was a familiar face and she needed to extricate herself from Hunky Boy's creeping hands without coming off as too much of an American country prude.

"Jeremy!" she called and he turned to her. His face broke into a grin and he left his conversation with a very intense young man without a backward glance and walked over to her.

"My darling!" Jeremy spoke a few abrupt words in French to Maggie's couch mate which prompted the young man to bolt off the couch and Jeremy sagged into his seat next to her as if he were exhausted. "Are you enjoying the party?" he said. "You have met our hostess?"

"Just a second ago," Maggie said. "Wow. You fashionistas really know how to party. It hasn't let up in hours. How do you keep it up?"

"I assume you mean that metaphorically?" Jeremy wiggled his eyebrows at her and Maggie laughed. The champagne had gone to her head just enough and she was at that point in the evening when the music and the thick press of bodies was exactly right.

"Have you seen Stan?" she asked. "He disappeared as soon as we got here, like two hours ago."

"I saw him in the kitchen a little bit ago," Jeremy said. "Have you met the ferocious Tasmanian Devil himself yet?"

"I have no idea who you are talking about."

"Denny Davenport? Oh, that I will be the one to introduce you to him! Stan will thank me. He hates the bastard but you simply have to know Denny."

"Well, naturally, I do."

"And Diane?" Jeremy began scanning the room. "I'm surprised she hasn't come over and introduced herself. We all of us know you, darling Maggie, Stan has talked about little else since he knew he would be reacquainting himself with you."

"So his visit to St-Buvard was not a spur of the moment thing? I kind of got the impression that it was."

"Well, by all means, whatever impression you got, is what it was," Jeremy said. "Nope, can't see her. She might've gone home early. She has a kid on the west coast she can't seem to take two steps without talking to or talking about. Probably back at her hotel Skyping the little dear even as we speak."

"You don't have children, Jeremy?"

"Oh, you are a funny girl! And Stan didn't tell me you had a sense of humor. No, horrid creatures, children. But some people swear by them."

Maggie laughed.

"So you're enjoying yourself, I hope?"

"Oh, yeah, this is great," Maggie said. "I'll be able to go back to my country mouse ways and live on the memories of these three days forever."

"Why settle for memories?" Jeremy asked and Maggie, in her slightly drunken mood, was reminded of something Stan had said to her just last week about memories. "Why not live like this all the time? Life is too short for compromise."

"Like this?" Maggie waved a hand around the room. A few people were standing but at this point in the evening most were seated and either nuzzling each other or engaged in intense conversations. "Not sure I could do this too many times in a year."

"Well, the rest of it then," Jeremy said. "Paris. I don't know how you can survive living in the country like you do. It's perfect for some people but for me..." He shrugged. "I would rather die."

"Yeah," Maggie said. "The country's not really my thing either. But I'm stuck there," she said. "What can I do?"

"What, indeed?" Jeremy said, leaning past her to reach for another glass of wine and then handing it to her. "You only have one life, my darling," he said. "The good news is that we all get to choose how we spend it."

"Is everyone in Paris this wise?" Maggie asked. "Or is it just the constant flow of champagne that makes it seem so?"

"Maybe you're just in the mood to hear the wisdom," Jeremy said.

An hour later, at a little after three in the morning, Maggie was ready to go. She had not even caught a glimpse of Stan the full time she had been at the party and was nearly at the point of worry. She had switched to *l'eau gazeuse* thirty minutes earlier.

"Hello, are you waiting for me?"

Surprised at the voice by her shoulder, Maggie turned to stare into one of the most physically beautiful faces she had ever seen.

Closer to her own age, the man had brown hair, hazel eyes with thick lashes and a full sensuous mouth which spoke very comforting American English. At this point, she had stopped being startled when people acted like they knew her, but his beauty was still something remarkable. He was obviously a model of some kind.

"Hi," she said. "No, I'm looking for my uncle. We came together and I'm ready to go home."

"Stan Newberry, right?"

"I guess everybody knows that." Maggie smiled wearily. "I didn't realize he was such a party animal. Last night when we went out, he was ready to retire by ten."

"I can see you might have the effect on men of making them want to retire early," he said, drilling her with a very sexy grin, "only not alone."

Maggie laughed, not sure how to react to him. She felt a little flushed. He was *extremely* good looking. A girl stumbled over to them and fell into his arms and Maggie couldn't help but note that he was strong too. He held the girl effortlessly in his arms, laughing at her antics like a fond uncle. Maggie noticed his hand on the girl's bottom. *Not too avuncular, then*, she thought.

"Time to go, Teddy," she slurred. "We'll need a taxi. There's no way I'm walking six blocks in these heels."

"Take them off, sweetheart," he said to her, giving her a quick kiss but his eyes were looking at Maggie. He swept the girl up into his arms to her squeals of delight. He made a half bow at Maggie, the blonde model squirming sexily against his chest. "Until we meet again," he said, "which I have no doubt we will," and gave her a wink.

Maggie watched the two leave the crowded party and couldn't help but wonder who he was. Turning back to the noise and heat of the party, Maggie thought she caught a glimpse of Stan in the crowd but by the time she worked her way in that direction through the wall of bodies, he had vanished. Deciding not to be a drag on his fun, Maggie downed another glass of champagne and set up camp at one end of the couch. An hour later after a continuous stream of largely gorgeous people—men *and* women—had stopped to chat with her, she was past ready to go. At one point, she wasn't sure she hadn't dosed off.

"I would be happy to escort you to your hotel," a voice said near her head.

She jerked awake, and saw that she was still holding her champagne flute.

"I can't leave Stan," she mumbled sleepily to Jeremy who was kneeling in front of her. He looked flushed and unsettled, like the champagne had stopped working.

"No worries, my darling." Jeremy said. "He specifically asked me to see you home."

"He did?"

"How to put this delicately? Your uncle has found his own way home this evening."

When Maggie looked at him in confusion, he added tightly: "To someone *else's* home."

"Oh." She felt even more tired than before. "It's just so weird that he wouldn't tell me, himself," she said.

"Darling, if you could have seen the delicious young thing he was chatting up, you would understand instantly."

Really? The picture of her kind, thoughtful and slightly elderly uncle chatting up anyone was hard enough to gel in her mind...let alone not coming to her and telling her to find her own way home.

"Thanks anyway," Maggie said, "but I think I'll just walk myself home."

"I really don't think—"

She collected her purse and her pashmina from the couch.

"Please tell Bijou good night for me, Jeremy," she said. "I know exactly where we are and Stan's apartment isn't four blocks from here."

Maggie knew she needed the walk to clear her head. And to cool down. She couldn't remember a time when she was this angry. It's true she didn't know Stan well but this behavior was beyond anything she would have expected from him. Maybe this was the tip of the iceberg of the reason why her family seemed to have cut off all contact with him.

As soon as she descended the long stairwell and emerged out onto the street, the quiet cocoon of Bijou's apartment building dissipated and Maggie was assailed by the noises outside. Directly in front of the ancient building a few people stood in the street looking up at the sky. There was a nightclub directly across the street and Maggie assumed the people had left the club and were on their way home. Two men and two women. All four dressed in what Maggie would have considered outlandish costumes if it hadn't been in the tail end of Paris Fashion Week. The two women stood on the curb while the men stood, bizarrely, in the middle of the street. As Maggie started to walk down the block, she noticed that the men were standing near a large pile of clothes centered in the road, almost as if guarding it.

Her pace slowed when she caught the men's soft voices under the sounds of the women on the curb. One of the women was crying.

"How the hell long does it take to get a goddamn ambulance here?" one of the men said in American English. When he spoke, Maggie found herself, without knowing why, moving toward them. The two men turned to look at her as she approached and she could see there was a third man kneeling in the street next to the pile of clothes.

Only not a pile of clothes.

Maggie gasped. She dropped her purse and ran to where the men were, pushing past where the two were standing. The man kneeling by the body looked up at her but she only had eyes for the broken body of her uncle lying at her feet.

3

The crouching man stood up as Maggie dropped to her knees in the street. Stan was lying on his back, his left leg bent at an impossible angle, the life seeping out of him in dark red rivers. His eyes fluttered.

"We saw him jump just as we were coming out of the club," one of the men said to her. "We called the ambulance. They should be here any minute."

In the background of her mind, she could hear the one woman continue to weep and she heard more people gathering. She knelt in the pool of blood and gently touched Stan's hand.

"Stan," she said. "It's Maggie. I'm here."

His eyes were not focused but his mouth moved. Maggie leant over him, careful not to touch him in case it mattered, and placed her ear close to his lips.

It was just a bare whisper of air with the last breath he would take, rumbling softly through his lips.

"Jimbo," he said.

Maggie froze in case he would speak again but the noise of the crowd that had formed around her would have made it impossible to hear in any case. When she pulled back to search his eyes, she felt her stomach tighten and then churn. His eyes no longer saw, his lips no longer moved.

A wave of heartbreaking sadness swept through her and gripped her tightly across the chest. She felt hands pulling on her and she realized that the paramedics had arrived. She allowed them to help her to her feet and watched them turn to Stan.

Maggie stood, covered in her uncle's blood, stunned and sick while the crowd in the street grew larger and noisier. Within seconds, she felt strong hands propelling her away from the scene, leading her to the sidewalk and pushing her into a sitting position on the curb. She knew he was speaking to her but she was having difficulty concentrating on what was happening. After a moment, she turned her head and vomited up all the lovely spinach puffs and *Veuve Clicquot* from her evening.

Two days later, Maggie sat on her uncle's couch and stared out his long floor to ceiling windows at the relentless afternoon rain. The days had passed in a blur of activity, weeping and intermittent boredom. Not surprisingly, Stan's apartment had stayed packed with a steady influx of loving friends. Stan was well known and well loved. The fact that he had died during Fashion Week meant everyone he knew was in town to pay homage and say goodbye to him. They treated Maggie as if she were the bereaved widow, clasping her hand, their faces streaked with tears, and giving their condolences and offers of shared sorrow. She was sorry to tell them, over and over again, that there would be no funeral in Paris. Her father had arrived that morning to escort the body home to Atlanta.

In a rare quiet moment when she and her father were alone and the apartment empty of sympathizers and mourners, Maggie turned to him and asked for the hundredth time, "How could this have happened?"

Her father handed her a demitasse of espresso from Stan's kitchen and sat down on the couch next to her.

"It's a tragedy," he said. "For sure Stan would be one of the last people on earth I would ever have imagined might kill himself."

"Dad," Maggie said. "I just spent three days with him. He was full of life and plans for his retirement. It doesn't make sense."

"Suicides generally don't," her father said.

"Are you sure you want to do all this back in Atlanta? Stan didn't know anyone there any more."

"His family is there," John Newberry said, sipping from his cup.

He looked suitably grim to Maggie but not particularly sad. He patted her on the knee. "Laurent couldn't come up?"

"I guess the harvesting couldn't spare him," Maggie said. "As he said, it's not like there was anything for him to do up here but hang around and drink too much and listen to a lot of people cry."

"He didn't say that."

"No, but he's clearly missing that sensitivity chip that would allow him to support his wife in her time of need."

"Did you ask him to come?"

"He should have offered without my having to."

Her father smiled tiredly, sipped his coffee and said nothing.

"Dad? Was everything okay between you and Uncle Stan?"

"We were not estranged, Maggie," her father said. "We just had busy lives."

"And really different lives."

"We lived on opposite coasts."

"Were you close as kids?"

"Not particularly."

"He was such a sweet man. I'm sorry I didn't know him better. I really liked him, Dad. I already loved him."

"Of course. He was your uncle."

"And a good guy, Dad."

"Look, Maggie. I'm very tired and I have to be up early tomorrow for my flight. Do you think you can close up Stan's apartment until after his will is read? That'll be some time next month."

"In Atlanta."

"Maggie, he doesn't have any children. Or a wife. If there is a favorite charity he wanted his money to go to, I will make sure it goes there. But all of that can be done from Atlanta, where he'll be buried next to our parents at Oakland cemetery."

"When was the last time he was even *in* Atlanta?"

"Trust me, sweetheart, at this point, it really doesn't matter."

THAT NIGHT, after her father had retired, Maggie agreed to meet Bijou and Jeremy at Stan's favorite bistro on the corner by his apartment. Since it was her last night in Paris and she couldn't help but feel his friends were being cheated out of the opportunity to say goodbye to Stan at his funeral, Maggie was glad for the opportunity.

The restaurant was a favorite of Stan's. It featured stained glass windows and dark, polished mahogany walls with ancient wall sconces which punctuated the high walls to the ornate ceiling which was crisscrossed with heavy wooden beams. The waiters appeared gloomy and dour which Maggie couldn't help but think was appropriate for tonight. When she entered the restaurant, she was surprised to find it full of people waiting for her. Bijou jumped up as she entered and flung her arms around Maggie. As tall as she was, she had to hunch over to wrap her arms around her. She had been to Stan's apartment every day during the last four days and every time she acted as if she were learning of Stan's death for the very first time.

"Let her come in and sit down, Bijou!" someone yelled. "Move over, let her sit."

Maggie felt a warm, strong presence materialize behind her and she looked up to see Ted standing there, his hand gently pushing the small of her back.

"Come on," he said. "We have a drink for you and the love of all of Stan's friends to envelop you."

"Thanks, Ted," she whispered, grateful for his arm as he guided her to the booth full of Stan's dearest friends. One by one, they stood and kissed her in solemn greeting. Jeremy, Ted, Diane —the American department story copywriter—and, of course, Bijou.

"Thank you, all of you," Maggie said. "I'm so sorry to be taking him home when I know here is home, wherever his friends are who he loved so much—"

Jeremy burst into tears and Diane, who was sitting next to him, gave his shoulder a perfunctory pat without looking at him. When Maggie first met her, she thought she was a mousey kind of woman. Quiet, shy, nondescript in every way. She looked sad but Maggie couldn't help but think there was something mechanical or staged about her show of grief. She scolded herself for thinking such a thing.

"We're a mess," Jeremy said, wiping the tears from his cheeks and pulling out a large handkerchief. "We're just a wretched mess." His shoulders shook as he cried into the handkerchief and Diane continued to absently pat him.

"We ordered brandy." Ted pushed an old-fashioned glass toward Maggie. "Have you eaten?"

"I have, thank you," Maggie said. Over the last few days she had heard bits and pieces of all of their stories and their connections with Stan. Ted had found a loving mentor in Stan whose blog had supported and promoted him during the hey day of his modeling years and of drug abuse. Ted had said repeatedly during what had passed for a wake at Stan's apartment that Stan had saved his career, if not his life.

Everyone had similar stories.

Maggie couldn't help but think it strange that no one seemed to have any trouble with the idea that Stan killed himself. These were his friends. They knew him better than she did. She took a sip of her brandy and looked at each of their faces. Jeremy continued to sob and blow his nose. It was difficult to ascertain anything with him beyond his show of grief. Bijou looked sad, it seemed to Maggie, and perhaps a little distracted. Maggie noticed she looked up frequently to look at the door as if expecting someone else to join the party. Diane was a conundrum. She looked sad but that could just be how she always looked. Maggie couldn't help but wonder, if she was so close to Stan, why he had never mentioned her when he talked about the friends he wanted Maggie to meet. She glanced at Ted who was watching her. Neither had he mentioned Ted.

"Has anyone talked to the police?" Bijou asked the group, her eyes resting finally on Maggie.

"They'll only talk to the family," Jeremy said, sniffing. He, too, turned his gaze onto Maggie.

"They're still investigating," Maggie said.

"Looks pretty straightforward," Ted said. "Witnesses said they saw him launch himself from the balcony."

"Well," Maggie said, "They said they saw him fall."

"You think he was pushed?" All heads turned to face the newcomer attached to the voice. A tall black man in his mid forties stood silently next to Ted, causing the younger man to jump when he realized he was there.

"Jeez, Denny," Ted said, clapping a hand to his heart. "You need to get squeakier shoes or something."

"Who would murder Stan?" Jeremy said, scowling at the newcomer. "Except maybe you."

Denny held his hands up as if to fend off any further verbal assaults from the group.

"I come in peace," he said, his mouth twisted into a smirk. "I saw you all sitting here and am simply offering my condolences."

"Bullshit, you venal bastard!" Jeremy said, struggling to stand at the table. "If anybody is happy that Stan's gone, it's you. Now you have no competition in the blogosphere. None! He was a pain in your ass and now it's clear sailing for Denny bloody Davenport."

Maggie watched Diane try to pull Jeremy back to a seated position in the booth. She murmured something to him and succeeded in getting him to sit back down.

"You're the niece?" Denny said to Maggie.

She nodded, recognizing that she pretty much instantly disliked him.

"So sorry for your loss." He gave a snappy little half bow, the smirk never leaving his face, turned and left.

"What a bastard," Ted said as the group watched Davenport exit the bistro into the night. "He's dancing in the street now that Stan's gone."

"*Ça ne fait rien*," Bijou said, signaling the waiter for another round of drinks. "Whether he is happy or bereft, it changes nothing."

"What's the deal with him?" Maggie asked. "I never heard of competing bloggers before."

"Oh, it's done a little differently in the fashion world," Diane said. "Denny and Stan both have pretty big followings and what they say can actually affect a designer's year."

"You mean like if Stan says Ralph Lauren's winter collection looks like the Goodwill bag lady, Lauren's ready-to-wear will suffer at the local Macy's?"

"It's not quite that simple," Diane said. "But it could affect reputations if not sales."

"Plus, both Denny and Stan are able to monetize their blogs," Ted said. "They don't take money for a positive review—or at least Stan wouldn't—but everyone knows a positive mention in one of their posts could translate into increased business. Not the big designers, but certainly the newcomers, the accessories people. That sort of thing."

"Stan was very good about launching new talent," Jeremy said, shaking his head and staring at the tablecloth in front of him. "He was always discovering someone new and introducing them through his blog."

"That's true," Ted said. "I can name two people who directly attribute their success today to public praise from Stan's blog."

"I had no idea," Maggie said. "I didn't know he was still into the whole fashion thing. I thought he was retired."

"He retired from *buying*," Jeremy said. "But he could no more give up his blog than stop breathing." As soon as he realized what he said, he burst into tears. Diane patted his shoulder.

Maggie turned to Bijou. "And there wasn't room for *two* fashion bloggers?"

"They crossed swords in their blogs," Bijou said. "It was now a part of their...?" She looked to Ted who spoke quickly: "Their brand," he said.

"*Oui*," Bijou said. "It was their brand that they were contentious of each other."

"It made for even more delicious reading," Ted said. "In fact, I disagree with Jeremy. I think Denny will find that having the floor all to himself will not be half so entertaining as having someone of Stan's caliber to spar with. And so, not half so profitable."

Diane twisted her body away from Jeremy's noisy sobs and leaned toward Maggie.

"When are you taking the body back to the States?" she asked.

"My father's taking him back tomorrow morning," Maggie said.

"And the reading of the will?"

Maggie felt a chill come into the little bistro.

"Immediately after the funeral," Maggie said. "Family only, in my father's lawyer's office."

"I see."

"Are you expecting Stan to leave you something in particular?" Maggie asked, wondering what in the world Stan ever saw in this mousy, unfriendly and decidedly unfashionable woman.

Diane picked up a napkin and folded it up carefully in front of her. Maggie couldn't help but notice that she appeared to be drying perspiration from her fingers.

"You never know," she said, looking away.

THE NEXT MORNING, Maggie said goodbye to her father and saw him leave for his sad journey back to the States with his only brother. She emptied out the refrigerator and locked up her uncle's apartment before leaving herself. She had already given, at least temporarily, Stan's half-feral tomcat to the woman living in the apartment next door. Since the animal spent more time roaming the streets of Paris than it did curled up on a rug in Stan's apartment, Maggie felt the change wouldn't be too drastic for him. In any event, she intended on checking on the cat the next time she was in Paris—probably when she came up to list the flat after the will was read.

The train trip from Paris to Arles was just under four hours and Maggie spent most of that time staring out at the brown autumn countryside of southwestern France. Even though a part of her felt like she was leaving tragedy and sadness behind, she was surprised to realize she felt worse with every mile that took her away from Paris.

Laurent was waiting for her at the train station. When she saw him, she felt her usual mixture of love and amazement that this big, handsome man was hers. Laurent moved with no hint of self-awareness, no obvious clue that he was someone that most women took a second look at. Six foot four, broad chested and long-legged, he moved like a native American, graceful and sure —even when he was just placing luggage in the back of a sedan.

"A good trip?" he asked after he'd taken her into his arms for a welcoming hug.

"Pretty good," Maggie said, relaxing into him and feeling some of the stress of the trip dissipate. "How's everything at home?" She hadn't spoken with him in a couple of days. It made her realize that *she* always called *him*. In the absence of that effort, communication ceased.

"Two of the pickers were arrested yesterday," he said as he started the car up. "Your father gone?"

"This morning."

Laurent placed a large hand on Maggie's knee before putting the car into gear. "*Ça va*, Maggie?" he asked.

"Yes, Laurent," she said. "I'm okay."

"A bad trip."

"Yes and no," Maggie said.

Laurent began the forty-five minute drive to St-Buvard and their home.

"I mean, it was terrible, of course about Stan. Not sure I'll ever get over that. I got to him seconds after he fell. Did I tell you that?"

Laurent nodded.

"But being in Paris was good for me."

Laurent looked over at her and then focused on the road. "*C'est bien*," he said.

"Did I tell you what he said to me? What his last words were?"

"Jimbo?"

Maggie turned to look at the foliage of the Provençal countryside. Everything looked so primitive and tiresome after the lights and fast pace of Paris.

"Just doesn't make sense," she said. "Who is Jimbo?"

"You are sure it is a person?" Laurent said.

Maggie turned to look at him. This was unusual. Laurent

didn't normally engage in these kinds of questions or word play. He was a straightforward kind of guy, Maggie thought. Not much like the old Laurent, she thought, who thought nothing of lying his ass off to bilk some rich heiress out of her fortune.

"What else could it be?" Maggie said. "You think I misheard and maybe it was *Jumbo*? That's even more mysterious."

"Perhaps it was a French word," Laurent said, pulling off the A47 to the smaller two lane road that led to St-Buvard—the one that Maggie always feared would be the death of her if she ever met up with one of the ubiquitous drunk French drivers on it.

"Stan wasn't French," Maggie said. "Why would he say a French word?"

"Sais pas," Laurent said.

They drove in silence for several minutes. Maggie wondered what it meant that she felt sadder and more unhappy the closer she came to her home.

JEREMY STOOD at the woman's apartment door, his silk ascot neatly knotted at his throat, his eyes bloodshot from tears and what could easily appear to the most casual observer as a seriously committed drug habit.

"It's just that I know Stan mentioned that he gave you a key to his flat," Jeremy said to the frowning woman standing in the door of her apartment. "And I wouldn't ask if it weren't an absolute emergency that I get in."

"*Pourquoi ne demandez-vous pas à sa nièce*?" the woman asked. *Why don't you ask his niece*? Jeremy's French was poor but he understood her well enough.

"I wish I had done so," he said. "*Mon erreur*. But the poor cat should not have to suffer for my negligence. *Le chat? Comprenez-vous*?"

"Le chat est en bon état."

Dear God, could this woman be any more difficult?

"Well, I really need to see that for myself," Jeremy said.

"*Non.*" The woman began to shut the door and before he knew he was doing it, Jeremy thrust out a hand to stop it from closing.

"Please!" he said. "Just give me the damn key!"

"Je vais appeler les flics!" I'll call the cops!

Jeremy took a step back and allowed the woman to slam the door in his face. He stood staring at the door for a moment, his heart pounding in his chest, when he heard the plaintive mewing coming from behind him. He turned to see Stan's big orange and cream tabby sitting on the bottom tread of the stairs regarding him coolly.

MAGGIE SAT at the dining room table with Danielle Alexandre. She and her husband, Jean-Luc, had brought over a large *pissaladière* that they had enjoyed for lunch with one of Laurent's early wines. Laurent loved *pissaladières* but Maggie always found them too salty for her taste. The men, not surprisingly, were wandering the perimeter of Laurent's vineyard.

"Again, I am so sorry about your uncle," Danielle said to her in English.

"Thanks, Danielle," Maggie said. She had not always been able to appreciate her neighbor. A good thirty years her senior, Danielle spoke English poorly and although pleasant, had always behaved, it seemed to Maggie, as a traditional French housewife —one from the nineteen fifties—might. When her first husband went to prison for torching Laurent's vineyard four years earlier, he divorced Danielle in a surprise move that gave Maggie new respect for the man. Danielle had long been in love with Jean-Luc. To Jean-Luc's credit, when Danielle became available he wasted no time in courting and marrying her.

"You will go home for the funeral?"

Maggie noticed Laurent's tall form through the French doors

as he and Jean-Luc walked together. There had never been a time when Laurent did not prefer to be walking his land, touching his vines and thinking or talking about them. She marveled that this was the same man who had lived by his wits for so many years lying and stealing. Until he had inherited *Domaine St-Buvard*, he had never owned an apartment or even a new car. To discover that he could be so passionately connected to the land—she wondered if that came as much a surprise to him as it did her.

"No," Maggie said, turning back to her neighbor. "There's really no point. I wish we could have it in Paris," she said. "Or San Francisco. Both places Stan had friends. He grew up in Atlanta but hasn't visited in years."

Danielle gave her a questioning look.

"It's the family homestead," Maggie explained. "It's where my grandparents are buried, where Stan was born. It's right, I guess, that he be laid to rest there. I'm just sorry that so many of his friends won't be able to say goodbye to him properly."

"It sounds like he had many friends."

"He really did. He had a retail fashion blog that was respected and read worldwide."

"Blog?"

"Yeah, never mind. Anyway, I didn't know him that well until the end."

"You found the body, Laurent says."

"Kind of," Maggie said, her glance once more darting out the door to find Laurent. "Stan spoke to me just before he died."

"*Vraiment*?" Danielle gasped. "What did he say?"

"Jimbo." Maggie shrugged.

Danielle frowned. "*Jambon*?"

"Well, maybe," Maggie said. "But Stan was American. Why would his last word be French?"

"It's a mystery," Danielle said. "Like Rosebud, *oui*?"

Maggie laughed out loud. "Good Lord, Danielle, that is just

about the last thing I would have expected out of your mouth. How did you know about *Rosebud*?"

"Jean-Luc and I saw *Citizen Kane* last year with French subtitles."

"You and Jean-Luc?"

"He hated it."

"Good," Maggie said, laughing. "The world can now continue on its axis. I could no more imagine Jean-Luc watching *Citizen Kane* than I could endure a Jerry Lewis movie marathon."

"Jean-Luc loves Jerry Lewis!"

"My point exactly!" Both women laughed.

When the door to the back garden opened, Maggie felt an icy blast of cold air and turned to see her husband and Jean-Luc stomping the wet leaves off their boots onto the terrace tiles. Jean-Luc was peering into the house to locate Danielle sitting in the very spot he had left her. Maggie noticed that when Jean-Luc looked at Danielle, his whole face lit up.

"Nice walk?" Maggie called to them from the table. Before they could answer she turned to Danielle. "I hated to miss all the excitement of the harvest this year. Who knew that Paris Fashion Week would be the same week that we'd need to harvest the grapes?"

"It was exciting," Danielle said, looking lovingly at her husband as he moved quickly to the table to slide into the seat next to her.

Maggie had made a concentrated effort to get along better with Jean-Luc. She had never liked him and during their first year she'd been right not to trust him. But in the intervening years, he had proven himself to be a good and loyal friend to Laurent—and Maggie, too, when she let him.

Laurent leaned over to give Maggie a quick kiss which surprised her. Not normally given to overt signs of affection, Laurent certainly wasn't known for it in front of other people.

"Help me in the kitchen, Maggie?" he said as he walked out of the dining room.

That didn't sound good. Laurent never needed help in the kitchen. Maggie hopped up and ran after him. She grabbed his sleeve.

"What is it?" she asked. "Something happen?"

Laurent ran his fingers through his long brown hair, a gesture she had seen him do a hundred times in the past—usually when he was frustrated or trying to stall for time.

"The Paris police called a few minutes ago," he said.

Maggie turned to look at the landline phone in the living room which had not rung all afternoon.

"My cell phone," Laurent said. "While I was out with Jean-Luc."

"What is the matter with those people?" Maggie said with exasperation. "They couldn't call *me*? I gave them my cell number. Unbelievable!"

"Does it matter, Maggie?" Laurent said, a weariness in his voice that she had heard before. "It is what they said that is important, yes?"

"Fine, so what did they tell you?" As long as she lived in France she would never get used to being erased from any equation—especially by the police—in favor of any conveniently available husband.

"They say it is suicide."

"Okay, that is total bullshit," Maggie said hotly.

"But not a surprise," Laurent said. "Will you start the coffee? I will get the tart." He moved to the refrigerator.

"So they are not going to do anything to find out what happened to Stan?"

"They have concluded their investigation, Maggie," Laurent said. "Use the full cream, not the half and half."

Maggie went to the sink and filled the coffee carafe with water and set it on the counter. She turned back to Laurent.

"Some investigation," she said. "You know they didn't even ask me any questions?"

"You were wanting to tell them about your uncle's last word to you, yes?"

"Well, if you were doing an investigation, wouldn't you want all the information you could get? They just saw someone smashed on the pavement and they thought the first thing that anybody would think."

"The cream, Maggie?"

Maggie turned to the refrigerator and pulled out a jug of cream and put it on the counter while Laurent ground the coffee beans. She waited patiently for him to finish.

"When did they call?"

"Five minutes ago."

"Unbelievable."

Laurent scooped the ground coffee into the filter and poured the water into the reservoir. He pushed the button and turned to her and pulled her into his arms.

"None of this is a surprise to you," he said into her hair. He kissed her cheek and held her chin to look into her eyes.

"I know," she said.

He watched her for a moment and then turned and handed her the tart. He patted her on the bottom as if to propel her out of the kitchen. "I'll be in momentarily with the coffee," he said.

Maggie brought the tart to the dining room and set it down in front of Jean-Luc and Danielle who both immediately oohed and ahhed. Maggie couldn't help but think of how easily distracted the French could be when food was involved. The thought nearly made her smile.

Nearly.

"Danielle says your uncle was an important person in Paris fashion circles," Jean-Luc said. Maggie glanced at Danielle who was handing out the stacked desert plates.

"Sort of," she said. "He had a blog that seemed to be widely read."

She saw him look at Danielle and mouth the word *blog*? Danielle shrugged.

"And now Laurent tells me the official investigation is over and they are ruling it a suicide," Maggie said.

"I am so sorry," Jean-Luc said, turning his attention to the slice of tart that Danielle was in the process of cutting for him.

Laurent appeared with a tray of coffee cups, sugar bowl, creamer and a silver coffee pot.

"Laurent, this looks marvelous!" Danielle said. "Where did you get the berries this late in the season?"

Laurent poured a cup of coffee and handed it to Maggie. He smiled at her and she tried to read the unspoken text. Was it: *don't talk about this now?* Or: *I feel your pain?*

As usual, she had no idea.

"They were frozen," he said.

"*Incroyable*," Danielle murmured taking a bite of the tart. "You are a magician, Laurent. Truly."

THE NEXT MORNING, Maggie wrapped herself in a thick cashmere throw and tiptoed into the living room. Her little dog, Petit-Four, a small poodle mix that she got in the first few months she came to St-Buvard, dropped from the bed and padded after her. Maggie curled up on the couch and set up her laptop on the pillows in front of her. Attracted by the glow of the computer screen, Petit-Four nestled herself in the crook of Maggie's arm facing the laptop as if waiting for the show to begin.

Maggie opened up her Skype application and dialed in Grace's number. She glanced at the kitchen clock. Eleven thirty in the morning here should make it right about Grace's kids' wake-up time in Indianapolis.

The screen expanded to show Grace's face, her hair combed and styled, lipstick on, earrings in place.

"Wow," Maggie said. "You look good for five thirty in the morning."

"Darling!" Grace said. "Is everything okay? Your dad got home okay? No problems?"

Grace had only been gone from Maggie's daily round a little over six months and still Maggie wasn't used to being without her. She was convinced she never would be.

"Yes, yes," Maggie said, shifting on the couch and pulling a dog toy from underneath her. "Everything's fine," she said. "I mean, he's exhausted but full steam ahead for the funeral and so forth."

"You still not coming home for it?" Grace turned her head to look at someone and spoke in a clipped tone. "No, ma'am, you sit right back down and finish that oatmeal. You are not eating snack bars for breakfast. Sorry, Maggie."

"No worries. How're the girls?"

"They're fine," Grace said. "Taylor is her usual titanic pain in the ass..."

"I assume that's not her you just spoke to."

Grace grinned. "No, that was the good one."

"And you swear you don't talk like this in front of them?"

"Maggie, darling, when you have children of your own some day, you'll realize how wonderfully resilient they are to the relentless mistakes and flaws of their parents."

"So that's a no?"

"I do my best, Maggie. How's that? I have to say I long for the day you put your hand to parenting. You'll be so good at it, you'll probably write books about it, until the day your perfect child enters her teen years and accurately informs you of what a truly crappy mother you are."

"I take it you're speaking from personal experience?"

"It doesn't matter," Grace said. "I am reliably informed by

Taylor's psychiatrist—and my own, for that matter—that it's just a stage."

"God, Grace, I didn't know things had gotten so bad. Was it leaving France, do you think?"

"Who knows? She was pretty difficult even in France if you recall. I think it's just being Taylor. Enough of that. You didn't interrupt my calming morning rituals to hear about the joys of parenting. What's up?"

Maggie sighed. "The Paris police have decided that Stan's death was a suicide."

"I see."

"Grace, there is no way he killed himself. No way."

"Well, what then? An accident?"

"It could be an accident."

"Okay, Maggie, it's early here and I have little monsters to get to school."

"I think somebody killed him."

"Based on what?"

"Based on it doesn't make sense that he would be on the balcony alone in the middle of a party."

"And if he wasn't alone..."

"Then he must've been pushed."

"Wow, pretty big leap there, Maggie. Excuse the image."

"How about I just feel it in my gut?"

"Maybe he had too much to drink and fell over?"

"How do you accidentally fall over a balcony railing three feet high?" Maggie said.

"I don't know," Grace said. "Three feet isn't very high. I'm sure I could manage to fall over it. But you still can't do anything about how the police ruled or the fact that Stan died."

Maggie chewed her lip and rearranged the dog in her lap.

"Maggie?"

"I feel like I have to do something."

"Do something? As in *investigate*, yourself?"

"Yes, Grace, I guess that's exactly what I mean. I can't accept that the world thinks Stan killed himself and I can't live with the idea that somebody out there will go unpunished after what he did."

"Laurent know about this?" Grace said. "Does he know you're thinking about strapping your Sherlock hat back on?"

"Nope."

"How are you two doing these days?"

"Peachy."

"Okay, now you really need to give me more than that. Everything was so good just a few months ago."

"He had the harvest last week."

"And that's always stressful because he's so preoccupied but you were in Paris during all that. And by the way, darling, can I tell you how totally pea-green I was to know that you were at all the shows? And you never would go when I lived in France!"

"Okay, let's stay on topic, here, Grace, okay?" Maggie said. "I really don't think I can let Stan's death rest without digging into it a little more."

"Don't you think you ought to give your marriage a little attention?"

"I can't do anything about Laurent's obsession," Maggie said.

"Well, you could do a little something about your reaction to what you perceive as his obsession."

"Now you're starting to sound like your shrink."

Maggie heard a muffled shriek in the background on Grace's end and she saw Grace turn her head and listen.

"I think Taylor's trying to brush Zou-zou's hair," Grace said. "Last time she did that blood was involved."

"Guess you better go."

"Guess I'd better. Maggie, talk to your husband, please. Laurent is such a good guy and he adores you. Talk to him."

"Yeah, okay, I will," Maggie said. "Go tend your babies, Grace. Love to Win."

"I'll tell him. Let me know what happens next, darling."

"You know I will. Bye, Grace."

Maggie clicked out of the application and sat on the couch for a quiet moment with the warm laptop on her knee and the dog nestled in her arms. She had a very strong feeling that something big was just about to happen.

And that it was *she* who would make it happen.

4

Laurent drove the Renault through the village of St-Buvard in the direction of the wine co-op on the far side of Aix. It was an hour's drive but he was lucky to have it at all, he knew. Being able to sort and crush his grapes at the co-op, and to bottle and distribute the wine from there made his livelihood possible. Without the co-op, his life's work simply could not happen.

It was distressing to see Maggie unhappy but he had learned long ago that what he did or didn't do had little effect on that. A pity that Grace had to leave France last year. While, on the face of it, one might never meet two more different women, they had found a common connection that was as inviolate and resolute as any two best friends could have. When Maggie had Grace to turn to, she was happier with her life with him.

He wished Maggie would find a hobby, like Danielle and her quilt-making. He wished she did not turn to him to fulfill every moment of her desires, or look to him to relieve her boredom. She once told him: "I wish we could always act like we just met." For himself, he was relieved that that time-consuming and often confusing part of their courtship was behind them.

His phone rang and he scooped it up.

"You are at the co-op?" Jean-Luc asked without preamble.

"Not yet," Laurent said, watching the last of the bright red leaves drift down from the trees that lined the two-lane road. "Nearly."

"Bernard has a contact in Lyons who may be interested in contracting with you for a dozen cases a week."

"Does he state terms?"

"No, he didn't want to overstep."

"I'll call him."

"It would be good, Laurent," Jean-Luc said. "It's a restaurant. Could open the door in Lyons for you."

"I am fine as I am, my friend," Laurent said.

"But you'll call him."

"I said I would."

"*Bien.*" Jean-Luc disconnected and Laurent couldn't help smiling as he tossed the phone back onto the seat. The man would always be looking out for him. If Laurent ever allowed himself to feel the kind of affection one man felt for a beloved uncle, that would be how he felt toward Jean-Luc. The thought reminded him of Maggie's uncle and her recent shock. Perhaps he had not been attentive enough to her in this. In his experience, if he did not anticipate the emotional heights to be reached *before* Maggie reached them, there was always trouble.

After Maggie finally got dressed for the day, the first thing she did was go to the French doors off the bedroom that led to the small stone balcony which afforded a panoramic view of the vineyard. Pulling on a thick wool sweater against the chilly autumn morning, she stood barefoot on the balcony and scanned the horizon for any sign of Laurent. The vines snaked across their stakes and poles, stripped of their fruit, and looking as depressing and barren as a thousand naked crucifixes. Laurent was nowhere to be seen. Of course, she reminded herself, he would be at the co-op, triaging the harvest and getting the grapes ready to be crushed. The co-op winery had no mechanical sorting equipment, which was fine with Laurent, Maggie knew. His wine was not a mass-produced product. It was lovingly hand-created, grape by perfect grape.

She sighed and retreated into the bedroom to change clothes for the day. He would be gone until past dark and then he would probably go straight to the café to drink and talk with the other *vignerons*—as if he hadn't seen enough of them all day. Maggie tried to imagine having a difficult child like Taylor to battle with all day long—and the child's father never home to help out, like Grace's husband Win was always doing. *What are the odds I'd get a good one?* she found herself thinking as she made her breakfast. *And if I didn't, it'd be too late to do anything about it. Just forge ahead with eighteen years of misery until the blighter finally left home.* Maggie sat on a kitchen stool and ate a piece of buttered toast with Laurent's homemade jam.

The afternoon stretched long and empty before her. She washed her coffee cup and put it away in the cabinet and then looked at the kitchen. It was absolutely pristine. Scrubbed until it sparkled with every dish linen and cooking spoon in its place. Laurent liked his kitchen just so. Like his vineyard. Like his life. She found herself marveling again at how he had turned his life around from when she first met him. Had he always been this precise kind of person? Is that even possible in the kind of life he had lived?

As she passed through the living room looking for a *New Yorker* magazine she hadn't read yet, her cell phone rang. She didn't recognize the number but the calling code said Paris. *Maybe those idiot police had decided to talk with her after all?*

"Hello?" she said.

"Maggie?" It was a woman's voice. "This is Bijou, *oui*?"

"Oh, Bijou! How are you?"

"Oh, not very well at all, Maggie. Not at all. We are none of us doing well. Are you coming back to Paris?"

Maggie sat down in the living room and watched the vineyard as it was pelted by a sudden downpour.

"I wasn't thinking about it," Maggie said. As soon as the words were out of her mouth, she realized that she had, on some level, been thinking of little else.

"Jeremy is so screwed up over Stan. We all are. We thought you might be coming back."

"Now that Paris Week is over," Maggie said. "What is it y'all normally do? Shouldn't Jeremy be heading back to California?"

"He says he won't go. He says Stan died in Paris and so he will stay in Paris."

"Well, he's emotional, is all," Maggie said. "Might do him good to stay on a little longer until he processes it better."

"What means *processes it*?"

"Nothing. Just a stupid American phrase I shouldn't have used."

"So, will you come back? You could stay at Stan's apartment."

I could, couldn't I?

"I don't know, Bijou, I'll think about it."

"Ted asked me to call you. Although we all want you to come."

"I gotta go, Bijou," Maggie said. "I'll let you know if I come, okay?"

"Okay. Maggie?"

"Yes?"

"The funeral is today?"

Maggie didn't have the heart to tell her it was really more of a graveside memorial service with just her parents in attendance. When she thought of all the friends Stan had—all the people who loved him—to think of him being sent to his final resting place with just two people to pray over him—and them virtual strangers—was just impossibly sad.

"It is," she said.

"I loved him so much," Bijou said, her voice thick with emotion.

"I know, Bijou. Take care of yourself, okay? I'll call if I come."

"*Ciao*, Maggie."

Maggie disconnected and sat staring out the window hearing the high whistle of the Mistral seeming to invade the very bones of the house.

She was going back to Paris.

HE SURPRISED HER.

Not only did he *not* go straight to the café after the co-op, he'd picked up takeout at her favorite Indian restaurant in Aix and was busy warming up the vindaloo and uncorking the wine when she came back from her late afternoon walk with Petit-Four. As soon as she rounded the last bend in the long and looping gravel driveway of *Domaine St-Buvard*, she saw his car parked in the garage and knew he had chosen to spend the evening with her. It had rained on the last half of her walk to the village and since going back to the village or forging ahead home both afforded the same degree of drenching, she just put up her collar and trudged home in the downpour. When she entered the house through the kitchen door, Petit-Four instantly shook herself, spraying water everywhere.

"Why does she wait until she is inside to do that?" Laurent growled as he grabbed a towel.

Assuming he was going to wipe down the mess the dog had created, Maggie was surprised when her husband draped it around her shoulders and, used it to draw her closer to him. Then he gave her a long kiss on the mouth.

"Drowned rodent?" Laurent said, his face still near hers.

"Rat," Maggie said, grinning and pulling back to dry some of the rain from her hair.

"There is time before dinner if you want to take your bath," Laurent said. "I'll bring a glass of wine up to you."

"Did I misread my calendar?" Maggie said, moving through the spicy aromas in the kitchen. "Is it my birthday?" She dropped the towel on a table in the hallway and trotted upstairs to her bedroom. After she'd stripped off her wet clothes, leaving them in a pile on the bathroom floor, she slipped into a hot bubble bath. The fragrance of lavender wafted pleasantly in the now steamy bathroom. When Laurent appeared ten minutes later with a glass of red wine, she had already relaxed nearly to the point of dozing off.

"Don't drown," he said, setting the wine on a small table next to the tub.

She reached out and touched his hand. "Help keep me awake," she said slyly.

He leaned over and kissed her, his hand reaching into the bath to draw her to him.

"You're getting all wet," Maggie murmured. "Either get in or help me out."

"Lady's choice," he said, this deep brown eyes glittering with intent.

An hour later, they sat in bed wrapped in bathrobes and duvets and dining on chicken *vindaloo* and *samosas*.

"When was the last time we ate in bed?" Maggie said, licking her fingers.

Laurent topped off her glass of wine and leaned back against the headboard.

"It's always too much trouble," he said, taking a sip of his wine.

Maggie gave him an inquisitive look. "But it wasn't too much trouble tonight," she said.

"It was worth the trouble tonight," he replied.

Maggie reached for her own wine and said nothing.

"Have you heard from your father today?" Laurent asked.

She shook her head. "I'm assuming it's done. The time difference makes it impossible to know real time."

"Are you sorry you didn't go back for it?"

"To Atlanta?" Maggie looked at him. "It would've cost a fortune to go back without a week's advance purchase."

"Even with a week's advance purchase," Laurent said. "But we have the money."

Maggie was trying to figure out where, if anywhere, this was going.

"I didn't need to go back," she said. "We're still going home at Christmas, right?"

"If you want."

"If I want? Laurent, you promised!"

"Of course, which is why we are going back."

"For a month."

Laurent sighed and put his wine down. "I cannot be gone for that long," he said.

"I don't believe this." Maggie wrenched her bathrobe tight around her. "You're not staying the whole time?"

"Not if the whole time is a month, no."

"May I ask why not? The harvest is done, the planting won't start for months. What possible reason could you have?"

"It is too long for a visit," he said. "My life is here, my home is here. I would ask that you come back with me, *cherie*, but I understand if you cannot."

"You know how there's nothing for you in Atlanta? Nothing for you to do?"

Laurent nodded warily.

"Well, that's what St-Buvard is for me."

"*St-Buvard* is your home," Laurent said. Maggie thought she detected a dangerous tone under the words. For a moment, she caught a glimpse of the man Laurent used to be.

It was on the tip of her tongue to retort that *Atlanta* was her home but something stopped her. Maybe it was the look in his eye, or maybe it was the knowledge of what she needed to tell him next that made her not poke around too energetically into any snake holes.

"I want you to do what you feel comfortable doing, Laurent," she said, trying to sound as reasonable and mature as she could.

"*Merci*," he said, sipping his wine and watching her warily over the rim of his glass.

"Same as I must do with regards to the botched investigation into my uncle's death in Paris."

He sat up quickly. "No," he said.

"Well, I would hope you would let me go with your blessing since it means so much to me..." Maggie said, her heart pounding through her words. *Had she ever directly defied him?* There were times she worked around him without his knowledge but she had never engaged in open warfare with him.

"That is *logique idiote*," he said. "Would I let you drink petrol if you were convinced it would help you to fly?"

"There is no real reason I shouldn't do this and every reason I should, even if it just helps me to better adjust to what happened."

"You barely knew him!"

"That's only part of what I'm talking about, Laurent. Besides, you don't need me here."

"You are my wife. I want you here!"

This was a first. She had never heard him yell before, least of all at her. She found it extremely unnerving.

"*Why* do you want me here? You're gone all day long and half the time the evenings too."

"If I had an office job in Atlanta, I would be just as gone and you would not complain."

Did he have a point? Was it not the time he spent from her that bothered her? Was her real problem that he was so happy doing it?

"Does it matter that I think I need to do it?" she said.

"No. You think many things. Often they are just silly."

"Dear God, do you even care how offensive you sound?"

"You will not go, Maggie. You will accept the police ruling and you will stop turning our lives upside down."

"Well, none of that is true," Maggie said, feeling stronger and more resolute by the minute. "I am definitely going, in fact, first thing in the morning, and I will *not* accept the police ruling because it's bullshit and as for turning our lives upside down, you're never here so I can't believe I have that power."

The two of them stared at each other, both fuming.

Maggie began to slowly collect their dishes from the bed. She decided she needed to stop talking and let him come round in his own time. The more she talked, the greater chance there was that she would say something she was sorry for—something that had nothing to do with her wanting to go to Paris.

"If you go..." Laurent said, raising Maggie's hopes that he was allowing the possibility of her leaving, "I will consider it an informal separation."

Maggie froze. "What do you mean, *informal*?"

"I will consider us separated," Laurent said flatly, his eyes cold and hooded as he regarded her.

"Why do you have to do that?" Maggie said, sagging onto the bed, the dishes in her hands. "Why can't you just let me take a few weeks to investigate this on my own up there, satisfy my doubts and come home, no damage done?"

"Because I have been down this road with you before," Laurent said, looking away. "Your *investigating* always ends up with you getting stitches in your head or standing in front of madmen holding pistols in your face."

"This won't be like that," Maggie said.

"Are we adding lying to the list of new things we are doing, Maggie?" Laurent asked redirecting his gaze at her. "Or have I just not noticed up until now?"

"Do I ask you to live a totally risk-free life?" Maggie asked.

"Weren't there times when you did what you had to do in spite of the consequences?"

"*Quoi que*," Laurent said, grabbing his pillow and standing up to signal that they would not sleep together tonight. *Whatever.*

"Laurent, please don't," Maggie said moving to grab his arm.

He pulled it from her grasp. "You want to have your way and Laurent smiling, too," he said. "But you can only have one, Maggie. I think I know which one you will choose."

He stared at her for a moment and when she didn't answer, Maggie thought the fire went out of his eyes and he only looked sad. He turned and left the room, leaving her alone with the dirty Indian dishes and the little dog looking expectantly from Maggie to the doorway.

5

The view from Stan's balcony off the Rue Galande was nothing short of breathtaking. Maggie marveled that she had been so busy with her uncle during her week with him that she hadn't fully noticed before. Situated on the Île de la Cité and less than a block from the Cathédrale Notre Dame, his Saint Germain apartment building in the Latin Quarter had been built in the 19th century during the time when the street was alive with infamous cabarets. Now it was full of bustling shops and cafés. Her first night staying there with Stan she had trouble sleeping due to the noise from the street life.

From where she sat this morning at the tiny bistro table on her uncle's balcony, she could see the famous Gothic cathedral with its flying buttresses. She had arrived midmorning, her legs shaky from the three-floor walk up to Stan's apartment and her mood unsettled by the gravity of what she was doing. Laurent had driven her to the train station early. But instead of a kiss goodbye at the platform, he offered only a hurt and resolute stare as she dragged her bags from the car and into the station.

The first thing she had done after unpacking her suitcase was to leave a note on the apartment next door, letting Stan's neighbor know that she had returned and would take back the cat—at least temporarily—whenever the neighbor liked. She saw a bowl of cat kibble in the darkened hallway and wondered if Stan's cat had agreed to the temporary custody arrangements or had insisted on making his own.

Now, as she drank a Diet Coke on the balcony, Maggie allowed herself to feel the mixture of many different sensations. The little apartment was quiet. Made quieter by Petit-Four's absence, Maggie thought. She had opted to let Danielle care for the little dog while Maggie was in Paris. She already missed her.

The weariness of her trip was made worse by the emotional upset that her parting with Laurent had been. She had to believe that he would forgive or understand in time—once she had returned and all was well. In the meantime, she thought it probably best to push thoughts of him—and the state of her marriage—to a quiet, infrequently visited corner of her mind so that she could work on the matter she had come to Paris to address. Another reason for her prolonged stay on the balcony was her resistance to be in Stan's apartment without him. She had promised her father that she would sort and pack Stan's belongings in preparation for the sale of the flat but it was way too soon to think about all that.

The other thread of emotion that was tangled up with her sadness and guilt over how she left Laurent was the undiluted delight that she felt at being back in Paris. As she sat and looked at Notre Dame, she remembered visiting it as a young girl with her mother and her sister Elise. She remembered the summer she had spent in Paris between her sophomore and junior year of college. She remembered the café she sat in on the Rue de la Paix when she learned the shocking truth about Laurent and the death of her sister's only child. She remembered a tumble of weekend jaunts with Grace. The very spirit of the city infused her with a thrill and level of excitement that she knew could never be replicated by any place else or anything else.

She was in Paris. And whether the memories were good or bad, it was awesome.

JEAN-LUC SLAMMED SHUT the trunk of his ancient Volvo and turned to see his wife disappear into the house. He smiled as she suddenly turned—as if wanting to catch one more last glimpse of him, too—waved and shut the door between them. For happiness to have come to him at this point in his life was a miracle that Jean-Luc would never stop being grateful for. That Danielle of all people could love him had reawakened his belief in God.

"Ready, Jean-Luc?"

Jean-Luc turned his attention to Laurent, sitting in the passenger's side of his station wagon like a hulk squeezed into a bumper car. They had made plans to ride to the co-op this morning before Laurent's wife had decided to piss off to Paris. If either of them had had any sense, they would have changed their plans and gone in separate cars. Jean-Luc settled into the driver's seat. He wasn't good at this, he knew. But he loved Laurent like a son. Like the son he would never have. To see the American making him so miserable—it was all Jean-Luc could do not to tip his hand and reveal how much he distrusted her.

"Is the sorting done?" he asked.

Laurent grunted with what Jean-Luc deciphered to be an affirmative.

"Did you call Bernard about the Lyons business?"

"I haven't forgotten, Jean-Luc." *That was Laurent telling him to get off his back*, Jean-Luc thought.

"Any word from your wife?" he asked. "She arrive safely?"

"I assume," Laurent growled.

"While I have yet to be separated from my own beloved," Jean-Luc said. "I am sure I would call to confirm that she arrived without stress or mishap."

"Maggie has lived on her own in the world long before she

married me," Laurent said, staring out the window at the barren fall landscape. "She is perfectly capable of dealing with any travel inconvenience."

"Oh, yes," Jean-Luc said. "As I'm sure *ma belle* Danielle is, too. She is not helpless. She has lived a lifetime without Jean-Luc. I was thinking more along the lines of loving support," he said. "Not as a travel agent would give, but as a husband."

"Speak your mind, Jean-Luc," Laurent said. "I tire of the hedging."

"If you didn't want her to go," Jean-Luc said, "then you should have made her stay."

"It's not that simple," Laurent said.

"And if you allowed her to go—as you obviously did because she left—then this..." Jean-Luc waved a hand to indicate Laurent's behavior, "...makes no sense."

Laurent looked at him as if trying to understand his words.

"She is shopping in Paris?" Jean-Luc asked. "Women love to shop."

"No," Laurent said. "She is not shopping."

"It is another man, then?"

"So, shopping or a lover, those are her options?"

Jean-Luc shrugged. "What else?"

"Maggie doesn't need to run to someone else," Laurent said, turning to look back at the forlorn countryside, "She just needs to get away from me."

"Is it you or St-Buvard she flees?"

"What's the difference? Would Danielle leave you because she didn't like the town you lived in?"

"Unimaginable."

"*Exactement*."

There didn't seem much more to say or if there was, Jean-Luc had no idea what it might be. "*Bien*," he said.

It was going to be a long drive.

. . .

Maggie picked up her cell phone just in case she had accidentally set it on mute—although she knew she hadn't—and had missed Laurent's call. She reasoned that if he wasn't going to kiss her goodbye after weeks, maybe a month's separation, he probably wasn't going to call her to see how she was doing. She knew him well enough to know he wasn't given to idle or staged gestures of affection. And right now, he was mad. Madder than she had ever seen him. And unfortunately, Laurent's brand of mad was silent and distancing. *We could probably use a good old fashioned knock-down drag out fight*, she thought with surprise. He was so controlled—due to years of needing to keep himself in check as if his life depended on it—that a serious fight with him was akin to a slow, deadly smolder. Maggie found herself wondering what would be left when the fire finally went out.

"*Allo*? Madame Dernier? *Allo*? Are you there?"

Maggie got up from her balcony chair—it had gotten too nippy for sitting out there anyway—and hurried to the front door.

"Oh, Mademoiselle Bonnet!" she said. "I was out on the balcony and didn't hear you. Were you knocking long? You got my note, I see."

The woman—no more a Mademoiselle than she was a springer spaniel—winced in what Maggie decided to believe was a smile and edged into the apartment.

"It is cold in the hallway!" she said, hugging herself. "I have been knocking for several minutes. Please, call me Genevieve."

"Please come in," Maggie said. "Can I get you a cup of tea?"

"Yes, that would be very nice," the woman said, openly gawking at the interior of Stan's apartment. "It has been a long time since I was inside Monsieur Newberry's apartment," she said. "The last owner was a very good friend of mine who died, unfortunately."

"Oh, I'm sorry," Maggie said as she turned on the electric kettle in the kitchen and took two ceramic mugs from Stan's cabinets. As she piled sugar cubes, napkins and spoons on a little tray, the woman stood in the kitchen doorway.

"The cat has found another home, I'm afraid," she said, watching Maggie dump a small pile of store-bought cookies onto a plate.

"I figured he might," Maggie said. "I saw the bowl in the hallway. At least you tried. Thanks."

"A man came last week asking after the cat."

"Really?" Maggie poured the water over the teabags in each of the mugs and picked up the tray. "Let's go into the living room," she said.

The apartment was extremely small but room enough for one person. Maggie set the tray down on the tiny coffee table between two armchairs.

"I wonder who it was," she said.

"He wasn't really interested in the cat, Madame," the woman said, taking a mug from Maggie and dropping two sugar cubes into it. Maggie handed her a spoon. "He wanted the key that Monsieur Newberry had given me."

"I didn't know you had a key."

"Oh, yes." She pulled the key out of her pocket and laid it down on the coffee table. "Unless you would like me to keep it," she said.

"Did you let the man into the apartment?"

"Never! I could tell he was lying about the cat. He tried to prevent me from closing my door! I had to threaten to call the police."

"Interesting," Maggie said. "If you don't mind, I think I will hang on to the key, at least for now. Had you ever seen him before, this guy?"

"Of course, many times." The woman was looking around the living room with great interest. "He was Monsieur Newberry's lover. He was often here. But if Monsieur Newberry did not trust him with his own key...Pfutt!" She made a face as if to say: *to hell with him.*

Maggie drank her tea and watched her visitor closely. She didn't look like she was intentionally dissembling. She looked like the typical nosy, busybody neighbor interested in spreading gossip or preening because she believed she had special information. In Maggie's experience, people like that were usually very useful in an investigation.

"How long will you be staying?" Genevieve asked, slurping her tea loudly.

"I'm not really sure. Long enough to pack up my uncle's things."

"You will sell the apartment?"

Maggie stared at her and then looked through the window to the hazy image of the Cathedral barely discernable in the distance. Until this very moment it hadn't occurred to her that she might not sell it. She looked around the flat. It was small. It was well-located. It was bright. It was perfect. She turned back to her visitor and grinned.

"Probably," she said, sipping her tea and feeling for the first time in a long time—at home.

THAT NIGHT, as she assembled a simple meal of store-bought quiche and a salad in the tiny galley kitchen, Maggie revisited Genevieve's words. *Was it Jeremy who came demanding entrance to Stan's apartment?* She thought there had been something between them and while there had been no overt proclamations to confirm it, she had assumed that both Jeremy and Stan were gay. *But why would Jeremy need to get into the apartment?*

She looked around as she set her plate down on the small dining table off the kitchen. *Was there something here of value beyond Stan's TV, stereo and computer?* Her eyes fell on the closed laptop on top of the bookcase next to the dining table. *Was there something on the computer that Jeremy needed? Or perhaps just didn't want anyone else to see?* She hadn't opened her uncle's computer yet. She assumed it was password protected and hadn't felt up to the endless guessing that would be required on her part to crack it. The police had told her that there were ways to get into a computer after someone's death and that they would assist her in doing so if she needed that. She chewed her quiche and eyed the laptop. *I'm almost positive I do*, she thought.

The day's light had faded fast and Maggie ate her meal staring out into the inky black void that had been such an extraordinary view all day. She thought about turning on the TV but in her experience, trying to watch French television was even worse than being lonely and bored.

She tried to gather her thoughts for how she would proceed in determining the truth behind her uncle's death. It made sense to search his apartment first, she thought, since it was right here. And that included whatever was on his laptop. Then, she would reach out to his friends to see if the week since his death had altered anything in the way that they remembered him or how they appeared to her. It was helpful, she thought, that Jeremy had decided to stay in Paris a little longer. Especially if the reason he had decided to stay had nothing to do with grieving Stan and everything to do with covering up a crime.

Reminding herself not to line up her suspects before she had some actual clues to underscore the effort, Maggie picked up her dish to take to the kitchen when her cell rang.

It was Laurent.

"Hey," she said.

"You are arrived safely, I see," he responded coldly.

"Yeah, I did, thanks," she said, reseating herself and pushing her dinner plate away on the table. "Everything okay there?"

"Why wouldn't it be?"

"Laurent, I am so sorry about all of this," Maggie said. "But I really need to be here. My father has asked me to pack up Stan's flat to get it ready to sell—"

"Non."

"Well, yes he did. He wants me to—"

"At least you can be honest about why you are there," Laurent said with more heat than Maggie ever remembered hearing from him.

"I *am* being honest," she said.

"*Non*. You are not there for that reason. You are there to be investigating like all the times before."

"Well, that's partly—"

"And you are there to not be here."

Maggie let the phrase sit for a moment. To argue with it would be to lie and she owed him more than that.

"I can't explain why," she said. "I'm sorry, Laurent. It's something wrong with me."

"Je sais," he said. *I know*.

"I'm not asking you to change who you are," Maggie said. "But I need more than what I've got in St-Buvard."

"More than what you have with me," he said, flatly.

"I'm not cut out to be a farmer's wife!" she blurted.

"That would mean you are not *cut out* to be my wife," Laurent said. "Because I am a farmer."

"I would never ask you to give up your vineyard for me."

"If you make that the reason you leave me, that is exactly what you are asking."

"I'm not leaving you, Laurent! Would you quit calling this a separation? I'd rather be miserable and making quilts in a dirt hut than leave you!"

"Did you ever think how living with someone who is always miserable and wishing to be somewhere else might feel?"

"I..." Maggie felt her eyes sting and her throat close up with the effort not to cry.

"If what I want makes you miserable," he said, almost reasonably, "I am not truly loving you or caring for you."

"Laurent, don't say that."

"*D'accord*," he said. "I am glad you went to Paris. It is best for both of us that you are there."

"Now you're just being mean."

"*Non*. I am being honest with what I see and what I feel. Isn't that always what you are asking of me?"

"I love you, Laurent," Maggie whispered, her eyes clotted with unshed tears.

"*Quoi que*," he said. *Whatever*. And disconnected.

6

Maggie closed the heavy door to the apartment building and stepped out onto the narrow street that was lined with shops and would, in a few blocks, empty out onto Quai Saint Michel. From last night's noise and the trash she stepped around, she could easily imagine the students, tourists and general bohemians sleeping late this morning. It was nearly November and the wind whistling through the close alley was mean and insistent. Maggie pulled her collar up against it and tucked her head. Coming in yesterday from the train station, she had noticed the *boulangerie* on the corner. It had been doing a brisk business then—people collecting their *batons* for *le dîner*. This morning the shop still looked busy but Maggie was refreshed and ready to begin her day—even if that meant speaking a foreign language to the typically sour counter help. *Or maybe that's just in St-Buvard*, she found herself thinking, as she pushed open the beautifully ornate wooden door into the shop and was greeted by a smile and a sing-songy "*Bonjour*, Madame!"

"*Bonjour*," Maggie said, her own smile involuntarily prompted by the proprietor's friendliness and the heavenly aromas of the bakery.

This is why I love Paris, she found herself thinking as she selected several sweet rolls for her breakfast. Due to an unfortunate series of deadly events, her own village of St-Buvard had not had a bakery for going on three years. A traveling bread truck made the rounds twice a week and was, in fact, one of the primary café topics of disgust and complaint by literally every soul in the village. *Was there any place as welcoming and delightful as a Paris bakery?* Maggie "*au revoired*" the chatty bakery counter woman and stepped back out into the crisp morning air. She walked briskly to the courtyard in front of Notre Dame, grateful for the lack of tourists this time of year, and settled on a stone bench to eat her breakfast.

He came up on her at the exact moment she had a good excess of custard on her bottom lip.

"Allow me," he said, handing her a paper napkin with a flourish.

Maggie took it and squinted up at him.

"Hey, Ted," she said. "You stalking me?"

"Is it stalking because I happen to see you leave a shop I often frequent and followed you to this spot where you obviously need my services?"

"Yeah, that's pretty much the textbook definition of stalking."

"May I join you?"

Maggie scooted over on the bench. "How did you know I was back?" she asked, dabbing at her lips with the napkin.

"I didn't," he said. "I was surprised to see you this morning. You're staying at Stan's?"

Maggie nodded. "I needed to start clearing out his place," she said. "To sell."

"Need any help?" he asked.

Maggie wondered, for a moment, if it could've been *Ted* instead of Jeremy who tried to strong arm Genevieve. But no, she said he was Stan's lover. And Ted was clearly, and totally straight. In spades.

"Maybe," Maggie said. "I loved the stories you told about Stan at his apartment."

Ted nodded. "I didn't know him as long as the others," he said. "But what we had was for keeps."

"Yeah, he had that effect on a lot of people."

"I still can't believe he's gone."

"I know."

"Do you want to have dinner tonight?"

"Tonight?"

"You have plans?"

"No. I…I'm not sure."

"You're not sure if you have plans?"

"No, I'm not sure I want to. You know I'm married, right?"

Ted laughed. "Oh, like that means anything in Paris!" he said.

"Are you joking?"

"Yes, yes, I'm joking. I wouldn't dream of hitting on a married woman."

"*Now* you're joking."

"Sorry. But I'm just as happy to go to dinner with you to enjoy your company and nothing more. Not to worry."

"Can I take a rain check? I really need to get to the bottom of Stan's apartment. He was incredibly neat and tidy but still—it's a lot of stuff to decide what to do with."

"How about I bring groceries to your place and make you dinner?" Ted clapped his hands together as if this was just about the most brilliant idea he could imagine. "Then you could work and I would feel like I was helping but still not intruding."

Maggie had to admit the plan had its merits. For the slightest of moments she found herself wondering what Laurent would be doing tonight.

"What would you make?" she asked.

. . .

MAGGIE SPENT her afternoon stacking and sorting all of Stan's home office. She intended to leave the laptop until last. When she taped up the final box, she allowed herself to take a break and sat on the couch, her shoulders aching from the position of being hunched over most of the day.

It was amazing how you could get to know someone, she marveled, *just by going through their things.* The first hour, she felt like she was invading Stan's private world, but by the time she started to become more efficient about what was worthless and what wasn't, she had become hardened to the special little notes he might scrawl in the margin of some book or the collection of museum magnets he seemed incapable of passing up. She was thankful that he had been so organized. She had been instructed by her father not to discard anything—regardless of how worthless it may appear—until after the will was read lest it was some treasure that he had bequeathed.

Regardless of how streamlined she became with the task, it was a sad day's work. She found herself looking forward to Ted's arrival and that first sip of wine that would signal the end of the hardest part of her day. She glanced at the clock. He would be here within the hour. She scanned the results of her labor. *Was there anything here Ted shouldn't see?* she wondered. Everything looked straightforward—the evidence and detritus of a man who lived alone, who loved books, clothes, his friends. Her glance fell on the laptop. *But that may well tell a different story,* she thought.

Before heading into the bedroom and, eventually, her bath, she picked up the computer and slid it under the couch. Not the greatest of hiding places, she admitted, but at least someone would have to be actively searching for it to find it.

And that would tell a lot in itself.

JEAN-LUC PUSHED AWAY from the dining table. He had already gained twenty pounds since his marriage. A bachelor's life had left little room for any excess culinary enjoyment if it meant making it himself. Jean-Luc cooked minimally and never had enough money to waste on restaurant meals. He watched his beloved Danielle as she swept the dirty dishes from the table, a lightness in her step which meant she had prepared a surprise dessert for him. Jean-Luc loosened his belt another notch.

They lived on her money, in her home. After a lifetime of odd jobs—many of them underhanded—and usually seasonal, Jean-Luc had little to offer her but his love. His complete and undying love. And his respect. All of which she had no experience with in her previous marriage. It was more than enough for her. He listened to her as she hummed in the kitchen, readying whatever presentation she was creating for his delight. He swore he would not let his pride interfere with their happiness.

"Have you talked with Maggie since she left?" he called to her.

Danielle popped her head out the kitchen doorway. "She has only been gone a day," she said. "Close your eyes, now!"

Jean-Luc dutifully closed them and tucked his hands into his lap. A prior surprise had ended up down the front of his shirt when he'd blindly brought a hand up to scratch his nose just when his beloved was placing an oversized wedge of cream pie in front of him.

"Open your eyes!"

When he did, he gasped in true delight at the marvel of burnt sugar crisscrossing the top of one of his very favorite delights: *crème brûlée*.

"Do you like it?"

She knew he loved it. For a moment, tears threatened him as he looked at her beaming face, so happy to please him, so full of love for him.

"I love it, *mon amour*," he said hoarsely, reaching out to take her hand as she sat back down at the table. "How is it that I deserve you?"

She smiled and handed him a spoon to crack the hardened top of the custard.

"Why did you ask me about Maggie?" she said.

Jean-Luc shrugged. "Laurent thinks she has left him."

"No! I thought they were getting along well."

Jean-Luc spooned past the hardened sugar surface of his dessert to the creamy depths within. "He is convinced she wants to divorce."

"For what possible reason?" Danielle looked truly strickened.

"He says she hates the country. Hates being married to a farmer."

"That makes no sense," Danielle said. "He must be misunderstanding. Men do so often."

"Perhaps you could talk with her?"

"Yes, of course. Do you mean call her?"

Jean-Luc sighed. "I am very selfish to always want you here," he said. "You used to go to Paris often."

Danielle took his hand in hers. "While you are here, I am not lured by anything Paris has to offer," she said.

He smiled, a tinge of guilt for all that he had when Laurent was in such pain.

"Laurent's wife does not feel the same."

"You want me to talk with her."

"I don't want you to, no," Jean-Luc said. "But Laurent is being stupid and prideful. He will not stop her and she cannot be allowed to simply go."

"I'll leave tomorrow," she said.

"Perhaps," he said, feeling his recent euphoria beginning to slip away. "Perhaps the weekend is soon enough."

She squeezed his hand. "I am the luckiest woman in all of France," she said. "And you are a good friend to Laurent. In spite of himself."

"I know," he said, missing her already. "It is quite a sacrifice."

. . .

Maggie moved out to the balcony where Ted was smoking and handed him his brandy snifter. Dinner had been lovely. Not too fussy, more assembled than cooked. Maggie noted with pleasure that the kitchen was still neat and orderly.

"Quite the chef," Maggie said, as she sipped her own brandy and smiled at him before turning to look at the mesmerizing view of the Cathedral lit up, its buttresses in majestic flight spotlighted in the dark.

"Not really," Ted said, turning to her. "Unless you call putting cheese, olives, roasted peppers and cold chicken on a baguette cooking."

"I call it delicious," Maggie said. "And I thank you. The wine was good too. All of it was lovely."

"You get a lot of work done today?"

"A decent start anyway."

"That's good. Where in the States did you say you were from?"

Maggie looked at him and smiled. "Atlanta," she said. "And you?"

"Nome."

"God, as in Alaska? I don't think I've ever met anyone from Alaska."

"Not surprised. There's only, like, nine of us."

Maggie laughed. "So how did you break out? Someone with your looks, you must've been a statewide celebrity."

"Yeah, it actually wasn't a benefit, being good looking in what is still, basically, a frontier environment."

"I can imagine."

"I mean, here's me, interested in acting and fashion and literature in a state that is all about fishing and trekking and flying and crap."

"Must've been hard."

"You have no idea."

"So?"

"Well, I headed off to school in California."

"Where they prized what you had to offer."

"I'm more than a pretty face, Maggie," he said with mock seriousness.

Maggie laughed. The wine and the brandy combined with the bracing air and the invigorating company helped ease the unhappiness out of the day for her. She sat down in one of the outdoor chairs.

"How'd you end up in Paris?" she asked.

"This led to that," he said, sitting down next to her. "I got into modeling which turned out to be so much easier than acting."

"No memorizing."

"Exactly. And then I started writing because I had a lot of time on my hands between modeling gigs."

"You're a writer?"

"I am. I've got two romance novels with an American publisher and now I only model when I want. Usually just Paris Week, to keep my hand in."

"That is so cool."

"You're not a writer? I thought Stan said you were."

"I wonder why he said that. Although, to tell you the truth, since I've been here, I have been writing down the odd scene or description. It's almost like I'm thinking about writing a story on some subconscious level."

"That's often how it starts."

"And you never married?"

"Boy, that was a jump!"

"Well, I guess it was the thought of you writing romance novels that made me wonder. Most romance novels are written by women, aren't they?"

"I'm not gay, Maggie."

"No, I know," Maggie said, hurriedly. "Or, at least, I didn't think you were."

"I was married once a long time ago," he said. "It wasn't for me."

"It's hard," Maggie admitted, her glance stealing back to the darkened façade of Notre Dame.

Without warning, Ted leaned over and kissed her. Maggie pulled away, spilling her brandy in the process.

"Ted, no," she said. "I can't do this. I thought you understood that."

"Can't fault me for trying," he said, grinning.

Maggie stood up. "This friendship won't work if I have to be on guard against some move of yours, Ted. I'm married and very happily."

"Sure, okay, sorry about that," he said.

Maggie brushed at her sweater where she'd spilled her brandy.

"Why don't we go inside so you can attend to that?" he said, standing, too. "I may not know a lot, but I do know a few things about the care and repair of clothing."

That made Maggie smile. As they reentered the apartment, Ted passed Maggie on the way to the kitchen.

"Do you have cotton towels?" he asked. "And *l'eau gazeuse*?" He went to the refrigerator. At the same time, Maggie noticed that one of the little drawers to the coffee table was half open and she tried to remember if she had forgotten to shut it.

"Whatever I have is in the kitchen," she called to him as she set her brandy glass down and moved to the couch. She started to close the little drawer when she noticed a four by six inch photograph sticking out.

Had she done this in her hurry to get ready? She thought she had emptied this drawer. She pulled the picture out and looked at it. It was a photograph of her uncle taken many years earlier. He stood with his arm around an attractive young woman and something about the way they stood made Maggie think it was not a platonic relationship. Looking closely at the woman she was surprised to realize that it was Diane. Much younger, with a smile on what was now a permanently frowning face, and dressed downright provocatively in a mini skirt and tight sweater. Maggie turned the photo over. Someone—and she did not recognize the scrawl as her uncle's—had written the date: 1994. And one word: *Asshole!*

7

Jeremy stood on the street corner watching the day's fading light extinguish and then cloak the street in varying shades of gray. When he'd seen Ted go into the apartment hours earlier—with a bag of groceries!—it had been difficult to believe that Stan's niece was actually using Stan's home as a *pied à terre* from which to date someone known to everyone in town to be the randiest, most promiscuous man in all of Paris. Finally, after a very uncomfortable ninety minutes whereupon he was finally forced to buy a sandwich and anchor a café table on the street corner, he saw the two of them emerge from the building to sit on the balcony.

Stan's balcony. The very balcony that he, Jeremy, had spent so many pleasant evenings laughing and talking with Stan. Now Stan was gone for good and so were those evenings—or any hope of future ones. And his niece was simply picking up the baton and carrying on as if nothing had happened. Had Stan left the flat to her? Had the will been read yet? Did she know something? Did she suspect him?

His phone vibrated against his chest and he plucked it from an inside pocket.

"Oui?"

"Where are you?"

"What do you want, Bijou?"

"Did you know Stan's niece is in town?"

"I did."

"Well, I cannot imagine how. I just heard from her."

"She called *you*?" Jeremy involuntarily turned away from the balcony to focus on his conversation with Bijou.

"Earlier this evening," Bijou said. "She wants to see everyone."

"And so she called *you*?"

"I called her when she was in the country, did you know that? I told her that I thought she should come back to Paris."

"You did what?!"

"Jeremy, are you drunk? Where are you?"

"Why did you want her back in Paris?"

There was a pause. "Well, why not?"

"Because she does not accept the police report on Stan's death, that is why," Jeremy said, turning back around to look up at the balcony. It was empty. "She thinks he was murdered."

"Well," Bijou said, "maybe he was. Did you ever think of that? Makes more sense than him jumping to his death in the middle of a party."

"You're just angry because it was *your* party," Jeremy said, furious with himself for missing the part where the two went back inside.

Bijou hung up on him.

It didn't matter, he thought. *Now comes the interesting part.* If he was right about what happened next, he would not see Ted emerge from Stan's apartment building until very early tomorrow morning. He signaled to the waiter and ordered a whiskey. Before it came, his phone chimed and he looked at the screen to see that Bijou had sent him a text.

It read, "*Tomorrow at Le Bal. 8 p.m.*" Before he could reply, he was stunned to see Ted approach his table from across the street.

"*Bon soir*, Jeremy," he said, hunching his shoulders into his heavy jacket as if that would keep him warmer against the cold night. "Dining alone?"

Jeremy's mouth gaped in surprise as Ted waved to him and trotted down the sidewalk in the direction of his own apartment.

Another chime from his cell phone, still in his hand, alerted him to yet another text from Bijou. This one read simply: "*Putain*."

THE NEXT DAY, Maggie was up early. Pulling on jeans and her heavy wool coat against the chill winds whipping around the sharp corners of her street, she ran down to the corner *boulangerie* for her usual bag of sugar powdered and drizzled breakfast. The neighborhood bistro had just opened its doors as she walked back to her flat so she went in for a large *café crème*, wondering when the French in Paris had started offering take-out coffee. The café in St-Buvard still professed to be outraged by the whole concept, forcing anyone with a caffeine fixation to actually sit and drink it out of ceramic cups while watching the world go by. Maggie knew her uncle had a perfectly serviceable espresso maker in his kitchen but she was sure it would take longer than she had in Paris to figure out how to work it.

She planned on spending her day finishing up with Stan's paperwork, boxing up his photo collections, and packing his clothes. He had two closets full of suits, sweaters, shirts and shoes. Assuming that many of the pieces were vintage and therefore valuable, Maggie would wait until after she heard from her father before she decided what to do with them. It occurred to her that some of his friends might like a tie or handkerchief as a treasured memento.

Especially whoever pushed him off a balcony to his death, she thought as she taped up the last box. Stan knew everyone at that party, she was sure of it. He wouldn't have gone onto the balcony with a stranger—not with Maggie downstairs and not knowing a soul. He went with a friend. A friend who killed him.

The question was *which one*?

At lunchtime, Maggie pulled out the remnants from last night's supper. She felt good about how she had left things with Ted. She liked him a lot and could really use a friend in Paris, but she didn't need the complications he seemed only too willing to create. She felt she had been honest with him and direct. Now it was up to him, she thought as she smeared a long swathe of mustard on her sandwich.

When the phone rang she realized her first thought was always going to be that it might be Laurent.

It wasn't.

"Hey, Maggie," Ted said. "Did I catch you at a bad time?"

"Not at all," she said. "Just enjoying the rerun of last night's supper. Thank you again."

"Oh, good," he said. "Listen, you did say you wanted Diane there tonight, right?"

"That's right."

"I just wanted to double check that you don't want to do this one at a time," Ted said. "This group feeds off each other. You won't get the same level of cooperation together that you would separately. That's especially true with Jeremy."

"Well," Maggie said, doubtfully. "I guess you have a point."

"How about we call off Diane and Jeremy and just do me and Bijou tonight? You can do the other two another time."

"Good idea, Ted. Thanks," Maggie said. "I'll text them but if you talk to them first..."

"No problem."Oh, and Ted?"

"Yeah?"

"How about we make it just me and Bijou tonight?"

"Oh."

"I mean, you and I already talked last night..."

"Absolutely. No problem. Good idea."

"Thanks, Ted," Maggie said. "And thanks again for dinner last night."

"*Pas du tout*," Ted said, a little crisply, Maggie thought.

Le Bal was not unlike any of a hundred Parisian brasseries. It was at least three hundred years old and had been in service as a place for people to gather and eat and drink for almost all of that time. It was dark with gleaming brass fixtures and ancient chandeliers which hovered over most of the tables. Maggie chose it as a good place to meet because it wasn't right in her neighborhood but not terribly far either. Plus, it was just far enough off the beaten tourist path—even though the season had deflated now that Paris Week was over—not to be too populated by English-speakers.

As Maggie waited for Bijou, she was determined to conduct the whole interview—for that was exactly what she considered the evening to be—in French. She had been pleasantly surprised to realize that her language skills had improved to the point that they had. She and Laurent spoke a mixture of French and English at home but she had made a point of speaking more French with him than she had her first two years in France when she had stubbornly refused to speak any. The only slight downside about her new found pride in her language mastery was the fact that she was often received by Parisian shopgirls as speaking what she could only describe as hillbilly French. The *patois* of the region of France which St-Buvard was a part was very different from the beautifully precise French spoken in Paris. She felt that the reaction she received was better than if she had been caught speaking Americanized French—or not bothering at all—but she was still enduring that famous uptilt of the Gallic nose for her efforts.

"*Bon soir,* Maggie!" Bijou waved to Maggie from the door, stopping only long enough to embrace and vigorously kiss at least two patrons on the way to Maggie's table. Maggie stood and the two kissed cheeks before Bijou shrugged out of her coat—a full length silver fox that did amazing things for the model's complexion.

As if she needed any help, Maggie couldn't help but think. Bijou was so striking that there was no chance any companion would ever be noticed, let alone favored in comparison. Maggie watched as every head in the restaurant, women included, turned to gawk at Bijou. *And this in a city where fashion and beauty permeate,* Maggie thought.

"So smart to get rid of the others," Bijou said sitting down on the same side of the table as Maggie.

"Ted's idea," Maggie admitted.

"Ted wants to sleep with you," Bijou said, her large blue eyes widening as if this was shocking to her.

"I'm married," Maggie said, holding up her hand with her wedding band on it.

"Okay," Bijou said, shrugging. Suddenly she leaned over and touched Maggie's hand. "I have a terrible secret to reveal today," she said in a hoarse whisper, then looking side to side to see if anyone were listening. As far as Maggie could tell, every single person within listening distance was openly staring at Bijou as if they were somehow included in the conversation. Bijou appeared not to notice.

"About Stan?" Maggie asked, feeling the hand that Bijou held start to sweat.

"Yes, about Stan," Bijou said. "Of course. It's why we're here, yes? To find out who killed Stan?"

"So you think he was pushed, too?"

"Of course! The police are so stupid. Stan was *pushed.*"

Maggie's confidence in her language skills flagged. "Can we

speak in English, do you think, Bijou?" She indicated the openly listening diners. "Perhaps it will confuse our audience."

Bijou switched easily to English, her voice still a whisper: "I am sleeping with the enemy," she said dramatically.

"You mean the killer?" Maggie said excitedly. "You know who it is?"

"No, the enemy," Bijou said, sitting up straight and signaling the waiter. "The one everyone hates. The one Stan hated."

Maggie held her tongue and waited.

"Stan knew and it sickened him." Bijou made a shrug as if to say that this must be accepted. "But I could not stop it."

"So you are in love?" Maggie asked.

Bijou burst out laughing. "Oh, funny! So funny! I see why Stan enjoyed your company so very much. No, I am not *in love*, Maggie."

The waiter came to take their orders and Maggie found herself barely able to wait for the man to leave before she leaned toward Bijou.

"Okay, who is it?"

"You cannot guess?"

Fighting her natural impatience, Maggie smiled and shook her head.

"It's Denny, of course," Bijou said.

"Denny." *Crap. And she was hoping to like Bijou.*

"You are disappointed in me."

"What? Oh, God, no. I mean, you don't need to worry about what I think."

"But I do," Bijou said, lighting a cigarette.

"I don't think you're allowed to smoke in here," Maggie said.

"Stan was so mad at me, he could barely speak to me. *Tu sais*? He died and he was so angry with me."

"Oh, Bijou..." Maggie tried to determine to the best of her ability—which history had shown wasn't stellar—if Bijou were faking her present unhappiness.

"*Non, non,*" she said. "We had not made up. He died hating me."

"I'm sure he didn't hate you, Bijou."

Yeah, this was when these investigative interviews got away from her and turned into ad hoc therapy sessions which she was absolutely not qualified to conduct. Nor did she want to. Maggie fought down the annoyance that had begun almost from the moment Bijou joined her at the table. *I don't care if he did die hating you,* Maggie thought, watching Bijou puff on her cigarette while surrounding diners made energetic gestures of waving away invading smoke at their tables. *Were you the one who pushed him?*

A loud voice boomed out from behind Bijou, "I am not so sure of that!"

Jeremy appeared, quivering with rage. His heavy winter coat made him look larger and more imposing than the last time she had seen him. His face was red from emotion and the cold, his bloodshot eyes darted from Maggie to Bijou and he worked his lips as if rehearsing his next lines before speaking.

Bijou jumped up from her chair and slapped him before he could speak again. Inexplicably, a few of the surrounding diners began to clap.

"You bastard!" she shrieked at him. "You encouraged him! He would have forgiven me long before...before—"

"Before he flung himself to his death because of your crass betrayal?" Jeremy's French pronunciation was a little awkward, even Maggie could hear that, but his vocabulary was good.

Bijou gasped dramatically. "I did not kill him!"

"Maybe you didn't physically push him. I don't know," Jeremy said, looking at Maggie now as if performing for her. "But it was the heartsickness over what you had done that carried him over the railing that night!"

"You cretin!"

"Shut up, both of you," Maggie said, her annoyance finally

winning out over her attempt to be civil to these two. "Jeremy, sit down or leave. I don't care which. Same goes for you, Bijou."

The waiter approached with Maggie and Bijou's drinks and frowned at Bijou. He muttered something about her cigarette and she angrily stubbed it out in the butter dish on the table.

"I will not stay," she said, grabbing the coat off her chair, the blood red talons of her polished nails stark against the fur. She stared daggers at Jeremy. "At least I feel guilt over my part in Stan's death," she hissed at him before turning and, without a goodbye or backward glance, sauntered out of the brasserie like it was the downhill run on a fashion catwalk.

Jeremy sat down in her chair, his coat still on.

"What the hell, Jeremy," Maggie said, shaking her head.

"I'm sorry," he said, looking forlornly at Bijou's still-smoldering cigarette on the dish.

"Why are you even here?" she asked.

He looked at her, his grief and pain nakedly on display across his face.

Doesn't mean he didn't kill him, Maggie reminded herself, trying not to flinch from the sight. *Could be guilt I'm seeing, not sadness.*

"I needed to talk with you about this idea you have that Stan was murdered."

"Because you're so sure he wasn't?"

Jeremy reached out and stamped Bijou's cigarette out until the ember died completely.

"Stan had a lot of issues," he said evasively, "more than you were aware. He had things that ate at him."

"Like what kind of things? You mean about being gay?"

Jeremy looked at her, startled. "He talked about that with you?"

"He did not. What things, Jeremy?" she asked. "Had he slept with a politician? Fathered a love child? Taken steroids during a bike race?"

"Things I am not at liberty to tell."

"Whatever secret you feel you are keeping for Stan cannot harm him now," she said. "Unless you are also keeping it for yourself."

"It has nothing to do with me."

"Then who can it hurt to reveal these secrets?"

"That is not for me to decide."

"Okay, I don't have the energy for this crap. If you say Stan had secrets that were insidious enough to make him want to kill himself but you don't want to reveal what they were, then I guess we're done."

"He wasn't murdered."

"I disagree. I knew him all of four days and I knew he wouldn't kill himself."

"I knew him three decades," Jeremy said fiercely, "and I tell you it has been a long time coming."

"At a party with all his friends and the niece he hadn't seen in twenty-five years."

Jeremy looked a little uncomfortable. "People in distress do not always have the leisure to pick the time and venue when their despair reaches its apex," he said.

"Did you try to get into Stan's apartment last week?"

Jeremy looked at her. "What?" he asked.

"Stan's neighbor said you came by last week to try to get the house key from her."

"It wasn't me. I haven't been to Stan's since you left."

Maggie dug a photo out of her purse and slapped it down on the table. "I found plenty of photos of you when I was going through Stan's things, Jeremy, to be able to show her and ask if the guy who tried to force his way into her apartment was you."

Jeremy looked at her with his mouth open and then reached over to take a sip from Bijou's drink. He glanced at the photo on the table.

"I just needed to get something," he said quietly.

"Want to share with me what that was?"

Jeremy looked at her and she could see his lip curl ever so slightly. “So now you don’t trust me.”

“That’s what happens when you lie.”

“I’m sorry about that,” he said. “I guess I may have one or two secrets of my own.”

“Yeah, that’s what I’m starting to see,” she said, regarding him coolly.

8

Later that evening as Maggie walked back to her apartment—and she was surprised at how quickly she began to think of it that way—she found herself more confused than before the evening started. Both Jeremy and Bijou had been significant question marks to her before tonight. She knew them only slightly better now but they continued to hold their cards close to the vest.

They both have something to hide, she thought. *Was it the same something?*

As she approached Pont Neuf she thought of how ironic it was that the name translated was *new bridge* but it was, in fact, the oldest bridge in Paris. She walked quickly across it, noting that amorous couples were still in abundance on this bridge. She appreciated the carefully placed lights on the bridge which separately illuminated each of the carved stone faces along the top in great detail. *Was there another place on earth so in love with itself?* she wondered. She decided it was actually nice to see a city so proud of itself that it refused to allow such a mundane thing as darkness obscure an opportunity to showcase its beauty.

The weather had turned cold and Maggie flipped her coat

collar up against a chill that was inching down her neck. There was something else there too. A feeling of uneasiness. She glanced at the preoccupied lovers on the bridge and hurried her pace. The uncomfortable feeling was almost as if she could feel eyes on her. Eyes hidden in the dark, watching her.

As she turned the final corner of the block that held her apartment, she saw a lone figure standing under the street lamp.

"Danielle!" Maggie hurried to her friend and embraced her before she noticed the train case at her feet. "Why didn't you call me?" she said. "Have you been waiting long? Are you alone?"

"It's just me," Danielle said, goodnaturedly. "I ate at the corner café."

"Let's get you inside," Maggie said. "There's no lift, I'm afraid and the apartment is on the third floor..."

"I am not fragile," Danielle said.

Maggie grabbed her suitcase and found herself genuinely delighted to see her friend.

Danielle appeared impressed with the apartment.

"A two-bedroom in the heart of the Latin Quarter," she said as she settled onto the couch in the living room. "Your uncle was rich."

Maggie set down two cups of peppermint tea on the coffee table. She was glad Danielle rejected the offer of wine. It had already been a long night, and while she was looking forward to an in-depth conversation with Danielle—and that in itself surprised her—the day had been a long one and she hoped to postpone the more indepth talk until tomorrow.

"I'm finding out all kinds of things about him," Maggie admitted.

"The one who killed him?"

"I'm working on it."

"So you still believe it was murder?"

"More than ever. His friends, if you can call them that, are positively shifty."

Danielle laughed. "Well, if anyone can get to the bottom if it, it's you, Maggie. As I know better than anyone." Maggie smiled at her friend's reference to what was a singularly miserable time in the older woman's life. And although Maggie's sleuthing had, at that time, caused what Danielle believed to be the end of the life she had known up until then, it turned out to be the best thing that could possibly have happened to her.

"Thanks, Danielle," Maggie said yawning. "Although, you know, one thing Stan's group has got in spades—and it's actually something I hope to learn from them—is the ability to enjoy life for what it is." She laughed at the confused look on Danielle's face. "I can't explain it," she said. "But what do you say we do some shopping tomorrow and just forget Stan's problems and Maggie and Laurent's problems—I assume you and Jean-Luc don't have any problems—and just enjoy ourselves?"

Danielle laughed and looked fondly at her friend. "Sounds good," she said.

"You've called Jean-Luc to say you got in okay?"

"I was hoping to use your phone."

"Oh, goodness, Danielle! Why didn't you tell me? Jean-Luc is probably on his way to Paris right now!"

Danielle moved to the telephone on the side table. "Well, hopefully not," she said. "But it is nice to be missed. It is a new feeling and one I do not think I will ever tire of."

As Danielle dialed the phone, Maggie collected the empty tea cups and left the living room to give her some privacy. The effects of the long day and the late hour—and even Danielle's joy—had begun to weigh on her.

At approximately three in the morning, Maggie was awakened by the sound of the phone ringing in the living room.

Who the hell? Afraid the noise would awaken Danielle in the bedroom down the hall, Maggie stumbled into the living room and snatched up the receiver, her heart pounding. It occurred to her that if it was Jean-Luc, she was not going to be very pleasant.

"Yes?" she said into the phone.

"Leave it alone or prepare to die." The voice slithered across the phone line into Maggie's ear. She nearly dropped the receiver, she was so repulsed.

"Who is this?"

"Let the poor bastard die. Or join him."

The connection was broken. Maggie sank to a seated position on the couch, still holding the phone receiver in her hand.

"Maggie?"

She turned to see Danielle standing in the doorway of her bedroom.

"Is everything alright?"

"Everything's fine," Maggie said, trying to calm her racing heart. "Just a wrong number."

"Oh, okay."

"See you in the morning."

"Goodnight."

Maggie remained seated until Danielle closed her bedroom door. And then she hung up the phone. She had left the curtains open and could see a hint of light trying to come up from behind the darkened cathedral out the window. Morning was still several hours off but the light from the coming day had already started.

Stan's friends weren't just shifty, she found herself thinking. They were stupid, too. She got up and pulled the curtain across the balcony window and turned to walk back to her bedroom.

On the other hand, she supposed she couldn't really count Denny Davenport as one of his friends. The voice on the phone had been a distinct one. And the accent, definitely Australian.

. . .

The next day, Maggie pushed the threatening phone call to the furthest recesses of her mind. She was determined to let nothing spoil her visit with Danielle.

Danielle dressed provincially as if clothing were of no use or interest to her. Maggie knew she had her hobbies—baking, quilting and gardening—but she had always been shy and happy to let her first husband think and speak for the both of them. As Maggie learned from Laurent, Jean-Luc would not allow his beloved to follow him blindly and he sought her counsel and opinion on every subject from when the grapes were ready to harvest to which socks he should wear with his workman's jumpsuit. Maggie heard that Danielle had taken to this new way of interacting with a husband as if she had been waiting to do it all her life.

Their day was a welcome respite from the sadness and wall-to-wall busyness of Maggie's days in Paris up to now of cataloging and packing up Stan's apartment. The two went across the street to the *patisserie* for a leisurely late breakfast before taking the metro downtown to shop at Galleries Lafayette where they also lunched. It was the first touristy, just-plain-fun day that Maggie had had in over a year and she discovered that she badly needed it. She also discovered that Danielle was a sensible, intuitive woman with a slightly naughty sense of humor. Maggie couldn't remember the last time she had laughed so much.

After they had trudged home to the apartment, dropped off their purchases and bathed and dressed for dinner, they walked along the Quai Saint Michel until they came upon a restaurant that Maggie had heard about. It was a classic snapshot of Old Paris. Maggie was delighted to discover the restaurant a mere half a dozen blocks from her apartment.

"It's like that brasserie in *Midnight in Paris*," Maggie said. "You know the one? Where Hemingway and all of them go to?"

"I have not seen the movie," Danielle said.

"Oh, it's 1920's Paris," Maggie said, looking around at the interior of the restaurant, its ancient exposed beams in the ceiling, the beveled mirrors studding the walls and reflecting back the flickering wall sconces at each table. "A magical time," she said. "Like when Hemingway lived here. Paris is a writer's Mecca."

"You were a writer before you came to France?"

"Well, sort of," Maggie said. "I wrote advertising."

"So you are thinking of becoming a writer in Paris? Even though your husband lives three hundred miles south? A *place* is more important to you than your love?"

"Whoa, Danielle, slow down," Maggie said. "What Laurent does—his cooking—he can do anywhere. For me, that's not the case. My foreign language skills aren't good enough to find work outside my own country."

"Your French is much improved," Danielle said. "Jean-Luc and I were commenting on it just the other day."

"Well, thank you, but it's not so much improved that I could find a job in this country short of picking grapes. I need to *work*, Danielle."

"And Paris can give you that? What about the language problem *here*?"

"Paris has a huge ex-pat community," Maggie said. "If there was a chance anywhere in this country where I might fit in, it'd be here."

"But *cherie*," Danielle said patiently, "what is the point of living in Paris when Laurent is in St-Buvard? Why not just divorce him and move back to your own country where there is no problem at all?"

"No problem except I'd be living without Laurent."

"You will do *that* in Paris." Danielle leaned across the table and gave Maggie's hand a squeeze. "I do not mean to offend."

"I know you care about both me and Laurent, Danielle. So you can't offend me. Say what you think."

"For me, expecting to have everything I want is not a concept I have ever felt I had the luxury to indulge."

"I sound spoiled to you."

"You sound American. But the thing you will spoil forever is rare and hard to find in any country. To see you throw it away because it's not perfect makes me sad."

"I don't intend to throw it away."

"Maybe not but that will be the end result. You know your husband. Your actions will force *him* to act."

THE MEAL WAS EVERYTHING the perfect Parisian meal in a 1920's brasserie should be, Maggie thought, stifling a groan at how much she had eaten. *How did the concept of heavy starters work with a fashionable French woman's quest to remain a size two?* she wondered. When she was single in Atlanta, she had often eaten only fruit for breakfast, yoghurt for lunch and a glass of wine with her fat-free grilled chicken salad. Laurent's look of horror when she related this to him convinced her that he would rather see her fat than repeat the culinary habit of the single girl. *If that was the case*, she thought, *tonight he would be very proud of me.* They started with a bottle of Côtes-du-Rhone. Maggie noticed the St.Laurent Chateauneuf-du-Pape on the menu and it made her sad for a moment. She and Laurent had shared a personal joke about that wine on more than one occasion.

Tonight, she threw dietary caution to the wind and then took a stick and beat the tar out of it as she and Danielle both murdered a *Lyonnaise* each, with crisp greens and pancetta topped with poached eggs—runny and deliciously dangerous like the French do—before moving on to their main courses. Maggie had the "*Américaine*" *Bouillabaisse* although she couldn't help but compare it to Laurent's which had upon occasion nearly made her weep with pleasure, and Danielle had a Black Angus prime filet. Maggie always marveled how the French could take something so basic as a perfect cut of steak—and make it even better. Danielle ate her steak with roasted fingerling potatoes and wild mushrooms and the two ended their meals with a shared lemon grass *crème brûlée* and high-octane coffees.

When they left the restaurant, they left arm in arm, well-warmed by their conversation, the wine, the wonderful food and the lovely day they had spent together. And it was because Maggie was so contented and happy that she paid no attention to the other diners coming and going or the pedestrians surging along the busy sidewalk in front of the restaurant. She was anticipating a chilly but invigorating walk back to the apartment which she counted on to keep her at least nominally awake in the aftermath of the heavy meal and the busy day.

So she, literally, never saw it coming.

When Danielle hesitated in the middle of crossing the street, Maggie looked at her friend questioningly.

"I think I left my wallet on the table," Danielle said, turning back toward the restaurant. Maggie, feeling relaxed and slow in her movements, had no doubt that the wallet would still be there and so felt no need to hurry. She watched Danielle walk quickly back to the sidewalk and toward the entrance of the restaurant. Maggie was still standing in the middle of the street, when Danielle turned to her and screamed.

"Maggie! Look out!"

Maggie felt her own terror reflected in Danielle's face as she heard the sound of the car gunning toward her. Not taking the time to look to see which direction it was coming from, she launched herself onto the nearest parked car, leaving her purse and one shoe behind her in the street. The noise of the oncoming car was unbearably loud as she scrambled up onto the hood of the parked car, gashing her knee against its hood ornament in the process.

The sound of metal smashing into metal coincided with the terrible jolt that flung her from her perch onto the other side of the sidewalk when the speeding car rammed the parked car. In the back of her mind, she could hear Danielle screaming over the sounds of the roaring car. Her hands scraping on the sidewalk and her knee in agony, Maggie scrambled to her feet in time to see the car's taillights careen the wrong way down the narrow one-way street.

Danielle was at her side within moments. "Maggie!" She stood next to Maggie, panting. "You were nearly killed!"

Maggie was still staring after the retreating car although it had vanished from sight. She turned to Danielle and put a hand out to her. She could see she was shaking. Danielle took her hand.

"How did you happen to see it?" Maggie asked.

"I must have put my wallet in my coat pocket instead of my purse," Danielle said. "When I realized I had it, I turned back and that's when I saw the car...it was heading right for you."

Maggie limped to the front of the parked car to inspect the damage. It was significant. "Do you think it was some drunk?" she asked.

Danielle shook her head. "I...I don't know," she said. "Watching it happen...something about it felt...deliberate."

Maggie looked at Danielle, and Denny Davenport's ugly words returned to her. She felt suddenly very cold, the pleasure of the evening gone.

Danielle went to collect Maggie's shoe and purse from the middle of the road and Maggie found herself looking again in the direction that the car had gone.

The car that looked amazingly like the one that Jeremy drove.

9

Somehow, they salvaged the evening. Once in fluffy bathrobes, both of them, and Maggie's knee bandaged, they curled up together on the couch and sipped peppermint tea. Maggie seemed to be doing everything she could to steer the conversation away from what had happened that night. Because Danielle could see Maggie was trying so hard to pretend it didn't happen, she spoke only of the parts of the day that had been so pleasant.

When they finally parted to their separate bedrooms, Danielle knew that she had made a dear friend out of a neighbor and an acquaintance. It was a gift to be able to add to one's roster of friends at this age, she thought to herself as she readied for bed. And she had the wisdom of her sweet husband—and his obvious caring for Laurent—to thank for it. She prayed she could help open Maggie's heart to help her see her way to the other side of this treacherous game she was playing with Laurent.

The next morning, Maggie accompanied Danielle to the *Gare de Lyon* to await the train that would take her to Arles where Jean-Luc would be waiting to bring her home.

"I appreciate Jean-Luc letting you off the leash long enough to come see me," Maggie said as she stood next to Danielle on the platform.

"It was his idea," Danielle said.

"Really? I'm shocked."

"He loves Laurent," Danielle said, shrugging. "He wants him to be happy."

"Did he hope you would talk sense into me?"

Danielle laughed. "Perhaps," she said. "But, honestly, he believes that Laurent should throw you over his shoulder and bring you back to St-Buvard." Danielle laughed.

"Laurent is not like that," Maggie said.

"No, of course not," Danielle said. "My husband is from a different generation."

"I don't suppose I could ask you not to mention the incident last night to Laurent?"

"With the car? I'm sorry, Maggie. If it were for any other reason than your safety, I would do so happily. But he would consider it unforgivable for me not to tell him. And he would be right."

"Okay. It's just that it will only confirm to him that I shouldn't be here."

"What will it take to confirm it to *you*?"

"Danielle, you have to believe me when I tell you I love Laurent and I don't want to lose him."

"I believe you are in danger of doing exactly that."

"God! Why does it have to be so hard?"

Danielle picked up her valise. "Life is hard, *cherie*," she said, "which is why we need a good man beside us as we forge ahead." She kissed Maggie briefly on both cheeks. "I know you will find your way."

CLEARLY, Danielle didn't even wait until she was back in St-Buvard since Maggie's cell rang as she stepped back into her apartment.

"I can't believe she called you from the train," Maggie said. "It's not that big a deal, Laurent. Really."

"Someone obviously thinks your uncle revealed the name of his killer to you before he died."

"Jimbo?"

"If that is, in fact, what he said."

"That's crazy. Do I *act* like I know who killed Stan?"

"Perhaps they fear you will put two and four together?"

Maggie was silent for a moment. It was true. If Stan had revealed the identity of his killer to her, she was in danger—in spite of the fact she had not yet figured out who that person was.

"I guess it's possible they might try again," she said slowly.

"Why are you doing this?" Laurent said. Maggie could hear the anguish in his voice.

And things had been going so well up to this point.

"I think I am getting close," she said.

"And so, obviously, does the killer," he said.

"Would you let *my* killer get away with murder? Would you let him go on eating *foie gras* and enjoying life if you knew who it was?"

"You *don't* know who it is."

"I have confidence that I will. Look, Laurent, the day you start trusting the police to handle anything beyond taking bribes and fixing parking tickets is the day I start to cook four-course meals. Okay?"

Was that grunt she heard a muffled chuckle? Is it possible, he was unbending from his position just a little?

"I knew you would end up getting hurt," he said, rerouting the conversation back to the original line of attack.

"I didn't get hurt."

"This time."

So much for the hope that they were moving forward.

. . .

THE FOLLOWING WEEK, Maggie went out every night with Bijou. They went to the dance clubs, the bars, and all the late night bistros on the Left Bank. At the same time, Ted and she talked for hours about the manuscript he was working on. Maggie began to fancy herself part of a modern day Hemingway crowd.

She had to remind herself that what she was doing—while it didn't feel like investigative work—was at least as important as asking questions and tracking down clues. Going undercover to become a part of this group, to gain their trust—in so far as that was possible—was going to be more useful to her than lining people up and firing questions at them.

One evening after she had begged off going to the clubs with Bijou, Maggie made herself a simple cheese omelet, poured herself a glass of Pinot and sat down at Stan's desk in the living room in front of her laptop. She looked over the notes she had made during the week of bar-hopping with Bijou and Ted and realized that her observations and even direct snatches of dialogue that she remembered and captured were beginning to take a form that she could not have imagined. She read her notes from her computer screen and then printed them out on Stan's printer. In her excitement, she pushed her dinner plate away with most of the omelet uneaten, and reread her notes from the printer.

As she read, she realized that the week of talking and laughing and drinking and, yes, even flirting, had given her a boots-on-the-ground point of view that she hadn't anticipated. The notes—virtually useless at this point as far as helping her figure out who might be guilty or not—were invaluable as a testimony to the kind of life Maggie preferred. She was able to see—almost as an objective third party—that the life she was experiencing here in Paris was one that suited her. She was able to see that a veil of depression had lifted—at least a corner of it—on her world view and the kind of life she was trying on for size here in Paris with Stan's friends—was one that resonated with her and the kind of person she was. Deliberately shutting out any thoughts of what this might mean for her life with Laurent, Maggie focused on what her notes revealed about her life in this one week.

Suddenly, she saw that the notes also revealed something else.

Maggie got up from the desk and walked to the balcony window that faced Notre Dame Cathedral. She held her notes in her hands as she gazed out at the ancient church, half shrouded in the night's darkness and fog. She glanced down at what she'd written and realized that the way she had written her notes made the content read like a novel. She hadn't been aware that she was writing it like that, but when she looked at it closely, she could see the bones of a fictionalized mystery, complete with tension and character studies and a plot. As she turned to look back at the great Cathedral, she felt an overwhelming thrill vibrate through her at what she seemed to be creating that she had literally not felt since the day she had taken her first advertising copywriting job almost ten years ago.

As she stared out over her little piece of Paris, she felt such exquisite happiness and purpose that tears of joy filled in her eyes.

She was a writer. And she was finally writing.

LAURENT SAT in his car outside the café in St-Buvard. He had had one *pastis* in the café-bar before leaving the company of his friends—the other *vignerons* of the area whom normally he enjoyed so much—and felt a restlessness course through him that was unusual for him. He didn't want to drink. He didn't want to talk with his friends or to discuss the harvest or evaluate this year's grapes. He didn't want to go home to the empty house, either. And so he sat in the car, tapping his fingers against the steering wheel, and forcing himself not to think of her.

It had begun to rain while he was in the café and continued now in a cold downward drizzle. Since he wasn't driving, he didn't bother activating his windshield wipers but sat in the car and tried to see where he was going—where he and Maggie were going—through the opaque wall of rain in front of him and his own unnamed agitation.

As he stared into the gloom, he saw a shape take form from what looked like a pile of garbage humped on the sidewalk forty yards in front of him. Squinting against the rain, he flicked on the windshield wipers to see the shape morph into the wet and bedraggled form of a young woman staggering under the burden of a large backpack. He frowned and watched her. St-Buvard was nowhere near any likely hiking or backpacking trail. And with the harvest now two weeks over everywhere in Provence, transient pickers were long gone. He watched her stamp her feet as if that would somehow aid in removing the water from her clothes. She wore no hat and Laurent could see the rain had flattened her short dark hair in a spiky mass so that it was plastered to her head. She wore a leather jacket that seemed to provide little protection from the weather. Without thinking, he flipped on his high beams and the figure was illuminated in front of him. She turned to look in his direction and he flipped the headlights on and off. Without hesitation, she turned and walked toward him.

HE WATCHED her throw the remains of her baguette to the birds and then seat herself on the only available bench behind Notre Dame. He felt fairly certain she couldn't see him from this distance. Even if she could, he noticed she rarely looked up at her surroundings unless it was to stare off into space before snapping her attention back to her cellphone. Was she texting someone? Making notes about something? Not in a million years would he have expected old Stan to have had such a luscious niece. Ted leaned against the stone wingwall of the Pont de l'Archeveche and twisted his muffler tightly around his neck.

He was pretty sure he was unidentifiable but having her catch him following her twice would not help his plans any. A sour expression flitted across his face as he thought of Stan. While he could never sustain the whole father-I-never-had scenario back in California where people actually *knew* his relationship with Stan, it was still difficult to maintain it here in the face of his own constantly churning stomach at the misdirection. He didn't like starting things off with Maggie on a foundation of false assumptions or *hell, let's be honest, outright lies. Yeah, Stan,* he thought with disgust. *Old pal, old buddy. Go ahead and turn everything we all ever knew about you into a big ass lie. God forbid you could just die and take your secrets with you.*

She was moving now and Ted slid silently away from the railing of the bridge. *Would Stan have approved? Not likely*, he decided as he let Maggie put a few more yards between them before he stepped out of the shadows after her. But if Stan had ever done anything right, Ted thought, tucking his chin to further obscure his identity as he hurried down the bridge and watched her turn onto the Quai de Montebello, it was to bring this most delectable woman into Ted's life. And for that, Ted thought with a sudden realization that lit up his face and lifted his heart, he figured he could forgive the old bastard just about anything.

MAGGIE STACKED the printed out pages of her manuscript and set them on the coffee table. It was the day after she had discovered she was writing a novel without knowing it, and she had spent most of the day and part of the evening outlining and revising her prose. When the apartment phone rang, she was so distracted by the thought of the characters she was developing in the manuscript, she failed for the first time to hold her breath and hope it would be Laurent.

"Hey, Sherlock, feel like taking a break?"

Maggie held the phone against her chin as she moved out of the kitchen into her living room. "Ted, you are not going to believe what's happened. I can hardly believe it myself."

"Something's happened?"

"Well, I was writing out possible scenarios, you know, about this whole Stan thing? And I guess I got the texture and sounds and feeling of Paris in the notes or something but when I read back over what I'd written—"

"—you'd started writing a novel," Ted finished.

"Yes! I can't wait to show it to you. It's only a chapter but I was up half the night writing it."

"That's amazing, Maggie," Ted said. "I can't wait to read it. You've never written fiction before?"

"No, never," she said. "It's about Paris Fashion week."

"Of course. And it's a mystery?"

"Yep, since that's what I seem to be in the middle of, you know?"

"How about I come over and read your first chapter? I can bring take-out."

Maggie glanced at the clock on Stan's desk. She was dying to have him read what she'd written.

"I'm tempted," she said. "But I haven't showered all day..."

"I don't mind."

She laughed. "But I do. Let's meet up tomorrow night, okay?" Maggie could hear Ted talking with someone on his end. "Ted?"

"Oh, it's only Bijou. She's upset you won't meet us at *Le Bal* tonight. Ignore her. Get your work done tonight. I'll prepare to be thrilled and amazed tomorrow night when I see your stuff. Really proud of you, Maggie."

"Thanks, Ted. Tell Bijou we'll do it tomorrow for sure."

"Will do, meanwhile, don't forget to get some sleep. The opus or work-in-progress can be a demanding mistress, trust me, I know."

Maggie laughed. "Tomorrow," she said. "At *Le Bal*."

"You got it."

Maggie hung up the phone and then turned and looked at her cellphone lying on the coffee table. It had been four days since she'd spoken to Laurent. Overcoming her pride, she had tried calling him twice, yesterday and today. Both calls had gone straight to voice mail.

Fine, she thought as she got up and took her teacup into the kitchen. *If he wants to play it that way. That's just fine.*

She washed out her supper dishes, rinsed her cup and placed them in the dish drainer. She snapped off the kitchen light and went to stand in front of the window again to look out at Notre Dame. It was lighted up against a backdrop of inky blackness. It occurred to Maggie that—unlike every other time she had stood gazing in rapture at the magnificent church—tonight it looked kind of creepy.

AT A QUIET CAFÉ two blocks away, Jeremy sat alone at a corner table, a glass of scotch in front of him and his cellphone next to it. His eyes darted around the darkened interior of the restaurant. He wet his lips and fidgeted with the paper napkin under his drink. As cool as it was inside the café he was annoyed to discover that he was actually sweating as he sat and waited.

When his phone began to vibrate, he thought he might, too. He grabbed it up and glanced at the screen before clapping it to his ear.

"Well?" he said in a hoarse whisper.

"I thought I'd wait," the voice said. "It's too soon."

"It's *not* too soon," Jeremy said, a tightness beginning in his chest. He could feel the perspiration dribbling down his back underneath his silk shirt and ten-ply cashmere sweater. "It's exactly the right time."

"Easy for you to say."

"I've arranged for her to go out with Bijou and Ted, I told you," Jeremy whispered loudly, glancing around at the other café patrons. "She'll be gone for hours."

"Did you see her leave?"

"I don't need to see her leave, you imbecile!" Jeremy wiped his damp palms against the worn tablecloth under his drink and then clutched his free hand in a fist. "I'm not staking out her goddamn flat. She's out, I tell you. Do it now." He jabbed at the button to disconnect and dropped the phone on the table next to his drink, ending the conversation and ending further argument. *Would he go? Would it be done by this time tomorrow? Would this nightmare finally be over?*

Jeremy picked up his drink, noticing how the ice rattled gently in his shaking hand, and drank it down in one gulp. The sensation burned all the way down bringing tears to his eyes. Just as well, he thought miserably, dabbing at his eyes with the shredded napkin. *Just as offing well.*

LAURENT SLID the omelet from the pan onto a dish and set it before the young woman. She was not unattractive, he thought, even after weeks of wandering the back roads of France, sleeping in ditches and hostels, eating whatever came her way. Her short hair seemed to magnify her big brown eyes which were heavily fringed with lashes. Laurent had always loved the gamin look on a woman. It made him feel protective. Maggie wore her hair long and usually twisted into a ponytail or pinned up in some way.

"Wow," she said, pulling the dish toward her on the counter. "Smells awesome. I can't thank you enough for letting me crash here last night." She picked up a fork and began eating. "Really saved me," she said around a mouthful of egg.

Laurent set a glass in front of her and poured one of his own wines into it.

"*Pas du tout*," he murmured, watching her with curiosity. She was Australian and hitchhiking her way across Europe alone. Even in this day and age, that was unusual for a woman. In response to Laurent's kindness of a dry bed and a meal the night before, she had eagerly offered up the pleasures of her body and had seemed, if not disappointed, at least surprised when he had refused the offer.

Laurent couldn't help but notice how quickly she bolted her food. Did she eat in a hurry all the time, he wondered? Or was she in a particular rush to get back on the road?

"I would be happy to work off my room and board," she said, taking a long sip from her wine glass.

Laurent shrugged. "I have no work for a girl."

"I'm stronger than I look," she said. "I'd prefer to work for my keep."

"You wish to stay longer?"

"If that's not a problem," she said looking directly into his eyes. "I've pretty much been on the move now for weeks. A few days in one spot would be a treat."

Laurent nodded and turned back to his kitchen.

"*D'accord*," he said. "I'll find something for you to do."

MAGGIE WOKE up feeling as though she'd been shaken by the shoulders. An invasive hum had started somewhere in the background of the dream she was having until she realized she was no longer dreaming. As she sat in her darkened bedroom she ran the sound back through her memory tapes in her head and realized it hadn't been a hum at all. The noise that woke her had been a single, stealthy creak.

A creak that her apartment had not make on its own.

Fighting an overwhelming urge to bolt from the bed, Maggie forced herself to sit still and listen, her heart pounding so loudly she could barely hear anything else.

Someone was in the apartment with her.

10

Her mouth was dry and she felt a crawling sensation on her skin as she strained to hear the sound repeat in the hall. Within seconds, she heard it again: the sound of a heavy tread on the uneven boards under the carpeting in the living room.

She looked around her bedroom. *Was there anything she could use to defend herself?* She grabbed up her cellphone from the bedside table and swung her legs out of bed. Her breathing was coming in rapid pants that she was sure the burglar could hear; it sounded as loud as a roar in her own ears. Not knowing what to do but afraid to wait for the handle of her bedroom door to turn, Maggie dropped the phone on the bed and grabbed up her curling iron—the only weapon she could find—and silently opened her bedroom door. She saw her hand shake as she reached for the door handle. She moved into the hallway, mindful of which boards creaked. It occurred to her that if she could just make it to the kitchen, she had a wide assortment of weapons to choose from there. The thought gave her strength as she crept down the darkened hallway.

As soon as she stood nearly in the opening to the living room, she saw him. He was tall and dressed totally in black. He was standing in front of her desk. She measured her path to the kitchen: just four steps to her left. Then without realizing she had made the decision to act, she burst from the hallway and ran for it. She sensed rather than saw him pivot sharply in her direction. The knives were kept in a wooden block holder on the counter and her fingers quickly wrapped around the largest chef's knife at the top of the holder. Sliding it free, she turned to face him.

She was surprised to see that he wasn't just dressed in black, he *was* black. Denny Davenport stood in the middle of her living room with her laptop under his arm. Maggie waved the large knife in front of her.

"You!" she said.

Without a word, Denny twisted around to grab up a table lamp, ripping its cord out of the wall and heaving it in her direction. Maggie screamed and fell back against the refrigerator trying to dodge the lamp. As she caught herself from falling into the broken shards of the ceramic lamp as it crashed to the floor of the kitchen, she could see him fumbling with the front door handle.

Was he crazy? She'd seen his face! Maggie clutched the knife to her chest, immobilized, as Denny jerked open the front door and disappeared down the hall at a run. She ran to the door and slammed it shut behind him, then turned and hurried to her bedroom where she grabbed her cellphone and rang the police.

Why did he want her laptop? As she waited for the French police call center to process her request for a *gendarme*, she walked into the living room and tried to calm her racing heart. She could see the beginnings of dawn peeking through the mantle of heavy clouds outside the window, revealing the top twin spires of Notre Dame. Turning her focus back to her living room, she noticed the corner of Stan's laptop just barely visible where she had slid it under the couch. Her stomach did a slow flip as she realized the truth. It wasn't *her* laptop Denny had come to get.

"I CANNOT BELIEVE that happened to you!" Bijou popped a large ham-stuffed mushroom cap into her mouth and shook her head. "*Incroyable*! What did the police say? Have they arrested him?"

"I don't know," Maggie said, watching Bijou carefully for any sign that she might have known beforehand about the break-in attempt. "They're not really keeping me informed."

She sat with Bijou, Ted and Jeremy in the large corner table at *Le Bal*. She had asked Ted to extend the invitation to Diane too, if she was in Paris, which nobody seemed to know for sure. So far there was no sign of her. After last night's break-in, Maggie had decided to stop playing like she was a part of this crowd with their thinly veiled secrets and fashion entrenched code words and start dealing with them like they were all suspects. In her mind, she suddenly realized, they all were.

"So he took the wrong laptop," Ted said. "He got the one with your story on it?"

Maggie looked at him with surprise and then grinned. "I had it on a jump drive," she said. "I brought it."

Ted laughed and toasted her with his wine glass. "Now you're starting to act like a writer," he said. "Recognizing what's really important. May I presume to see it?"

Maggie dug it out of her purse and handed it to him. "Be honest," she said.

"Brutally," he responded, tucking the key into his top shirt pocket. "And I'll guard it with my life."

"Yeah, that too," she said, grinning. "It's my only copy until I can get my laptop back or pick up another one."

"Unbelievable," Jeremy murmured. "He looked right at you and didn't care that you recognized him?"

Maggie nodded. "Yeah, I thought that was strange too," she

said. "But then I started to think: what else was he going to do? Kill me? Running was really his only option."

"Unless he is the murderer," Jeremy said.

"I thought you didn't believe Stan was murdered," Maggie said.

"I have to say, I really don't know what to believe anymore," Jeremy said quietly.

"Well, I'm not sure whether I can tie Denny's trying to steal Stan's laptop as a motive for him killing Stan," Maggie said. "Didn't we all agree that Denny came to the party late and left early?"

"He still doesn't have an alibi for the time of Stan's...you know," Ted said.

"Well, it's certainly fishy," Maggie said. "If the cops don't arrest him, I'm going to go talk with him."

The table erupted in noise and dissention. "No! You can't!" "That would be crazy!" "He's *dangereux*!" Maggie shook her head and waited them out.

"I am going to talk to him," she said firmly. "He doesn't appear violent—"

"You said he threw a lamp at you!" Ted said in exasperation. Maggie felt a wave of familiarity when he said something so much like Laurent might say.

"Well, I choose to believe he was trying to delay me, not nail me," she said.

"Based on what do you believe that?" Jeremy said. "The man is an animal and capable of anything."

"Speaking of the night of the party," Maggie said, turning to face Jeremy. "There's something I've been meaning to ask you and I never seem to get a moment alone with you."

"Ask away," Jeremy said, sticking a cigarette in his mouth and patting his vest for matches.

"You can't smoke in here," Maggie said. "What's the matter

with you people? You know you can't smoke in restaurants any more."

"Your question?" Jeremy said, removing his cigarette and taking a sip of his Scotch instead.

"Why did you tell me that Stan was going home with someone as the reason he didn't say goodbye to me?"

The table became very quiet as Ted and Bijou both turned to look at Jeremy as one.

"You said that?" Ted said. "You told Maggie that Stan was leaving with someone else?"

"I know what I said, Ted," Jeremy hissed. "We don't need a reenactment, thank you. Although if anybody could ham it up enough to dramatize it, I'm sure we could look to you for that."

Ted flushed a dark red but said nothing.

"I'm waiting, Jeremy," Maggie said.

"Look," Jeremy said to the whole table. "It's very simple. Stan and I had words at the party—actually about a certain someone he was interested in—way too interested in for my comfort level if I can be honest—and...and I am not proud to admit it but I was just petty enough to take some comfort...some enjoyment, really...out of giving you wrong information. I knew it would upset him...must I go on? I feel as bad as I can feel about that particular ruse, bred from my own bad temper—"

"And jealousy," Ted said.

"Yes, Ted, and jealousy." Jeremy looked down at his hands. "Can you imagine how I felt when it turned out to be the last interaction I had with him?" He looked up at Maggie and she saw his eyes swimming in tears.

She took a long breath and deliberately hardened her heart to the sight of his guilt and his grief. She knew he was devastated to lose Stan. But just because he loved him, she reminded herself, didn't mean he didn't kill him.

An hour later, after Bijou and Jeremy had both left, Maggie took a moment to relax with Ted and talk about their separate writing projects. He, too, was using Paris Fashion Week as the setting for his current romance novel.

"It's always easier to write what you know," he said as he paid the bill and gathered up his coat.

"How is it people write so easily about time-travel and space aliens then?" Maggie said as they emerged from the brasserie onto the cold Parisian street. *Le Bal* was not close to her apartment and while she had taken the Metro to get here this evening, she was looking forward to walking home. With Ted.

"Well, writers are notoriously crazy," Ted said with a straight face. "A few whacked-out dreams of space alien invasions is as good as reality for them. Trust me," he said. "I may know a lot about the catwalk and can write about it easily, but I have never met a heroine in real life as perfect as the ones I create."

"Oh, really?"

"My heroines are feisty and feminine, loyal to a fault and always ready to jump into the sack."

"And your heroes, Ted?"

"Same thing. Total fiction. It's not possible in real life to be the kind of people that readers want."

"I guess you're right."

"Hate to burst your bubble." He laughed. "But men who are protective and strong and forceful without being overbearing or downright rapists? They don't exist." He shrugged. "I know my readers—who are all women, by the way—don't want to believe that. But it's true."

"Which one are you?" Maggie asked teasingly.

"Oh, me? Well, I am a model for my heroes, of course." He shrugged and took her hand and put it on his arm as they walked down the sidewalk. "I mean, how else could I know so well what my women readers want if not for the fact that I am strong and protective and all that other good stuff?"

Maggie laughed. As they walked, Maggie found her thoughts drifting relentlessly back to Laurent. He would be the brooding hero type, she thought. *Or is it just the language barrier that makes me think so?* She and Ted walked in companionable silence for a couple blocks and then he stopped abruptly and she felt his hand tighten on her arm.

"Wha—?" she began to speak.

"Shhh!" He pulled her quickly into the dark shadows of the street under the shuttered storefronts. Maggie could feel Ted's body hard and unyielding against her own. She felt a panicked need to remove herself from his grasp—getting tighter by the moment—and was seconds away from bolting back into the light of the nearest streetlamp when he turned her deftly in the direction of a side alley.

"Look!" he whispered.

An open door cut a large wedge of light into the darkened alley and she could see two men standing in the entrance. The doorway itself was giant, looking at least fifteen feet tall. She instantly recognized Denny standing in the doorway who was greeting his visitor.

Maggie drew in a sharp breath and Ted held up a finger to his lips. She nodded and looked back at Denny. She and Ted stood silently watching until her knees began to shake with the effort to remain totally still. Her legs, covered in sheer stockings, were already numb with the night cold. When the man Denny was speaking to began to enter the doorway with Denny, he stopped and turned to look around the alleyway as if to make sure no one saw him. Maggie stifled her gasp when she saw his face.

It was Jeremy.

11

Maggie pulled the *duvet* up around her neck and shivered. *How could she be surprised?* Jeremy had already been caught red-handed trying to get into the apartment—probably for the very thing that Denny was after. The fact that the two of them were working in concert shouldn't be that big a shock.

She could tell Ted was surprised, too. Unusually silent on their walk back to Maggie's apartment, he hadn't even asked to come up for a nightcap.

What were the two after on Stan's laptop? Maggie glanced at it sitting on her bedside table. *What was on it that was so important to both Denny and Jeremy?* With renewed vigor and determination, she had spent an hour after she returned to her apartment trying to crack the password on the machine but to no avail. Whatever was there would have to wait. Besides, Maggie wasn't absolutely sure she would recognize the incriminating information when she saw it. What could it be that both men were willing to go to such measures to retrieve?

She checked her cellphone for the time and decided to call Laurent again. It was starting to feel deliberate to her as she listened to his phone ring and then go to voice mail. While it was true he had never been tethered to his phone like most people were these days, he certainly looked at it more than once every two days. *He will have noticed that I am trying to reach him.*

In frustration, she tossed the phone down on the bed and then quickly grabbed it back up again and punched in Jean-Luc and Danielle's number. If anybody knew anything in the whole of St-Buvard, it would be Danielle.

"Hello?" Danielle's breathless voice answered and Maggie had a bad moment thinking she might have caught her friend at an inconvenient time.

"Danielle?"

"Maggie!" Danielle's voice was animated and cheerful. Maggie frowned. *Too* cheerful for eleven thirty at night on a Tuesday. "I am so glad to hear from you. How is everything in Paris?"

Now Maggie *knew* something was wrong. Danielle was too frenetically happy to be believable.

"It's good, Danielle," Maggie said. "Listen, I've been trying to get a hold of Laurent but no joy. Have you seen him around? He's alive, right?"

"Laurent? No, no, I have not seen him."

Suddenly, Maggie's stomach lurched with a roiling nausea. Her friend's clumsy attempts to dissemble flashed a message as clear as a billboard on the A4: *Laurent is done with you.*

"Okay," Maggie said, now finding herself fighting tears. "Because I've not been able to reach him."

"Well, I am sure he is just busy, Maggie," Danielle said with enthusiasm. "There is always so much to do in the vineyard, you know?"

Not right after the harvest there isn't, Maggie thought. *Even I know that.* "That's true," she said. "Well, I'm sure I've just caught him at a bad time. Everything okay with you and Jean-Luc?"

"Yes, yes, wonderful," Danielle said. "Everything's fine."

"Okay, well, that's great, Danielle," Maggie said. "Give my best to Jean-Luc."

"I will of course," Danielle said.

Maggie hung up and sat in bed staring at the cellphone in her hand, her tears finally released and struggling down her face.

Jean-Luc came up behind his wife and put his hands on her waist.

"That was Maggie?" he asked.

Danielle nodded, her shoulders sagging with the weight of her worry, her lie. "This is all just so sad," she said to her husband. "She's worried and Laurent is not returning her calls."

"You did warn her."

"I did." She turned in his arms to face him. "But even I could not imagine he would take another woman into his bed this soon."

Jean-Luc shrugged. "You did warn her."

The next morning, Maggie decided she would spend the morning shopping and walking. She hoped to exhaust herself physically. Ignoring the work that visibly awaited her in the living room—in fact just about everywhere she cared to look in Stan's apartment—Maggie dressed warmly in cotton tights and long boots, and a snug wool tunic that caressed every curve she had. Where she was going today, she did not want to look like a tourist or an American. Before leaving, she peeked into the hallway of the apartment building to see if Genevieve was lying in wait for her. Her neighbor was a nice enough lady but Maggie had learned the hard way that she was nearly impossible to get rid of and Maggie was too afraid of offending to drop any effective hints.

A folded piece of paper was jammed into the hinge of

Maggie's door and she could see a big and looping *G* on it that could only mean *Genevieve*. Jamming it into her coat pocket, Maggie bolted for the stairs.

Deciding against the Metro, she hurried down the Quai Saint Michel, then crossed over Pont Neuf to the Right Bank. She paused as she always did to take a moment to enjoy the sight of the Eiffel Tower in the distance. It never failed to buoy her spirits and remind her where she was.

On the far side of the Île de la Cité, she decided to walk up the Quai de George Pompidou between the river and the Tuileries in order to avoid most of the crowds clustered in the courtyard of the Louvre. Hurrying past the booksellers—most still open for business even this late in the year—Maggie halted at the Pont des Art and scanned the bridge as it spanned the Seine. Like many of the bridges across the river that featured chain link railings, this one was covered in locks of every size and shiny finish. As Maggie waited for the traffic light to change in order to cross the street, she found herself watching the lovers on the bridge. One couple, typical of every other couple who was lured to the bridge, held their lock between them and kissed. Maggie watched them as they gazed into each other's eyes and spoke their private words. They looked so young, so sure that their relationship would be the one to last. She watched as the couple kissed again, snapped their lock to the bridge ties, and then flung the key into the river. She could hear the girl's squeals of delight.

Would that it were that easy, sweetie, Maggie thought as she turned her back on the couple, now holding hands and walking across the bridge toward the Louvre. Maggie and Laurent had been to Paris many times but it had never occurred to her to ask him to put a lock on the bridge together. If Laurent was anything, he was a realist, she thought. Although he had never commented on the practice, she was sure he found the whole idea asinine. She shook herself out of thoughts of him.

Plenty of time to think later, she told herself as she crossed the street. She moved quickly into the Jardin de Tuileries and across it to the Rue de Rivoli and on to the Rue de Castiglione. Her first official day of playing hooky instead of attending to the tasks of why she was in Paris, Maggie felt free yet at the same time desperately wished she had a girlfriend.

Forcing herself to slow down, she slipped into a *patisserie* with bistro tables and ordered a *café crème* and an almond *macaron* nearly as big as the palm of her hand. She sat by the window and watched the shoppers stream past. Without realizing she was doing it, she pulled a pad of paper and a pen from her purse and started jotting down observations on the people she saw—how they dressed, their pinched or worried expressions—and she tried to imagine if they lived here or were tourists. *Were they unhappy because they had some crisis playing out at home? An unruly unwed teen? A wandering husband? Or were they not particularly unhappy at all?* Maybe after forty years of living combined with indifferent skincare, their faces had simply relaxed into the visage of frowns which had nothing at all to do with what they were thinking or feeling. She took a relishing bite of the *macaron* and instantly thought of Laurent. He was always encouraging her to try new things—especially food. He would be pleased to see her eating *commes les francais* instead of scouting out the nearest Starbucks.

It was incredible that he wasn't taking her calls. Had he just stopped caring?

As she put her pad back in her purse she saw the note from Genevieve sticking out of her coat pocket. It read *Please knock on my door. I forgot to tell you something that happened the week before Monsieur Newberry died. I believe you will find it very interesting. G.*

Maggie put the note in her purse and collected her things. It was probably just a ruse to trap Maggie in her apartment for a long hour of chit-chat. As she left the shop, stashing the other half of her *macaron* wrapped in a paper napkin in her purse, she felt her phone vibrate. She answered it while she walked up the

Rue de Castiglione. She could glimpse the Place Vendome straight ahead.

"Hello, darling," her father said when she answered. She thought he sounded weary.

"Hey, Dad. Everything okay?"

"Your mother sends her love and we got Stan buried," he said. "It was a lovely service. Private and just lovely."

"Sorry I couldn't be there," Maggie said. "The will was read?"

"It was," her father said. "Not surprisingly, he left his money to some very eccentric characters back in San Francisco."

"Anybody we know?"

"None of that lot in Paris," her father said. "He left dribs and drabs to charities and organizations he was interested in but the bulk of his estate—which turns out to be considerable, by the way... to a man whose name does not appear anywhere else in Stan's papers."

"Really? Who?"

Maggie could hear paper rustling on the other end of the line and she stood at the street crossing waiting for the light to change.

"Stan ever mention a John Newton to you?"

"Never head of him."

"Well, anyway, we've contacted his representative..."

"Aren't you interested in meeting him?" Maggie interrupted.

"Meeting him? No. Why?"

"Well, Stan left everything to him. So obviously the guy was important to him."

"If Stan had wanted me to know him, he would have introduced us," her father said. "Or at the very least, mentioned his name."

It occurred to Maggie that her father was hurt by Stan's secrecy. She understood. It must feel to her father like Stan didn't trust him to accept him for who he was.

"How about the Paris flat?" Maggie asked. "He leave it to the San Francisco dude, too?"

"That's actually one of the weirdest parts about all this."

"Really? He left it to someone else? Who?"

"Me."

Maggie laughed. "He left that awesome two-bedroom flat in the heart of the Latin Quarter to you. And you're not totally flabbergasted?"

"I am surprised," her father said. "But not stunned. Your uncle and I once spent a summer living in the Latin Quarter after college."

"I never heard about this!"

"Well, no reason you should. You don't tell me every single thing you get up to, do you?"

"Whoa, were you guys involved in white slavery or black market drugs or something?"

"I hope Laurent understands your sense of humor better than I do. Anyway, as I recall, that summer was a fairly uneventful experience for both of us."

"Clearly not, Dad," Maggie said evenly. "He left you a million dollar apartment in the heart of Paris."

"I suppose it might be Stan's way of telling me how much I meant to him—you know, when we were younger."

"Oh, Dad." Maggie felt the sadness and the lost opportunities welling up inside her father even from this distance.

LATER THAT AFTERNOON, after a full morning of exploration in both buildings of the Galleries Lafayette, and a studied raid on *Ladurée* that was bound to leave her a pant size larger, Maggie came back to the apartment to sit in front of her uncle's laptop with a long list of possible passwords. She tried the birthdates of everyone in the family, Stan's boyhood dog, anagrams of Stan's name and the store for which he had worked for thirty years, even the names of his friends here in Paris. Nothing worked.

She took a break a little after four to have a cup of coffee and sit on the balcony. She tried to make her thoughts float freely, hoping they would reveal the more salient clues of the case, but she just ended up thinking about what she might like for dinner.

Thinking a shower might help, she bathed and washed her hair, then sat back down in front of her uncle's laptop with her wet hair wrapped in a terry cloth turban and a colorful plate of assorted almond, raspberry and kiwi *macarons* in front of her. She bit into one of the creamy, intensely sweet cookie cakes, then turned back to the laptop and typed in *JohnNewton* in the password box. She was rewarded with the immediate presentation of her uncle's desktop.

Who are you, John Newton? Maggie found herself wondering in her delight as she clicked on a folder on the desktop labeled *Published Posts*. She had read some of her uncle's work before by finding it cached as backlinks on other fashion sites and blogs. Now, she scrolled down a series of Word documents, each labeled with a date. Her uncle posted once a week. She opened a few and scanned the posts.

This can't be what they were after, she told herself. These posts were all readily available on the Internet. This isn't the only place to find them. She herself had gone to her uncle's blog site and skimmed through his archive posts weeks earlier.

She stared at the desktop. *Something about what I'm looking at is very important to the person who killed Stan*, she found herself thinking. *If I can see it or recognize it for what it is, it must be the evidence that will indict the murderer*. She clicked open a folder entitled *Musings*. It was empty. She opened the photo library application thinking that perhaps it was an incriminating photo and was surprised to see that there were well over a thousand photos on the laptop—none of them organized in any way to allow her to easily view them.

This is going to take awhile, she thought, getting up to make herself a cup of tea. Her cellphone rang on her way to the kitchen and she glanced at the screen, hoping it was Laurent, but knowing it wasn't. It was Ted.

"Hey," she said. "I got into Stan's computer."

"You're kidding. How?"

"My Dad called to tell me that Stan left everything to some guy in California called John Newton. Ever hear of him?"

"No, but I really only knew Stan from Paris. His California cronies never came with him. Maybe Jeremy knows him. He's from California."

"Yeah, anyway, I tried his name as the password and it worked."

"Very clever detective work, Madame Dernier."

"Thank you. Problem is there is nothing of any value that I can see on the laptop."

"Did you check his photos?"

"Funny you should mention that. I'm in the process now."

"Need a break? I'm in the neighborhood."

Maggie laughed. "You're *always* in the neighborhood," she said. "Do you ever work?"

"I'll have you know I got my two thousand word quota in for the day," he said, primly. "Now I get to screw off."

"You write two thousand words a day? I'm impressed."

"You don't do that much?"

"Hey, give me a break. My laptop is sitting in a French gendarme's evidence room and probably will be forever."

"Good point. Why don't you just use Stan's now that you know the password?"

"You know? I think I will."

"So? Come play with me? I can be there in twenty minutes. *Ten* if I don't stop to put on my pants."

"As tempting as that is," Maggie said, laughing, "I'm going to pass. Besides, unlike yourself, I don't have any word count done today and now, thanks to you, I have a way to do it."

"Well, far be it from me to get between a writer and her word count," Ted said. "Catch you later."

Maggie poured herself a cup of tea and settled back down with the laptop. She counted eight folders on the desktop and opened each one up. In the last folder, she found another folder entitled "Last W&T." She clicked it open to find a pdf file of Stan's will. Since she already knew everything went to the mysterious John Newton, Maggie didn't get too excited with her discovery. She idly flipped through the pages to confirm that this was, in fact, her uncle's latest will. The date indicated it had been drawn up five years earlier so perhaps it *wasn't* the most recent version, she reasoned. She quickly scanned the document until she came to the point where she should have seen Mr. Newton's name. Instead, she saw the beneficiary to all of Stan Newberry's earthly possessions was one Diane Zimmerman.

"ALRIGHT, darling, let's see if we can do this detective business from long-distance. What do you have?"

Maggie adjusted the computer screen so she could see Grace better. "I have four solid suspects but I haven't ruled out anyone," she said.

"Okay, so in other words you haven't made any progress."

"Well, I know *I* didn't kill him," Maggie said. "Although I'm not too sure about you."

"Oh, it's great that you can joke about it now," Grace said. "Okay, first off, this Bijou character is highly suspicious."

"Based on what?"

"Based on the fact that she's a size zero and pigs down *profiteroles* and champagne twenty-four seven so I want her to spend the rest of her life in prison."

"That is so not helpful, Grace. Next?"

"Who are your suspects?"

"Jeremy, because he's been lying from the get-go. Because he's Stan's ex-lover and was in the process of being dumped by Stan. And because I have every reason to believe he tried to run me down with his car."

"Okay, that's good. Is he your number one suspect?"

"Absolutely."

"Number two?"

"This guy named Denny who was Stan's rival."

"He's the guy who broke into your apartment? And by the way, I cannot believe that he's still walking around after breaking and entering! What kind of justice are the French practicing over there?"

"I don't know. Anyway, he's in cahoots with Jeremy so it might be that one killed Stan and it's to the benefit of the other to aid and cover up. For some reason."

"I see. And the rest of your lovely crew?"

"There's Bijou, who is kind of mysterious but not an obvious suspect, although she *was* sleeping with Denny who is definitely a suspect. And then there's Diane. I found a will on Stan's computer leaving everything to her. That is about as serious a motive as there is."

"But didn't you say he gave all his money to someone else?"

"Yes, so there was obviously a later will but what if Diane didn't know that? It's a motive."

"Okay. What about your boyfriend?"

"If you're referring to Ted, he's not a suspect."

"I notice you didn't say he wasn't your boyfriend."

"He's not that, either."

"Well, why isn't he a suspect, pray tell?"

"Well, first, he wasn't even *at* the party during the time Stan was killed. He'd left over an hour earlier with some model. And second, I cannot tell you how helpful he's been to me."

"Which is exactly what the murderer *would* be in order to throw you off the track."

"He *loved* Stan."

"They *all* did except for the Australian dirt bag. So nothing else helpful on Stan's computer?"

"Not really. I even reread his blog posts for the last year. He was acid-tongued but this is the world of fashion. They're all pretty bitchy. Him not more so than anyone else."

"And no incriminating photos?"

"A lot of naked people," Maggie admitted. "But this is fashion —not to mention Paris. They don't consider nakedness something to be ashamed of."

"And his emails?"

"They're taking a little longer to slog through. He knew a lot of people."

A long wail emanated from the background on Grace's end and she sighed.

"I feel my reprieve is coming to an end," she said.

"Is that Zou-zou? Isn't she a little old for naps?"

"Bite your tongue," Grace said. "I take any break from the little dears I can get. If she's twelve and still taking naps, I'll thank God for it."

"Maybe you could enroll her in college by then and be rid of her altogether."

"Oh, just you wait, Aunt Maggie. Your time is coming. I for one can't wait to be on the front row to watch Maggie Dernier in the ever classic role of Perfect Mommy. Really. I can't wait."

"Yeah, well, you may have to."

"Really? Why? Something up with Laurent?"

Another wail—this one more insistent—made Grace turn her head away for a moment.

"You go, Grace," Maggie said. "We'll catch up later. You've been a big help."

"Get your confessions, darling," Grace said. "Screw the

evidence and the clues. You'll never finish collecting that stuff. Get the confession."

"I'm on it, sweetie," Maggie said. "Go rescue your baby from Nap Hell."

Maggie snapped off the monitor and picked up her legal pad. She looked at what she had written and frowned. She knew Grace was right. Clues and circumstantial evidence might be helpful back home but here the police would need an admission of guilt before they acted.

"I need to start making some people uncomfortable," Maggie said aloud. "Laurent is right. There's no easy way to do this."

The fact that she had no answers and didn't know what was going on wasn't important, she realized. Making people think that she did have the answers was the fastest way to flush the guilty party from the underbrush.

It was also, she knew, the most dangerous.

After an early dinner, Maggie locked up the apartment, loaded her bookbag with Stan's laptop in case she found a comfortable café where she could spend the evening, and emerged onto the street ready for a long walk to clear her head. It was cold but not unusual for early November. She found herself wondering as she walked what Thanksgiving would look like this year. *Would she be back in St-Buvard? Did Laurent want her to be?* She jammed her hands deep into the pockets of her wool jacket and turned onto the Quai Saint Michel. The wind from the river punished her as soon as she turned but she always found the view of the church in the river so refreshing and exciting that it was worth the pain.

Ahead, she saw the mighty twin spires of Notre Dame looming and beckoning. The cathedral was like a huge magnet, she found herself thinking. Ever since she was a child, when she came to Paris on shopping trips with her mother and sister, she found the cathedral personally attracting her. Even more than the Eiffel Tower, it spoke to her soul somehow. If she ever thought she could be persuaded to believe in reincarnation, she would have to believe she once lived in Paris in the shadow of Notre Dame Cathedral.

As she quickened her pace in an attempt to warm herself, Maggie felt her cellphone vibrate in her coat pocket. She pulled it out and squinted at the screen. It was an international call from the States.

"Hello?"

"Is this Maggie Dernier?" A very New York female voice mangled the pronunciation of her last name but seemed friendly enough.

"It is. Who is this?"

"This is Sheila Danvers," the woman said. "I'm an agent with Sloan and Danvers Literary Agency in New York. You're a friend of Ted Gilbert's?"

"Oh! Yes. How are you?" *Why in the world was Ted's literary agent calling her?*

"I'm very well, thank you, ever since I read the first three chapters of your manuscript *Fashionably Dead*, I've been dying to get the rest."

Maggie stopped walking. "You have my book? How?"

"From Ted. You didn't know he sent me your manuscript? Oh, that Ted is a naughty boy. But I hope you'll forgive him, Maggie, since I'm prepared to offer you a contract with my agency based on these first three chapters and I have to tell you that absolutely never happens with a work of fiction."

"You want to represent me?" Maggie turned to face the Seine and watched as the sun glinted off the cold green surface. *She was going to have an agent!*

"Yes, I do. And I also want the rest of the book as soon as possible. I think it will do very nicely at a couple of different houses I know of and I hope you have more in your back pocket because they are going to want a three-book deal on this little darling. Maggie? You still there?"

I have an agent! I'm going to have a publisher! Maggie held out her arms wide to the river and the magnificent cathedral in the middle of it to encompass her joy and amazement.

"Maggie?"

She put the phone back to her ear. "Yes, I'm here," she said, breathlessly. "I'm flabbergasted. But I'm here."

Twenty minutes later, she was sitting in her favorite café overlooking the Boulevard St-Germain des Prés, still vibrating with joy over what happened to her. *Oh, she would have to strangle that Ted!* She laughed and noticed a few sour looks from nearby French women trying to enjoy a quiet moment in the café.

Maggie looked around the café and watched the patrons as they ate. *Food was so important to the French.* She marveled as she watched them eat and drink as if performing some exquisitely pleasurable, revered ritual. And then it occurred to her: she would throw a dinner party. She would invite everyone she suspected *à la Ellery Queen*. She would gather them all together in a warm and disarming evening of fellowship and then she would confront the killer. Flushed with her decision and the seemingly perfect resolution to her up-to-now stalled investigation, Maggie ordered another plate of *pommes frites* and another cup of hot spiced wine. Without giving it much more thought, she rang Bijou's number and left her a message inviting her to come to Stan's apartment tomorrow evening for dinner. She was about to call Diane when another thought occurred to her.

Oh, my God! Laurent! He will flip *when he hears about the literary agent.* She jabbed in Laurent's number and reached for her mulled wine. The fragrance from the wine's cinnamon and oranges seemed to fill her senses as the luscious Côte de Rhône infused her with warmth. She felt pampered and invincible. *He can go ahead and not answer,* she thought happily. *I'll leave him the most glorious message that he will have to respond to. He will be so thrilled to—*

"Yes? Hello?"

Maggie stopped and for a moment, she didn't know what to say. A woman had answered Laurent's cellphone. A woman with an English accent.

"Is...is Laurent there?" she asked.

"I'm not sure where he's gotten to this morning. Can I give him a message?"

Her heart and her joy deflating like a balloon with the air let out of it, Maggie said, "No, thanks." She disconnected and stared at the cellphone in her hand. Her body felt suddenly very heavy and her shoulders sagged within her coat as a feeling of dread began to emanate slowly though her chest.

BIJOU WALKED over to the couch and sat down next to Jeremy. She leaned over and took his hand. He often could not stand her touch, she knew, and it was probably for this reason she often felt compelled to touch him. She waited for him to flinch or pull away. He did neither.

"I *tried* to get her to come out," she said softly.

Jeremy grunted and shifted on the couch but still did not extricate his hand.

"It's not my fault she wouldn't come."

"Denny was furious," he said. "I *promised* him you wouldn't let us down. He could have gone to jail!"

"I said I was sorry."

"No. No, you never did," Jeremy said, finally snatching his hand away and looking at her as if he only just realized how close she was to him. "And now we're all screwed. Thanks to you."

"You are angry," Bijou said, shrugging and examining her flawlessly manicured nails. "But I am not the author of this disaster. If anything, you and Denny have made matters worse."

"Which would *not* have happened if *you* had just gotten her out of the apartment as I'd asked you to." Jeremy jumped up from the couch and began to pace.

Bijou smiled. *In a way, wasn't this exactly what she had been hoping for?* Jeremy calm and controlled was not the man she knew. He was not the man she could so easily manipulate. Her intention in asking Jeremy to come by her flat today had been to pump him for information about Denny. The bastard was screening her calls and Bijou found it virtually inconceivable that it was because he was so soon tired of her. It must have something to do with Stan's death. She knew Denny and Jeremy were up to something and while it would be impossible to find out *what* from the intractable Denny Davenport, with the easily excitable Mr. Jeremy, there could be nothing easier.

"Can I offer you a drink, Jeremy?" she asked sweetly, rising to head to the kitchen.

"No, I don't want a damn drink," Jeremy snarled.

As Bijou walked to the kitchen, she noticed her cellphone on the dining room table was blinking, indicating there was a voice message. Thinking it might be Denny after all, she hurriedly checked her recent calls to discover the call was from Maggie.

"Jeremy," she said to him as she held up her phone. "Speak of the devil."

He stopped pacing and approached her, his eyes on her phone. "It's her?"

Bijou tucked the phone under her chin and listened to the voice mail. She watched Jeremy waiting impatiently for her to finish and she wouldn't waste his anxiety by giving him the news quickly.

"You are not going to believe this," she said.

"What? What did she say?"

Bijou could actually see that the poor man was nervous! He looked about to explode as he waited for her to tell him what the message was about.

"She's having a dinner party," Bijou said, placing the cellphone back down on the counter. "You said no to the drink?"

"Am I invited?" As soon as the words were out of his mouth, his eyes widened and he clapped a hand to his chest. He fished out his cellphone from his top pocket and read the tiny screen. "She just invited me," he murmured.

"Well, there, see?" Bijou said. "And you thought she didn't like you."

"She *doesn't* like me," he said. "I'm sure she thinks I killed Stan."

Bijou stopped in her turn toward the kitchen to look at him.

"Why would she think that?" she asked.

"For heaven's sakes, Bijou, don't you listen? Everyone knows that Stan whispered the name of his killer to her seconds before he died."

"And you believe *your* name was the last word on his lips?" Bijou felt very cold all of a sudden. She put out a hand to steady herself against one of the dining room chairs.

"It is entirely possible that it was," Jeremy said. "I told you, we fought just before he went upstairs. I was definitely on his mind in his last moments..." Jeremy pulled out a handkerchief and turned away from her as if overcome with emotion.

"So if she heard Stan say your name—"

"Exactly. She would believe he was announcing his killer when really he was probably just ...regretful."

How had she ever suffered this worm? How had she ever endured him? How had Stan? Bijou forced down the bile that Jeremy's words generated in her throat and turned back to the kitchen. If he didn't need a drink of something, she definitely did.

IT MIGHT MEAN SOMETHING. It might mean nothing. If Laurent did not call her back it either meant the woman did not deliver her message or that she did deliver it and it didn't matter to Laurent. *How could this be happening?*

Maggie sat in the café for a full hour, her earlier happiness over the agent gone.

Fine. If that's the way it is, then so be it. No holds barred, Laurent. Go live your life as I will mine.

The words felt hollow and she couldn't gather the emotion to fully feel them but it wouldn't stop her from acting on them. If he has moved on, then so would she. *Looks like this is your lucky day, Ted,* she thought as she gathered her purse and left a euro on the café table. From now on, since she clearly no longer owed Laurent further consideration for his feelings, she would do things based on her own assessment—not hampered by having to keep some lame promise to someone who didn't care anyway. She checked her GPS on her cellphone and reoriented herself from where she currently was and where she remembered seeing Denny's flat in the fourth arrondissement.

It's a terrible feeling knowing there is nobody to worry about you, she suddenly thought as she began walking in the direction of Denny's neighborhood.

Terrible and freeing.

Maggie walked quickly to the *le Marais* neighborhood. She had lost track of time sitting at the café and it was now well after nine. He might be out. He might have company. She hurried. A cold finger of dread traced down her spine as she became aware that there were fewer people on the streets here than she was used to in the Latin Quarter. The alleyways in the fifth were quaint, cobblestoned and full of jostling, laughing students and tourists. These narrow alleyways felt dark and sinister. On top of that, she had the very definite feeling that she was being followed.

12

"You have every bit as much to lose as the rest of us."

"In what way?"

"You know very well, Bijou," Jeremy said, trying to stay calm. "You wouldn't have this apartment, your couture wardrobe, that spiffy new car, none of it without—"

"Shut up! Don't say it!"

"And you'll lose it all just as fast. Worse, you'll go to prison."

"Goddamn Stan! Damn him to hell!"

"Not helpful, but I echo your sentiments. The problem is Maggie. You see that, right?"

Jeremy was exhausted with trying to make this stupid creature see reason. It almost made as much sense to strangle her, than to work this hard to bring her around.

"I think so," Bijou said, her shoulders slumping, her head drooping in defeat.

"Finally. Have you spoke with Denny recently?"

Ahh, there it was. She looked at him hungrily, her need filling her big blue eyes. He had been right to tell Denny to stop being available to her. Amazing how blind heterosexual men were to their own power with women when it was so clear to anyone else with half a brain.

"Have *you*?" she asked, her breath quickening with her longing.

"It was Denny who suggested we talk," Jeremy said. "He and I have looked at this from every possible angle. Now we need you. Denny needs you."

"Why doesn't he talk to me, himself?"

"He will, *cherie*. Just as soon as you and I nail down the basics of what we need to do. It won't be pretty. But will you do it? For Denny, if not for yourself?"

"Denny wants me to do this?"

"Told me with his own words."

"If I must, then I must," she said.

Jeremy sat next to her on the couch. "That's my girl." He took a long breath and reached out to pick up her flaccid hand in her lap. "It will be over before you know it and all will go back to the way it was before."

"Except that Stan is gone."

"Yes, except for that. But you'll be with Denny and that will be lovely, won't it? No more hiding? No more lying to Stan or having to endure his disappointment in you?"

Bijou's hands were limp and her face seemed to sag before him. She gave a long exhalation.

"I am going to drug her drink sometime during the dinner party," Jeremy said.

Bijou snapped her eyes to his face and he thought he could see her lips tremble.

"She will appear drunk, which won't be unusual for a dinner party."

"Ted—"

"Don't worry about Ted," Jeremy said, patting her hand. "Ted wants to seduce her. Once he sees that his chances are ruined for the night, he will be eager to see her collapsed in her own little beddy-bye so he can find sport elsewhere. You, perhaps?"

Bijou blinked her eyes at him in surprise. "You want me to sleep with Ted?"

"Only if it looks like he won't leave or has some gallant notion of spending the night on the couch so he can be perceived as an honorable knight mixing her orange juice and hair of the dog in the morning."

"You need him to leave."

"On his own or with your help. That's all you have to do. Make sure Ted leaves the apartment."

"What will you do?"

"Denny and I will take her, bundled in a rug, to a low point on the steps off Pont—"

"I don't want to know!"

Jeremy smiled. "No reason you should," he said. "It will be quickly done and all of us will awaken the next morning to a better day, a brighter future."

"You'll murder her like Stan was murdered."

"Why Bijou," Jeremy said, patting her hand. "What a terrible thing to say."

MAGGIE STOOD on the doorstep to Denny's apartment, her finger poised to press the button next to Denny's name on the apartment roster of mailboxes and stopped herself. *Was this madness?* Was the horrible breathless feeling of her heart pounding in her chest an indication that she shouldn't be doing this? *Paying an unannounced house call on the man who broke into her apartment less than a week ago?*

Oddly, it was the memory of her terror that night that galvanized Maggie to finally press the button. She actually found the need to restrain herself from tapping her foot in impatience as she waited for Denny to respond.

"Yeah?"

"It's Maggie Dernier. Let me in, please."

There was a pause and then the sound of a loud buzz as Denny unlocked the front door.

While grand and imposing from the outside as many Paris apartments were, the hallway in Denny's building looked downright dilapidated. Maggie stepped carefully over a large pile of garbage shoved up against the wall. Worried that things might start crawling in her direction, she took the ancient steps—smooth and steep from centuries of climbers—two at a time.

Denny was waiting for her in the doorway to his apartment. Maggie slowed her steps not to appear too eager and as she approached him down the hall, she could see as well as smell the cloud of *cannabis* wafting around him.

"Well, this is a surprise," he said, smiling at her and making a grand sweeping gesture with his arm to indicate she should enter his apartment in front of him. If she had hoped to catch him off guard, she could see he had quickly recovered.

"Thought we should talk," she said, entering his apartment as every alarm bell in her mind went off at full tilt. "Since you were in such a hurry last time we met."

"Hope that lamp wasn't valuable," Denny said and closed the door behind them. "May I offer you a drink? I'm sure I have a clean glass somewhere."

Dear God, what had Bijou seen in this guy?

"No, thanks."

"Sit?"

Maggie didn't see any place that wouldn't take major rearranging and housecleaning to make a possible seat.

"I won't be here that long," she said.

Denny walked over to the coffee table and picked a cigarette butt out of the ashtray. He put it between his lips and lit it with a lighter before Maggie realized it was the pot she smelled from the hallway.

"Okay, shoot," he said.

"What were you looking for that night at Stan's apartment?"

"A favorite baseball cap I'd left over there."

"The French cops don't see it as a B and E?"

He shrugged. "As you see."

"Why not?"

"They might have thought there was something between you and me."

Maggie frowned in confusion.

"You know," he said. "Like a past sexual relationship."

"Why would they think that?"

"I may have given them the idea."

That made sense. With the French, sex either explained everything or was at least a suitable alternative explanation.

"Did you push Stan off that balcony?"

"Not that I remember."

"What are you and Jeremy up to?"

She caught him there. For a moment his easy insouciance faltered.

"What do you mean?" he asked.

"I saw the two of you together. I was led to believe you hated each other."

"I don't give a damn what you were led to believe."

She stared at him and then eased her heavy book bag to the floor of the living room.

"How about we strike a little bargain, you and me, Denny," she said, pulling Stan's laptop out of the bag. She could see he was watching her carefully and she wondered just how stoned he was. "It's pretty simple, really. I give you something I think you want..." She nodded at the laptop. "And you give me something I want. Sound good?"

He licked his lips, not taking his eyes off the laptop. She wondered for one bad moment if he might just hit her on the head and take it.

"What do you want?" he asked, his former studied casualness gone.

"I want you to come to dinner at my apartment in two days time," she said. "Stan's apartment. The laptop won't be there then so you'll have to just come for the food and whatever else I have on the menu."

He looked at her and then back to the computer.

"And what do I get?"

She handed him the laptop.

"You get two minutes alone with this right now. Whatever you need to do, whatever you need to delete, I don't care. Two minutes. Do we have a deal?"

He reached for the laptop and kicked a pile of clothes and newspapers off the couch so he could sit down. He put the laptop on the coffee table and opened it up.

"Password?"

"JohnNewton."

Maggie turned away and walked to the one window in the room and looked out. The view was of the interior courtyard. The trees were leafless and the stones were grey and slick with this morning's rain. It didn't look romantic as so many Paris courtyards could. It looked depressing.

In less than a minute she heard him stand up and approach her. He handed her the laptop and smiled.

"So will it be black tie or can I just wear jeans?" he said.

That bitch! What game was she playing at? Inviting her to dinner? What were they, *friends?* Diane sat in her Marriott hotel room off the Rue Lincoln one street off the Avenue des Champs-Élysées and willed her hands to stop trembling. She glanced at her reflection in the mirror over the dresser and winced. She was too old for any of this. She had been born too old. She deleted Maggie's voice message and immediately wondered why she felt the need to do that. Was even her voice an affront to her? Or was it all just evidence of a terrible experiment gone terribly wrong now needing expunging?

Diane crossed to the window with its barely visible view of the famous boulevard. *Is there any way to believe that this isn't Maggie's fault? Maggie and her goddamn family's?* As irrational as that sounded even to her ears, Diane couldn't help but take some comfort in it. It had been coming for a long time, she realized. The showdown, the face off. All the implied rejection and self-righteous judgments, all of it, had been building to a head for years. Until now. Until this moment when she would finally be able to reveal all, avenge all.

Starting with Maggie Newberry, she thought fiercely.

She sat down on the bed and felt her anger settle in her chest like a lodged infection. *Damn you, Stan*, she thought staring out into the Parisian night, the glow from the beacon lights on the *Arc de Triomphe* clearly visible from streets away.

If you weren't already dead, I'd be forced to kill you all over again.

THE FIRST THING Maggie did when she locked herself into her apartment that night was to pour herself a large glass of Pinot Noir and compare the hard drive history after Denny had deleted his email to the duplicate copy she had put on her iPad, using it as a portable external hard drive. It took less than fifteen minutes to see what he had deleted. It was an email from over a year ago. Maggie hadn't read that far back yet. It was a reference to a very detailed and obviously successful exercise in embezzlement involving Stan's last employer, Gumps department store in San Francisco. In the email, Stan appeared ashamed of his involvement and refused to take the money they had stolen. Jeremy, Bijou and Denny took their share and divided up his. Denny reminded Stan to delete the email. *Nice, Uncle Stan*, Maggie thought wearily. *But was it motive enough to kill?*

After a solid three hours of scrolling through her uncle's emails, Maggie didn't feel like she knew him much better than before. She had run across a comment in one of his later blog posts which alluded to his love of the handwritten note for communications with his friends and so she wasn't surprised to find mostly business-related emails on his laptop. His Facebook page—she was mildly surprised to discover he had one—was infrequently visited and his Twitter account reduced to one or two tweets a month. She noticed several zingers from Denny via Twitter—none of which Stan had bothered to respond to.

There was a brief email exchange between Jeremy and Stan that ended with Stan reminding Jeremy he considered email the vilest form of communication and unless his phone dialing finger was broken, would not be amused to see more from him.

So strange, Maggie thought. Stan obviously spent a lot of time on the computer. His history cache showed he kept tight tabs on Denny's blog and often visited certain designer's websites for news. A few of the emails he received were from dressers and photography assistants who sent him unposed photographs of models with no make up on, designers wearing sweat pants and haute couture gowns that were safety-pinned to their living mannequins to make them appear better fitting than they were. None of it was particularly flattering, Maggie thought. But hardly worth killing for. While he was clearly a good writer—animated and playful in his word choice—and he definitely knew everybody in the business, it was also pretty clear that her upright and proper uncle could easily be defined as the TMZ of the fashion world. Not pretty.

But worth killing for?

Later that night, unable to sleep, Maggie sat at the little bistro table in the kitchen and sipped a cup of peppermint tea. Giving weight to the fact that it was after two in the morning and so contributing to her feelings of loneliness, Maggie couldn't remember a time when she felt more alone. Not even that first year in Provence when she was assured by Laurent that it was all temporary even though everything else she heard and felt told her otherwise. She glanced out the window at the ghostly outline of the cathedral, spotlighted by flood lights that illuminated all of its architectural details. When she visited over three years ago, she thought she missed home and Atlanta and her friends then to the point she was sure she would never be able to stay in France. From her present vantage point and this point in time, that younger Maggie seemed very immature.

She sighed, rinsed out her cup and placed it in the dish drainer. At least then she had Laurent. She had the promise of the best relationship of her life—the love of her life in fact. But what she had wanted then was drive-through banking and the convenience of parking at Lenox Square mall. While she had agreed to stay on in France, she had never really agreed to it in her heart. All of a sudden she felt a wave of guilt over what must have felt like a lie to Laurent. For her to say "I do," but really still be waiting for the loophole and the opportunity to go back was dishonest. It had always been "I do, *but...*" And Laurent had known that all along, lived with it and hoped against it getting worse. But the threat had always been there: the moment Maggie would choose to go back.

She stood in the doorway of the kitchen, her eyes full of unshed tears and her heart breaking. He had been right. This *was* a separation. Maggie was choosing her old life over her new one with him. He saw that. And she really hadn't until now. Her heart heavy with the realization of her responsibility of her own misery, she flicked off the kitchen light and turned toward the bedroom when she heard Stan's cat meowing in the hallway. The beast came and went and rarely actually entered the apartment, preferring to eat his meals in a dish in the hall. It was unusual for him to call attention to himself except for those moments he was demanding food. Frowning, Maggie went to the door, unlatched the chain, pulled the door open and fumbled for the hall light. The cat sat perfectly still, staring at her from the middle of the hallway.

Maggie wasn't sure whether to shoo him away or try to lure him in. She glanced up and down the hall but the cat was the only thing visible.

"What is it, you stupid cat? Go away. Or come in."

The cat stood, arched its back, and moved to sit in front of Genevieve's door. He turned to look at Maggie and let out a long howl that had Maggie bolting from her apartment to chase him away. *Damn cat would wake everyone!* As Maggie tried to shoo him back down the hall, she noticed that Genevieve's door was ajar.

What the hell? Maggie watched the cat scamper down the hall then turn and watch her as she stared at Genevieve's open door. Tentatively, Maggie pushed the door open with her foot.

"Genevieve?" There was no answer. *Should she just close the door? Was the poor woman passed out on the couch? Had she forgotten to lock up for the night?*

Or to even shut the door?

Maggie glanced at the cat again and noticed something she had failed to see before. The cat was making faint little pink tracks on the worn hallway carpet. Maggie felt her stomach clench before she even leaned down to confirm what she thought was seeing.

The cat's paws were bloody.

Maggie stood frozen in the hallway, trying to decide whether she should retreat to her own apartment and call the police or enter Genevieve's apartment, when the hall lights went out.

With panic rising in her throat, Maggie fumbled for the light switch which was on a timer. When the lights snapped back on, she instinctively pushed open Genevieve's door. The wedge of light from the hallway illuminated the woman's foyer where the trail of blood was easily visible and the trail of tiny cat prints led from the living room to the front door.

"Genevieve?" Maggie said again, louder. She took two steps into the apartment and saw her, slumped on the rug in front of the couch. The rug that was soaked black with blood.

13

Laurent leaned down to examine the withered rootstock. The cold air of mid November cut into his windbreaker as he knelt in the dirt. He looked down the long line of trussed and desiccated vines and felt a bleakness that matched the landscape. Never before had his land failed to lift and sustain him. Never before had he walked its perimeter or surveyed his kingdom without a sense of pride and satisfaction. This morning, he felt like his vineyard had betrayed him. The very thing that had given him so much pleasure--a purpose in this world--was now the very thing that was making it impossible to keep his wife.

Ruefully tossing down the broken vine, he scratched his head and looked back toward the large stone *mas* where the Australian girl still slept.

Did it always have to be one or the other? he wondered. *Was the universe truly set up such that one had to choose one love or the other? Did not some people have everything?* He thought of Jean-Luc happily tucked in with his beloved Danielle but shook his head.

What more could he have done? Was the price for his happiness —for Maggie's happiness—that he become her pet Frenchman living in a suburb of Atlanta, Georgia? The trained bear trotted out at dinner parties to cook and beguile and add to her collection of unusual souvenirs of a well-lived life? What about *his* need for a well-lived life? Must it include losing the woman—the only woman—he loved? Laurent rubbed his hands against his jeans and began to walk back to the house.

Had it only been Maggie's choice, he wondered? *Or just obviously her choice*? He realized it didn't matter. *Whoever* chose...the result was the same. Both were ready to walk away to get what they wanted. What they really wanted.

The recent evidence of Maggie's betrayal, revealed to him two nights earlier, hadn't been the catalyst or even the final nail in the coffin of their marriage. That had happened the day he had driven her to the train station in Arles and allowed her to get on that train to Paris. He wouldn't lay all the blame at her feet. He had played his part, too.

As he approached the house, Suzie stepped out on the stone patio. She was holding a large mug of the coffee he had made that morning. She stood wrapped in a bulky duvet, her bare legs seemingly impervious to the cold. Her young face radiated in a welcoming smile just for him. Laurent felt a tiny part of his burden lessen when he saw her and quickened his step.

Maggie decided she wasn't surprised by anything the French police said. In her experience with them, they seemed to consider instinct and personal experience equally as important as physical evidence or signed confessions. They had taken her statement, taped off Genevieve's apartment and left. Genevieve had been stabbed in the neck—that much Maggie could see for herself when she found the body. As to *when* it happened or how the killer gained entrance to the apartment—things Maggie would have imagined the police would understand were of interest to her, living right next door—this information was not forthcoming. Maggie decided it was likely because they just didn't know.

Was the murder related to Stan's death? Was it just a coincidence? If it wasn't a robbery, what was the motive? Maggie stood in front of her bathroom mirror and applied gloss to her lips before heading out to do the shopping for tonight's dinner.

Did the killer get the wrong apartment?

She gathered up her purse, checked the weather on her smartphone, and grabbed an umbrella. It seemed inconceivable to her that such a thing could happen—a next door neighbor was murdered while Maggie slept—and she was not calling Laurent straight-away to tell him. She grimaced. At best, Laurent would give her a healthy dose of I-told-you-so. At worst, she would have to relay the message via his new girlfriend. The nausea that she had felt intermittently since she first spoke to the woman on Laurent's cellphone threatened to overwhelm her. She sat down on the couch to catch her breath and give her stomach a chance to settle.

She still couldn't believe he had replaced her so quickly. *Where had he found her?* There were only village teenage skanks or old women in St-Buvard. He must have met her in Aix or Arles although why he would be in either of those towns...*unless it was for the food market...but who was there to cook for now that she was gone? Why would he have gone to the bother?*

A feeling of misery cascaded over her as she thought of the bother Laurent had always gone to in preparing their meals. *For her. What a cliché I am*, she thought. *Not appreciating his acts of love, his messages of affection. I wasn't just trying to learn French this year, she thought. As a newly wed, I should have been trying to learn the language of Laurent and his ways.* It suddenly occurred to Maggie that because she wasn't listening to his nonverbal expressions of love, his purely *Laurent* exhibitions of devotion, because she was comparing him to her former boyfriends back home, she never saw what he had been offering her.

She forced herself to stand up and shoulder her bag. *And now it was too late. Even if I went crawling back to him and begged for forgiveness, this woman would always be between us. This time would always be a beacon of the rift—the evidence of my lack of faith in his love. No, she wouldn't be able to get past it. Would he? If he thought she had been with another man? It was hopeless,* she thought, stepping out into the hall and forcing herself not to look at the taped off entrance to Genevieve's apartment. As she approached the stairs, she saw the cat sitting by his empty food bowl on the landing, eyeing her indictingly.

Bijou put down her cellphone and walked to the double bank of French doors of her apartment as they overlooked the Seine. She felt a sense of peace that she had not felt since many weeks before Stan died. She realized that now as she stood there, missing him, loving him, avenging him.

She spread her arms out as if giant angel wings hung at the ends of her fingers and she could leap from her balcony and glide over the river, across the Tuileries, and back over the Île de la Cité to alight nose-to-nose with the gargoyles of Notre Dame.

I am doing it for you, Stan, she thought with a tired smile. *It won't bring you back. I know that. But it will help me go forward without you.*

It occurred to her that she hadn't truly smiled since his death. The thought made her smile even broader.

As she turned back to the interior of her apartment, she saw that her phone was silently ringing. She picked it up, her smile even wider.

"Hello, Jeremy," she said.

"You ready for tonight?" he asked.

"I am."

"You seem to have made peace with what has to be done."

"I have."

"I guarantee you'll feel even better once it's all done and behind us."

"I know that, Jeremy," she said. "I understand that now. Is everything in order on your end?"

"Like ducks in a row. Everyone plays their part, it'll go off perfectly."

"Any special preparations I should do?"

"Just look irresistible tonight," Jeremy said with a chuckle. "Like you can't help doing anyway."

Bijou felt a wave of affection for him. He really was a bundle of contradictions, she thought. It was no wonder she a little bit hated him and a little bit loved him.

"*Je suis prêt*," she said. *I am ready.*

"I know you are, darling," Jeremy said smoothly. "I know you are."

MAGGIE CRADLED her cellphone and reached across her bedside table for the bronzer she had bought today. She squinted in the bedroom mirror. Her reflection came back to her as pale and frazzled. Not exactly the look she was going for as the hostess of this very important dinner party.

"Are you sure this is a good idea? Confronting the murderer like this?" Grace interrupted her thoughts on the other end of the phone line and Maggie looked away from the mirror.

"It worked for Ellery Queen," she said.

"...who is fictional."

"There will be six people here, Grace," Maggie said.

"Okay, you're citing safety in numbers? Because isn't it just possible that your uncle's murder was a group effort? I mean, one to plan, one to obfuscate, one to actually do the deed?"

"Even if that's true—and it's really unlikely—these people may hang out together but they can't agree on anything—nobody is going to risk implicating themselves by hurting me unless they're the actual killer."

"You think."

"Well, that's what the dinner is about, to find out for sure."

"So you don't know who the murderer is?"

"Well, I think I do. I suppose something could happen at the dinner to surprise me."

"You mean like you being stabbed to death while you serve the *hors d'oevres*? No wonder Laurent didn't want you doing this."

"Look, Grace, I have to stir things up," Maggie said in frustration. "If I don't goose these people, everything stays the way it is —Stan a suicide and some bastard just carrying on with no consequences for his actions."

"I get it, Maggie," Grace said. "I just don't remember you and I doing this direct confrontation thing when we were doing our sleuthing thing."

"Weren't you the one who said get the confession?"

"Yeah, but I guess I was thinking just be there when someone breaks down sobbing and tells all."

"That's what I'm trying to make happen at the dinner. I can actually use the others to help me corral the guilty party and break him down. It will work, Grace, trust me."

"And if it does work, how does this translate into a conviction in the light of day down at the police station?"

"I'm going to be secretly recording it."

"I'm worried, Maggie, is all," Grace said.

Maggie tossed down the tube of bronzer on the bed.

"Oh, please don't," she said with exasperation. "It's very safe and none of these people is a career killer. I'll expose the murderer—"

"Who *is* the murderer, did you decide?"

Maggie cleared her throat. "After careful examination of the facts—"

"You mean the very few facts you have available."

"Yes, Grace," Maggie responded testily. "I have determined that the murderer is Jeremy."

"Really."

"You don't sound surprised."

"Darling, I have no idea who it might be. Why did you decide it was him?"

"Well, even if it's *not* him, it'll stir things up and very likely prompt the real killer, if it's not Jeremy, to reveal himself."

"You have totally been watching too many *Closer* episodes."

"We don't even get that show over here. This is from basic deduction."

"Oh, dear Lord."

"Okay, Grace, I appreciate your support but I feel strongly about this—and I am the one on the front lines so to speak—and I have to get ready for the party."

"Anybody else but me know you're doing this tonight?"

Maggie paused.

"I take it by your silence that that's a No?"

"*Nothing* is going to happen, Gracie," Maggie said. "Nothing except the public discovery of Stan's killer."

"Okay, you have to know that that is *not* going to happen, right? Whatever goes down, you're not really anticipating the culprit, whether it's this Jeremy character or whoever, to fling himself at your feet with a tearful admission of guilt and, by the way, an involuntary applaud of your brilliant sleuthing."

Maggie felt her face flush with embarrassment. "I'm certainly not doing this for the ego gratification," she said hotly. "This is the only way to get the stupid French police to reopen the investigation. I told you that."

"Yes, you did," Grace said tiredly. "Please call me when they've all left, will you?"

"To confirm that I am still alive?"

"Something like that, darling."

"I'll call as soon as the last guest leaves and I have Jeremy's tear-stained confession in my little hand."

Maggie could hear Grace's long sigh.

"Call me, darling," Grace said with resignation, and hung up.

Maggie sat on the bed holding her phone and wondered with a slightly sickening feeling in her stomach what Grace would have said if she'd told her about Genevieve.

AFTER SHE PULLED the Camembert out of the fridge to bring it to room temperature, she spent an hour walking through her carefully choreographed presentation of bringing Jeremy to his knees. First, she intended to put them all at their ease as any hostess would and then reveal the purpose of the gathering. That should prove interesting--even entertaining—to all nonguilty parties. For Jeremy, she fully expected a loud and offended denial. Maggie surveyed her preparations with satisfaction and went into the bedroom to dress.

Two hours later, Maggie welcomed what appeared to be the last guest on her list into her apartment. She had set out two plates of olives and *gougères* on the coffee table and a tray of filled champagne flutes. She wanted to keep things simple. She had found a photo of Stan and Jeremy together with the manic scrawl on the back *I'll see you dead first*, which she was planning as her *coup de gras*.

She anticipated the look on Jeremy's face when she presented him with the photo—she intended to pass it around the group as the original was hidden safely away—and it was all she could do not to jump right to the incriminating photo and watch Jeremy crumble. But she knew she had to do everything in stages in order to get the rest of the crowd behind her. Every bit of her plan was working smoothly, including the slightly suspicious glances she was receiving from each guest except Ted.

Out the window, the descending sun drenched the facade of

Notre Dame like some highly expensive stage prop conjured up just for the evening. Everything was exactly as she'd planned with the exception of one thing.

Jeremy was not there.

Bijou sat on Maggie's couch next to Denny. She looked the picture of the moon-eyed lovestruck teen even down to the detail of nearly having her head resting on his shoulder. Ted stood by the French doors, clearly enjoying the sight of the sun going down on the cathedral and talking with Diane who stood opposite him speaking softly.

How can I do the Ellery Queen thing if my suspect doesn't show up? It was maddening! Jeremy had always shown every hint of feeling left out up to now to the point that the last thing Maggie would have believed possible was that he would blow off a dinner party hosted by her. She frowned. *Unless he thought he might be exposed tonight?* She shook off the thought. It's true Jeremy acted downright paranoid at the best of times but he could no more pass up a party—especially with this lot—than tell the truth when his life depended on it.

Maggie approached Denny and Bijou on the couch and was surprised to see Denny roughly disengage himself from Bijou and stand up.

"The toilet?" he said.

Maggie nodded in the direction of the hallway and wondered, briefly, if he might not just head on to the bedroom and rifle through her jewelry case. Bijou grabbed her hand and pulled her down onto the couch, spilling some of Maggie's champagne in the process.

"Come, sit, *mon vieux*," Bijou said.

"You doing okay, Bijou?"

"This is exactly what I would like to ask you, Maggie. You look so sad tonight. You look like you have lost your best friend...perhaps to your husband."

Maggie smiled sadly. "Yeah, that'd be pretty bad," she said.

"What is it?" Bijou asked. "What makes you so sad?"

Without realizing she was about to say it, Maggie found herself on the verge of telling Bijou everything about Laurent and the woman who answered his phone, about the separation and what a fool she had been. Instead, she fought to keep the words in and the tears from cascading over her lashes.

"Oh, Maggie!" Bijou said, running her hand up and down Maggie's arm. "It's about your husband, isn't it? Have you broken up?"

Maggie took a long breath to fortify herself and tried to smile.

"It's possible," she said, surprising herself that her voice sounded as strong as it did speaking the words.

"Oh, I am so sorry," Bijou said, looking very much like she was going to start crying too. "I hate sad stories. And this is so sad."

Maggie tried to shake herself out of the mood.

"Well, you know?" she said to Bijou before taking a swallow of her champagne. "There's nothing for it and that's not what this party is about so let's just leave it alone, okay?"

Bijou nodded and patted Maggie's hand. "Tomorrow we will drink wine, just us two, and sort it all out," she said. "If it can be salvaged, we will concoct a plan, okay?"

Maggie nodded, finding herself grateful for Bijou's simple answers.

"And if not, we will salve the pain," Bijou said.

At that moment Ted approached and knelt down by the couch.

"Hey, everything okay, you two?" he said.

"Just girl talk, Ted," Bijou said. "Unless you speak that language?"

Ted laughed. "Nah, I'll leave that to you." He caught Maggie's eye as if to ask: *is everything okay?*

Maggie took herself in hand and stood up with her drink. She patted Bijou's shoulder. "Tomorrow for lunch, okay?" she said. "And thank you."

"*Pas du tout*, darling," Bijou said, which just made Maggie sadder. Laurent always said that.

Ted took Maggie by the elbow and propelled her into the kitchen where the catered boxes sat ready to have their contents distributed to the six, now five, waiting dinner plates. He refilled his champagne glass as Maggie began to dish up the *cassoulet*.

"You did invite Jeremy, didn't you?" he asked.

"I did," Maggie said. "I'm as surprised as you are that he's not here."

"Well," Ted shrugged. "It's a better party for it."

Maggie grinned at him.

"It is," she said, "except he was kind of the centerpiece of my entertainment for tonight."

Ted blinked at her for a moment, frowning and then brightened.

"Ahhhh," he said. "So you finally think Jeremy's the murderer."

Maggie tonged up salad greens from a large store-bought cellophane bag and shook out the packet of blue cheese crumbs onto each plate.

"The French eat their salads after the main meal," Ted pointed out.

"I'm not French," Maggie said and then stopped. She turned and looked at him. "You're right," she said. "I'll serve it last."

"Hey, you can serve it whenever you want," Ted laughed. "Bijou's your only Frenchie and trust me she doesn't care."

"It's not that," Maggie said, setting the salads aside. "I don't think I've done myself any favors by sticking so rigidly to my vision of how things would be done back home. A little adaption would probably have been better in the long run."

"When in Rome?"

"Yeah, something like that."

"So I heard from Sheila that you have a minor bombshell to share with me tonight and I cannot imagine why you haven't said something by now."

Maggie stopped scooping up the *cassoulet* and swiveled toward him. "Oh, my God, Ted, how could I have forgotten!"

"I know, right?"

"It's so amazing and I'm totally over the moon about it, really. It's just that there has been so much going on..."

"Like your neighbor getting offed."

"Yes, can you believe that? And the police haven't been back to the crime scene or asked me to come down to give my statement or anything."

"Did you see something to make a statement on?"

"Well, no, but they don't know that. They should exhaust every avenue, you know? Really unbelievable."

"But back to Sheila..."

"I've sent her two more chapters—which she loved and now I have a New York literary agent. *Your* New York agent, in fact. I can't thank you enough for sending her those chapters."

"No problem," he said drinking down the rest of his champagne.

"Is Diane okay tonight?" Maggie asked as she peered into the living room. Diane was still standing at the French doors, hugging her arms as if she were cold and not talking to anyone.

"Yeah, why?" Ted said as he followed Maggie's gaze.

"She just acts so..."

"Miserable?"

Maggie looked at Ted for a moment as if she were getting an idea.

Ted frowned. "What is it? Spinach in my teeth? Awesome spinach puffs by the way."

"No," Maggie said, dropping the ladle back into the largest take-out container. "It just occurred to me that without Jeremy here there really is no point in continuing with this." She waved a hand to indicate the food sitting on the dishes on the kitchen counter.

"Wow. So it really was for his benefit. Want me to get rid of everyone?" Ted asked brightly, rubbing his hands together.

"I think you'd be doing all of us a favor," Maggie said, reaching for her champagne flute and refilling it.

THIRTY MINUTES LATER, Ted and Maggie were alone, sitting on the couch and picking at the duck *confit* and bean casserole. Denny and Bijou had left together, abandoning any attempt at romantic subterfuge. Diane left before Ted had even finished speaking.

Now, relaxed—if disappointed in the failure of her evening and her plan to reveal Jeremy as Stan's murderer—Maggie kicked off her shoes and tucked her feet under her. Ted was in the process of reenacting the scene earlier tonight where he asked Denny where his cat burglar clothes were and if he felt uncomfortable coming into the apartment through the front door instead of the window.

"He said he came in from your neighbor's balcony, by the way."

"Genevieve's? Did she know it?

"I thought you said she was out of town that weekend."

"You know, you're right. What a jerk. I still can't believe he broke into my apartment and the police did nothing."

"I can't believe you had him to your apartment for dinner," Ted said, looking at her over the rim of his wine glass.

"Well, it was all part of my really idiotic plan to force Jeremy into a public confession," Maggie said with a sigh.

"And you thought having Denny here would help that?" Ted shook his head. "Me, I always thought Denny looked guiltier than anyone."

"He has no obvious motive."

"Does anyone?"

"Good point. Anyway, I feel like I defused his interest in me by allowing him five minutes alone with Stan's laptop."

"You what?!" Ted nearly dropped his wine glass. Maggie was surprised at his reaction.

"Don't worry," she said. "I did it so I could see what, if anything, he deleted from it."

Ted mopped up drops of spilled champagne from the coffee table.

"And *did* he delete anything from it?"

"He did," she said leaning back into the couch and gazing out onto the image of the church through the windows, now hazy with a heavy fog drifting in. "But it wasn't worth killing over."

"In your opinion."

"That is true," Maggie admitted. "People kill for what you or I might consider trivial reasons."

"Can you share with me what it was?"

Maggie smiled. "It doesn't matter, Ted. And it only makes Stan look bad, too. Let's let sleeping dogs continue their slumber and your memory of him intact."

Ted's face relaxed. "I can live with that," he said. "I miss him."

"Yeah, me, too."

"So aside from the fact that Jeremy was a no-show tonight—"

"Which makes him appear even more guilty to me."

"But when you consider all the facts, it's possible that this whole party idea tonight might very well have been to trap the wrong man. Do you agree?"

Maggie looked uncomfortable. "I was fishing," she said. "I figured if I didn't flush out Jeremy, I might notice someone else looking guilty. I don't know. I guess I'm not very good at t his."

"What made you think to have a dinner party of all things? It's really kind of a strange tactic, don't you think?"

"It's how Ellery Queen did it. He would gather everyone in a room and then go around one by one and break everyone down until he got to the main suspect. It sounds so stupid when I put it into words. You're American. You probably have seen Ellery Queen in action."

"I have, in fact."

"I admit, at one point I imagined trying to explain it to my husband and that's when it really started to sound insane. I probably should have used that as some sort of gauge but because he's so against my being here and doing this, I left what I predicted his opinion would be out of the equation."

"So you didn't talk to him about it?"

"No. I decided I didn't need the ridicule or lack of support or whatever I knew I could count on from him."

"You sound bitter."

Maggie looked at him with surprise. "Do I?"

"And your husband sounds like a jerk."

"Well, he's not," Maggie said, her face hot with annoyance. "He's not at all. If anything, he's long-suffering," she said, beginning to feel the misery of earlier in the evening return. "Frankly, I'm beginning to think I didn't deserve him."

"Whoa," Ted said. "That's wild. You are such a gorgeous creature, Maggie, I can't believe there's a guy out there makes you feel like you don't measure up."

"That's *not* how I feel," Maggie said. "I'm just seeing some things I've done, or said in the past that were bratty and careless and how he never really called me on it. He just put up with it."

"And now? Sounds like there's an *and now* to this story."

"*And now*, he appears to have found someone who is a lot less work," she said quietly, sipping her wine.

Ted leaned over and kissed her on the cheek. "One thing I know, dear girl," he said. "Is that regardless of what you have done and said to your husband, I am here to tell you that you are totally worth the work." He leaned over to kiss her on the lips but she stopped him.

"No, Ted," she said. "I'm not ready for this."

Ted pulled back and examined her with a slight frown. "But maybe someday, you think?" he said. "I'm not wasting my time?"

"Is being friends with me a waste of time?"

"Well..." Ted scratched his chin and grinned. " If friendship is all I have to look forward to, I might invest a tad less time, I admit."

Maggie smiled tiredly at him. "No promises," she said. "I'm a long way from wanting anyone but Laurent."

"Even if he's cheating on you?"

Maggie looked back to the touchstone of the church outside the window. "I don't know," she said. "Maybe even then."

An hour later, Ted had gone home and Maggie was tucked into bed, exhausted but too wired to sleep. She glanced at her cellphone on the bedside table. *Was it really that easy for him to just write her out of his life?* she wondered with a deepening sadness. No phone call, no texts, no word from him in nearly three weeks.

Really, Laurent? Maggie buried her face in her pillow and cried as quietly as she could although there was no neighbor to hear or care. After a few minutes, she got out of bed, went to the bathroom and washed her face with cool water. She went back to the bedroom, grabbed her phone and the quilt off the bed and settled down on the couch in the living room to watch television with the sound muted. It was after three in the morning and she could still hear people laughing and talking at the bistros and bars in the alley below her apartment.

She looked at Ted's wine glass on the coffee table and smiled. *Thank God for him,* she found herself thinking. After the attempted kiss, he had quickly moved on to safer ground by encouraging her to talk about her manuscript. Maggie had surprised herself by how talking about the work totally distracted her from her situation with Laurent and the unsolved mystery.

Clearly, I should have been writing books all along, she thought wryly. Ted loved her prose but was quick to point out little habits she had exhibited that she would do well to quit. In some ways, she realized, talking to another writer was the first dose of true camaraderie she had felt since Grace left. Better in some ways, since she and Grace—although the dearest of friends—were so very different. Grace was polish and elegance and style and Maggie was quirky and neurotic and casual. She grinned just thinking of her friend.

But as good as it was to talk to Grace, she realized that even that wasn't as primal as connecting with someone who knew and felt the process of writing. The connection she had felt with Ted tonight wasn't sexual and it wasn't romantic although she admitted it could easily turn into that. It was a meeting of two like minds, of two creative spirits who knew how it felt to bleed from the fingertips when trying to fashion just the right phrase to elicit the desired reader response. Nothing against any of the other people in her life, but that connection was valuable to her. And new.

Ted had given her a list of websites to help with self editing as well as advice on dealing with their joint literary agent. Maggie still couldn't believe she had representation. She had always thought that took years of struggle and rejection. It had all happened so fast and so easily. A pinprick of regret touched her buoyant memory of the talk with Ted when she thought, for a moment, of what Laurent would think if he knew. *Would he be proud of her? Or would he just be grateful that she had finally found a hobby of her own to give him some peace?*

When she thought of that last point, she realized how far down a bad road she had come with Laurent. It struck her that she had developed an intricate web of resentment to match his wall of defensiveness over her neediness. Did she really think that the man she fell in love with in the south of France four years ago would only feel relief at her accomplishment? Relief to get her off his back? If that was true, it was her doing entirely. She had crafted that sad state of things, snarky comment by snarky comment. And, if by some miracle owing only to Laurent's strength of character and love for her it *wasn't* true, then she was only continuing a long line of injustices to him to believe it now.

Can people change? She sat up straight and looked at her cellphone. Was it really possible for her to shed the chronic homesickness—which she realized now was really just a grass is greener mindset—to accept and appreciate the goldmine of love and opportunities she had here in France with Laurent?

And if people can change, she thought, biting her lip, *is it too late to do it*?

Suddenly, as she watched the phone, the screen lit up with an incoming call. For one mad, hopeful moment, she thought it must be Laurent and she snatched up the phone and pushed *Accept* before she saw that it was only Ted.

"Hey, Ted," she said, trying to hide the deep disappointment in her voice.

"You still up?" She thought his voice sounded tense and it occurred to her a phone call in the middle of the night wasn't good no matter who it was from.

"Is everything okay?"

"Not really," he said, blowing out a long exhalation. "I found out why Jeremy was a no-show at your party tonight."

"Jeremy? Did something happen to him?"

"You might say that," he said crisply. "The cops fished his body out of the Seine an hour ago."

14

Jeremy dead? Did that even make sense?

Maggie thanked the cashier at her corner *boulangerie*, took the paper triangle that held her warm chocolate crepe and plunged back into the crowds on the Quai Saint Michel. The streets were full of more tourists than usual this morning, as Maggie elbowed her way to a bench in the park at the back of the cathedral. Even in November, the birds were a nuisance and never more so than in the square behind Notre Dame. Maggie watched the tourists tear off bread from their *fromage* sandwiches to lure the sparrows to alight on outstretched hands. She had been charmed by the bird feeding a month ago. Now she wondered if the tourists were also equipped with bottles of antibacterial wash.

She looked at the river, green and fierce in the cold weather. It was inconceivable to her that *that* is where Jeremy had ended up. He was always so cold, she thought. He was always so buttoned up, with a scarf against the chill. To have ended up at the bottom of the cold, cold Seine...She shivered and shoved her breakfast away, suddenly not hungry. Three bold pigeons landed on her bench and she shooed them.

Ted had found out through Bijou who had found out through, of all people, Jeremy's mother, who had called her in hysterics after being contacted by the Paris police. Maggie was impressed the police had contacted anyone at all. She wouldn't have been surprised if they'd just tagged him and shelved him away in some obscure morgue for nonnationals. Ted had also heard from Bijou by way of Jeremy's mother that the police considered it a mugging gone bad.

Of course they did, Maggie thought. *If it hadn't been for the rope around his neck, they probably would've chalked it up to another suicide.* She peeled a piece of crepe off and tossed it to the ground, which prompted a flurry of feathers as the pigeons fought each other for it.

If Jeremy killed Stan, then who killed Jeremy? And if Jeremy didn't kill Stan, what does his death mean to the whole investigation? It was not believable that his death was a coincidence. She turned and looked in the direction of Stan's apartment. It also was no coincidence that Genevieve was murdered.

But what did it all mean? How did all the pieces fit together? And if whoever killed Stan *also* killed Jeremy, why was the murderer still going around killing people? Was this a fashion serial killer or was he done now?

The worst of it, in Maggie's mind, was the fact that Jeremy's murder happened without question during the time she had everyone at her apartment—effectively giving everyone a very tidy alibi. *So was there somebody new she needed to be looking at for Stan's murder? Someone she hadn't met yet?* She ripped off a large chunk of the crepe and threw it to the birds.

She obviously was nowhere near finding the person responsible for any of these murders, she thought with disgust. Laurent was right. Grace was right. Danielle was right. She should never have come to Paris. She should have left it to the police. She was no closer to finding Stan's murderer and had only succeeded in tanking her marriage in the attempt. Maggie shredded the rest of the crepe and gave it to the birds, drawing glances of annoyance from a young couple who were trying to make out on a nearby bench and were now waving away birds drawn to the feast Maggie was dispensing.

Her phone buzzed and she looked at the screen to see that it was Ted. She pushed *Not Accept*. She wasn't in the mood to talk about it, rehash it, or analyze it. Without thinking, she punched in her parents' number in Atlanta. Her father picked up on the second ring.

"Hello, darling," he said with enthusiasm. "I was just going to call you. Everything alright?"

Maggie decided against mentioning the latest body count. She had really only called to hear his voice or her mother's. As soon as he spoke, she felt herself relaxing.

"It's fine," she said. "Just thinking about wrapping things up here and heading back to St-Buvard." Her words surprised her because up until that moment she didn't realize that that was exactly what she wanted to do. "Or some place," she added lamely.

"I'm sure Laurent will be glad to have you back," her father said.

I wish I were so sure, she thought, watching the pigeons continue to fight and peck at each other over the *crepe*.

"But I'm glad you called. I have some interesting information about Stan's will."

Maggie frowned. "Really? Like what? He decide to give a hitherto undiscovered yacht in Monaco to the League of Women's Voters?"

"Again, darling, I must confess to not understanding your wit," her father said but he was laughing. "No, I found out who John Newton is."

Maggie snapped her attention back to the phone call.

"I'm listening," she said.

"Well, I'm frankly astonished to have to tell you," her father said, deliberately revealing his information as teasingly slow as possible. "That John Newton is a sixteen year old boy."

"Okay, well, that's just perverse."

"It's not like that, darling," her father said with a hint of annoyance. "He is Stan's son."

"His *son*?" Maggie gave a gasp and her hand flew to her mouth as the surprise sank in. She smiled tentatively and shook her head in wonder.

"That's right. It seems that Stan impregnated a friend of his and whether as a result of a night of romance or through the aid of a clinic and a test tube I do not know, so please don't embarrass us both by asking. The short story is that you have a cousin."

"Short story is right," Maggie said. "We're talking O. Henry short story here. *Newton*?"

"My understanding is that Stan wanted to give the boy his name but was afraid it would complicate things if too many people knew he was the father."

"I am totally shocked, Dad," Maggie said, shaking her head. "Do we know the mother?"

"Turns out, we do," he said. "It's Diane Zimmerman."

Maggie looked out over the Seine and felt a few pieces of the puzzle click into place in her mind. "That kind of makes sense," she said slowly. "What about the will?" she asked. "The one I found on Stan's computer leaving everything to her?"

"It predates the one leaving everything to the boy," her father said.

"Are we going to get to meet John?"

"I think there's every reason to believe we will," her father said. "His attorney has conveyed to me the message that the boy is very interested in being connected with his father's people."

"I'll be damned. Old Uncle Stan. You little devil."

"It's likely he was just doing a good friend a favor," her father said. "But there you are. Take it from me, there's nothing quite like holding your own child in your arms."

"I just wish he felt he could have brought him home to us," Maggie said.

"It's possible it wasn't up to Stan."

"You mean Diane?"

"I don't have any other information as to that but she's there in Paris, isn't she? Maybe you could find out how she feels about John connecting with his father's family."

"I haven't been very friendly with her," Maggie admitted.

"And maybe you could amend that."

Maggie gathered up her *crepe* wrappings and shouldered her bag. "Yeah, maybe," she said.

AFTER A LONG WALK around the perimeter of the Île de la Cité trying to keep her thoughts in a line and her emotions from careening into those thoughts, Maggie let the start of a hard rain drive her back to the apartment where she climbed into sweat pants and a sweatshirt and wrapped up in a quilt on her couch.

Almost like I'm sick, she thought as she sipped a large mug of hot tea and stared out into the gloom of the rainy afternoon. Twice she fumbled for her cellphone to ring Laurent and both times she stopped herself. She was long past asking herself why *he* didn't call *her*. Danielle's scattered and veiled response to her on their last phone call made all kinds of sense now that it was clear that Laurent had hooked up with someone else. Pretty hard to be chatty and casual when you know your friend is being cheated on—and you told them it would probably come down like this.

Why hadn't she listened to Danielle? Or Laurent, for that matter? How was it possible that she had been so blind and so stubborn? No, she couldn't excuse herself for her blindness. Not when everyone around her was telling her that coming to Paris was a bad idea. Maggie just thought she knew better. As usual. And now she was paying the price for that arrogance. She looked at her phone. She was at fault. It wasn't up to Laurent to put it right.

What if his girlfriend answered?

Maggie took a long steadying breath and punched in his number. Every ring was like a knife in her stomach until she heard it roll to voice mail and she disconnected. She stared at the phone. *Had he screened her? Had the other woman*? She dropped the phone on the couch, put her face in her hands and cried her heart out.

THE BISTRO WAS one of the very oldest ones deep in the heart of the Latin Quarter, with Art Nouveau decor, brass fixtures, French posters, and waiters in long white aprons. When she first entered and seated herself, she crossed her ankles under her and sipped elegantly at her martini as if to strike a pose. How was it that all the celebrities were photographed looking so perfect, so *jejeune*? Well, the ones who *were jejeune* at any rate. Obviously, the ones who didn't bother with their hair or going out in public in last season's jacket—*those* ones simply didn't merit a photographer's interest. Bijou looked around the restaurant as if expecting a member of the paparazzi to jump out from behind the booths and start snapping her at any moment. She sighed and tightened her grip on her martini glass.

She would tell Maggie everything. Well, perhaps not everything. But enough. Enough that she would know how much she had cared about Stan. It was possible that Maggie didn't really know that yet. And of course, she would tell her that she and Denny had broken up. She took another sip of her drink, mentally rehearsing the words that would reveal how sorry she was to have broken his heart. If she didn't look careless and just a little *not* sorry, Maggie would soon guess who got whose heart broken.

"Bijou, you look beautiful. Have you been waiting long?"

Bijou knocked over her martini and began mopping up the spill with her napkin.

"Oh!" she said. "You startled me! *Merci*, Maggie. That is very sweet of you."

"Are you okay?" Maggie's brow was creased with concern as she sat down opposite her.

"Of course, I am okay!" she said shrilly, smiling too wide. "Why would I not be? Are *you* okay? That is the question, *ma chère*!"

The waiter approached and took Maggie's order for a glass of white wine. She turned back to Bijou.

"What is it, Bijou?" she said. "You're upset about something."

"I am not," Bijou said, pushing the wet napkin away from her on the table. "But Jeremy did just die two days ago!"

"And you hated Jeremy."

"I did not!" Bijou said hotly. She started to rise from the table but when she saw the look of alarm on Maggie's face, she forced herself back into her seat. "I'm sorry," Bijou said. "I'm a little upset."

"What's happened?"

Bijou couldn't help but marvel at the way Maggie asked the question. Her eyes looked so caring, so genuinely interested in Bijou's problem. *Americans*, Bijou thought. *They step over every line, push open every door—no matter how hard you tell them to stay back*. Her eyes filled with tears. *Just like Stan used to do*.

"Everything," she whispered. "Everything's happened."

The waiter came with Maggie's wine and a replacement martini for Bijou which he set in front of her while he deftly swept away the wet napkin from the table. He glanced at the unopened menu and turned on his heel and left the women in peace.

"Tell me," Maggie said.

Bijou shook her head. "We are to talk about your crumbling

marriage," she said. "I am supposed to be making you feel better about your life. Not the other way around."

"Friends are a two-way street," Maggie said.

"Yes?" Bijou reached out to Maggie and then snatched her hand back and picked up her martini glass instead. "Are we really and truly friends, Maggie? I hope so."

"Well, I think we are," Maggie said earnestly. "I hope so. Stan loved you so much."

Bijou nodded. "He did. And I loved him, too. So much."

"I know."

"No, you don't," Bijou said, her voice shaking. "I loved him so much that I killed for him." She watched Maggie carefully to see the reaction she was waiting for. The American nodded as if judiciously digesting the information.

"Really," was all she said.

"Yes, really," Bijou said.

"Maybe you'd better tell me about it."

Bijou made a face. "He thought I would help him after what he did. He never knew what Stan and I had together. Or respected it."

"Okay, I'm getting a little confused here," Maggie said. "Which *he* are you talking about?"

"*Jeremy*," Bijou said with a touch of exasperation. "I'm talking about Jeremy."

"Help him after he did what? What did Jeremy do?"

"You know."

"Push Stan off the balcony to his death."

"C'est ca." That's right.

Bijou watched Maggie take another sip of wine and then look over her shoulder as if trying to locate the waiter. *Oh, these Americans were very cool!*

"So Jeremy confessed to you that he killed Stan?" Maggie said.

"In so many words, yes."

"When?"

"Before your dinner party. He told me why it was that Stan spoke his name to you with his last breath."

"He thinks Stan said his name to me that night?"

Bijou nodded. "He tried to make it sound like it was because Stan just loved him so much but it was an admission of guilt. It was his twisted explanation for the very damning facts."

She watched Maggie pick up the menu and she felt like snatching it away from her and throwing it to the floor. *Did she not care what Bijou was telling her?*

"*You* even thought it was Jeremy," Bijou said. "Didn't you?"

Maggie nodded. "I admit I did," she said.

"And now because Jeremy is dead you think differently? You think Stan's killer is still alive? I am disappointed in you, Maggie. Up until today I thought that we were very much alike," Bijou said. "The only difference is that you want justice or some such idiocy." She stared at Maggie encouragingly as if expecting her to finish the thought. "And I want revenge," she finished. "It's a small difference, *je sais*."

Maggie stared at her. "Are you saying what I think you're saying?" She spoke slowly, as if she were trying to form the thought cohesively in her head but was struggling to make it gel.

Bijou smiled smugly because Maggie was not reading the menu now.

"Do you want to know what I feel?" Bijou said. "I feel *free* knowing that Stan's killer is dead. Because this is what I did for Stan."

Maggie stared down at the menu in her hands as if surprised to find it there. She looked back at Bijou who was still talking on and on about how much she loved Stan and how they could all sleep in peace tonight. Maggie thought Bijou sounded proud—as if this were all a competition for Stan's affections and she had somehow won. Maggie knew it wouldn't do any good to mention to Bijou that committing murder would hardly put her at the top of Stan's treasured people's list—or that the man was dead and so not likely to have such a list anyway.

Or that Maggie had just heard Bijou confess to murder.

La Prefecture de Police was situated on the Rue de Lutèce on the Île de la Cité. Built in the late 1800s under Napoleon Bonaparte, the imposing double-towered building had a long and colorful history, starting with the fact that it was originally a former palace that once served the Vichy regime during the German occupation.

When the call had come in from an administrative police *judiciaire* officer, Maggie had opted to walk to the headquarters as it was only a mile from her apartment. She found walking in Paris to be different from walking any place else in the world. The same distance on the track at her sports club in Atlanta took her an agonizing hour to labor through while the equal distance in Paris was a quick, mesmerizing jaunt down quaint and enticing alleyways filled with pistachio and chocolate shops, clever boutiques that only sold scarves, or tiny stores with culinary treasures she never knew she couldn't live without. Even the uneven walking paths over lumpy curbs and cobblestones didn't slow her down. In fact, they added to the pleasure of the experience.

The police lieutenant who had called her that day was brisk, clipped and efficient. She informed Maggie that she might have her stolen laptop back if she were to come down to the station for it. Maggie left her meeting at the bistro with Bijou after a strained and uncomfortable lunch. Bijou seemed completely oblivious to the fact that she'd confessed to murdering Jeremy. At least Maggie *thought* that's what she had done. When pressed for details, Bijou had simply smiled slyly and shaken a slow finger at Maggie.

"You are not going to solve me, Madame Dernier," she said. "I have

done all of Stan's friends the ultimate favor. I have done what they would not do. What the police would not do."

"Did you strangle him yourself?" Maggie asked. "Because as wimpy as Jeremy could be, he was still bigger and stronger than you."

Bijou had given her a look of amazement and scorn. "Do not be stupid," she said. But Maggie thought she looked a little sick when she said it. It was possible that Bijou wasn't really sure *what* she had done. It was also possible that Bijou had done nothing to Jeremy and this was all just wish fulfillment in an addled, emotionally confused mind.

Maggie wasn't sure Bijou wasn't a little mad.

The lieutenant at the station ushered Maggie to a long hallway and filled her lap with a clipboard and a sheaf of papers to be filled out before she could retrieve her property. Maggie filled in the first set of pages and quickly realized that the others were just different versions of asking for the same set of information. She wrote until her hand cramped. When she looked up, she was surprised to see the police inspector who had come to Genevieve's apartment when she was killed. The man was looking at her and frowning as if trying to place where he knew her.

Maggie smiled. "*Bonjour*," she said. "I'm from Genevieve Bonnet's apartment last month? Off of Quai Saint Michel?"

He approached her and nodded. "*Ah, oui*," he said. "That's right. The American. No more disturbances, I hope?"

Poor Genevieve. A violent murder in her own living room reduced to a "disturbance" for her many inconvenienced neighbors.

"No," Maggie said. "All quiet."

"You are not here for Madame Bonnet?"

"No, actually, my apartment was broken into the week before she was killed," Maggie said, nodding at the clipboard in her lap. "I'm recovering my stolen property."

"Paris is a big city," he said. "There is much danger."

No kidding, Maggie thought, not even shocked at the man's

insouciance. She could tell he was distracted and it occurred to her that that was often the best time to luck into information she might not normally be able to extricate from a valuable source.

"In fact," she said, "did you know I had a dinner guest murdered just a couple of nights ago?" She shook her head. "I'll *say* it's a busy apartment building. I'm from New York City and even *we* don't have that kind of action. Although the cops usually sort it out pretty quick."

He frowned at her. "A dinner guest was murdered?"

"Jeremy Hutten? I don't suppose that's your case too, is it?"

Surely, if it was homicide in the same arrondissement this guy would be aware of it?

The police inspector drew himself up to his full height of just under six feet and puffed out his chest. "That murder has been solved," he said, pursing his lips.

"Gee, that's great but don't you need to have someone in custody for that to be the case?" Maggie asked sweetly, baiting him.

"*Bien sûr*," he said, hooking his thumb in his belt looking like a parody of Barney Fife trying to look relaxed. "We have a suspect and we have a confession from the suspect."

"Oh, that was clever!" Maggie said. "Getting a confession from him so fast. I'm impressed." Her heart was pounding and she willed herself to look calm. She had him hooked but if he could see how excited she was at what he was telling her he would surely clam up.

"It was nothing," he said, shrugging. "We picked him up within hours, of course."

"Of course. Good job! A friend of Monsieur Hutten's, I wonder? Because he wasn't loved, I have to say. Just about anybody probably wanted to throttle him at any given time."

"Our suspect insists he was not an acquaintance," the detective said, preening with the information he had possession of. "He was simply hired to do the job." He barked out an ugly laugh.

"Clearly, the salary of a lowly dresser must be augmented in as many creative ways as possible."

"He was a dresser? From which house?"

All of a sudden, he gave her a suspicious look.

Damn. Too far.

"Give your information to the Lieutenant when you are done," he said. And without further comment, he turned and walked down the hall and disappeared into one of the many offices.

Maggie watched the now empty hallway and found her thoughts collecting slowly as if the burden of their inevitable logic would be too much to bear.

So it *was* Bijou. Which the police would quickly discover upon further interrogation of their amateur assassin.

Jeremy and now Bijou. Their lives forfeited or destroyed because of Stan's murder. She glanced at the wedding band on her left hand. What other collateral damage would register in the final culmination of this terrible business as they all headed down the home stretch?

15

The Jardin de la Tuilieries was beautiful any time of year, Maggie decided as she tossed a corner of her pizza to the little huddle of dirty pigeons and gulls who sat watching her hungrily. It was the last week in November—the day before Thanksgiving back home—and Maggie thought of the preparations her parents would be busy with about now. A wave of guilt and sadness crashed over when she thought of the four Thanksgiving day dinners Laurent had created for her—right down to the cranberry sauce and corn bread dressing which he had essentially considered a violation of his integrity as a Frenchman. But he had done it. Every year he had done it, even when the process of procuring a turkey, fresh or frozen, in the south of France had been harder than finding truffles in July. He had done it. For her.

Was there a statute of limitations on idiocy? she wondered. *Or blindness?* She wiped her fingers on a paper napkin and scattered the remnant crumbs of the pizza crust from her coat. Fact is, she was pretty sure she didn't deserve to have Laurent. In lieu of frustration or stubborn refusal at her idiotic, childish demands, he had gone underground. He possibly hoped that his resignation would be enough.

And of course, it hadn't been.

Sighing heavily, she pulled her cellphone out of her coat pocket and punched in Bijou's number.

"*Allo*, Maggie?"

"Hey, sweetie," Maggie said. Through the ferris wheel at the end of the gardens, she could see the obelisk on the Place de la Concorde which marked the beginning of the Champs-Élysées which stretched a famous mile to the Arc de Triomphe. Maggie could never look at that avenue without thinking of Hitler parading down it with his Nazi cronies thinking he had claimed Paris for his own. "I've got some news for you," she said into her cellphone.

"*Oui*?"

"There's no good way to say this, Bijou," Maggie said, hunching into her coat on the bench when a wicked slice of cold wind lifted her skirt and sent her long hair flying around her face. "The police have arrested the man you hired, you know, for Jeremy? And it's only a matter of time before they knock on your door. I'm sorry."

There was a moment's silence on the line.

"Bijou?"

"I am here," Bijou said tiredly. "I did not think it could be so easy."

"I don't really know," Maggie said. "But a tiny bit of digging by the police will probably unclog the info drain on that embezzlement thing you did with Stan and Denny. I'm not saying you should get rid of any evidence that links you to that because that would be wrong, but..."

"*Je comprends*, Maggie," Bijou said. "Thank you."

"Goodbye, Bijou," Maggie said. "Take care." She disconnected and sat for a minute looking at her phone.

Jeremy dead and Bijou's life ruined and Maggie still didn't

know who killed Stan. She looked back toward the Louvre and spotted Diane hurrying toward her, wrenching her drab brown wool coat tight across her chest against the cold wind as she walked. Not for the first time, Maggie found herself wondering if Diane ever *read* the fashion copy she wrote.

Diane scattered the birds as she came to a stop in front of Maggie.

"It's freezing out here," Diane said, nodding to Maggie. Her eyes looked as if she had been crying and her cheeks were red from the cold. "Can we move it inside?"

Café Marly overlooked the pyramid at the Louvre. The décor inside was typical of the kind of homespun Parisian brasseries that Maggie preferred. Silver candelabras were set on white starched tablecloths and patrons sat nearly elbow to elbow at long dining tables. Since Maggie had already eaten, she ordered a blueberry tart and coffee. Diane sat in front of a large wedge of quiche with a rocket lettuce salad.

Once out of her coat, Diane pulled her drab brown hair out of its clip and let soft curls bounce against her shoulder. Maggie noted with surprise that Diane's black knit dress, although plain, had a simple style that was pleasing. Diane dug in her purse and extricated a packet of *par avion* stamped envelopes secured with a large rubber band.

"They're old," she explained, pushing the packet across the table to Maggie. "We corresponded by email for the last ten years. But the years that you will be interested in are in there."

"I don't need to see them," Maggie protested. "My father said there wasn't a question of paternity."

"I guess I just wanted to clear up any notion that my son's father and I weren't a deeply committed, loving pair." She grimaced and emptied a sugar packet into her coffee. "I don't say *couple*, because of course we weren't that. We couldn't be because of Stan."

"But you loved him."

"And he loved me, too. Just not in the way I would've preferred."

"Why did you keep your son a secret from us?"

"Stan's preference." Diane shrugged. "I figured his family had an issue with him being gay."

"We didn't," Maggie said emphatically.

"In that case, I don't know," Diane said. "Possibly to protect John somehow. It's pretty much why we did everything."

"Is that why you changed his name to Newton?"

Diane nodded. "Stan wanted at least a piece of his name for John."

"My dad said originally Stan left everything to you." Maggie skirted around the fact that *she* had found the original will.

"I asked him to change it," Diane said simply as she sliced into her quiche. "I didn't want him doing it out of guilt for me or something. It needed it to be about John."

"Wow," Maggie said softly. "You're really something, Diane. I'm sorry I didn't get to know you better before now. I can see why Stan loved you."

"I suppose he did, in his way," Diane said. She smiled but her eyes were sad. "There are a few things at the apartment that I would like to have of Stan's. Nothing valuable except for what they mean to me."

"Of course." Maggie sipped her coffee and surprised herself by feeling a kinship with this woman, from whom before today she had felt nothing but animosity. "Tell me something about John," she said. "Does he look at all like Stan?"

Diane's face lit up as she pulled her billfold out of her purse and handed Maggie a small photograph.

"He's a sophomore in high school," she said, "so that photo is a little more formal-looking than how he normally is." She beamed as she pointed to the picture. "He's very much into sports—as I believe Stan was at that age—and he's extremely bright."

"He's handsome," Maggie said. She looked at the photo and could have been looking at a picture of her own father forty years earlier. The boy had long brown hair and deep-set blue eyes—just like all his Newberry relations. His nose was straight and his grin lopsided. Just looking at the photo made Maggie feel like she was getting a little piece of Stan back again. "There's a strong family resemblance," she said. "You must be so proud of him."

Diane nodded without speaking as she took the photo back. Maggie saw the love that Diane felt for the boy in the way she looked at the picture one last time before putting it away. For a moment, Maggie half expected her to kiss it.

"So you're okay with him getting to know the rest of us?"

"I have no family, myself," Diane said. "As a result I've raised John with no aunts, no uncles, no grandparents, no cousins."

"*I'm* his cousin," Maggie said.

Diane reached over and put her hand on top of Maggie's on the table. "I would love for him to get to know you—all of you," she said. "I know he wants that, too."

"What about you?"

Diane frowned. "What do you mean?"

"Are you up for joining the Newberry family too? The fact is, we're a big believer in package deals."

Diane put down her fork and turned to rummage in her purse once more before answering. She pulled out a large handkerchief and turned to Maggie, blinking back the tears that filled her large brown eyes. "I would like nothing more," she said.

LAURENT STOOD for a moment on the stone slab porch of his house. He reflected without irony that this was the very porch where the young English family had been murdered right after the war. It was a story that Maggie loved to tell, embellished only a little and retold with much panache and drama, particularly since she was the one who solved the mystery of the sixty-year old murder.

Four years ago he and Maggie had left Atlanta and moved to this village. Four years ago he had promised her he would make her happy and that living in this Provençal village would allow him to keep his promise to her. He turned and carried the heavy suitcases to the Renault and settled them in the trunk. He slammed the lid shut and looked at his *mas*. It was tall and proud, like the mysterious uncle who had left it to him four years ago. When the inheritance had first come through, he and Maggie had left their new life in Atlanta to come to this tiny village of St-Buvard with the intent to prepare the old *mas* to be sold. Along the way, he had faltered in his promise to return with her to her homeland. He knew she wasn't happy and yet he had hoped it could be. That it might somehow be.

From the first moment he had stood at this very spot—on land that was his own—he knew he belonged to it. He knew that all the ugliness and the lies, all the feints and the crimes he had committed to get himself to this point in time had been forgiven. *For how could God reward him so sweetly if that were not so?* He had Maggie—the surprise above and beyond them all—and he had *Domaine St-Buvard*.

He knew Suzie was getting impatient. But he couldn't help the temptation to memorize every rock, every stone, every curling vine of ivy as it vaulted the fieldstone walls of the farmhouse. A black wrought-iron railing framed a second-story balcony that jutted out over the front door. The three bedroom windows upstairs were tall and mullioned with peeling blue shutters. He should have painted them. He had told Maggie he would. But the grapes had demanded so much of him.

Towering Italian cypress and Tatarian dogwood flanked the front door. Hollyhocks, even in November, pushed out of the tangle of bushes lining the driveway, and the stone lion with one missing ear still guarded the edge of the terrace, its head cocked as if listening.

"Ready, Laurent?" Suzie called to him.

The wave of sadness hit him in the stomach first and then emanated upward toward his chest as he turned his gaze from the house to the fields. His fields. Twenty hectares planted with the grape of the region. His grapes.

"I'm coming," he said gruffly, shaking his head. He slid into the driver's seat and gave the Australian a quick, blank smile, then started the car. With much effort, he was able to drive away without looking back.

AFTER DIANE LEFT, Maggie walked slowly down the Boulevard des Capucines and stared at the restaurant across the street. A part of her brain knew she was coming here as her feet moved her to this spot. She stared at the famous restaurant and remembered the evening five years ago when she had travelled alone to Paris and had discovered what she believed was the ultimate betrayal by the man she loved.

Laurent. It was at *this* restaurant that she had learned the truth. The good and the bad. But the truth. And from that day forward nothing had ever been the same for her, for Laurent, or for her family. She watched the people scurry in and out of the *Café de la Paix* and remembered hearing that if you sat there long enough, the whole world would eventually pass by. She sighed, remembering herself five years younger and carrying all her doubts about the mysterious man she would eventually marry. And she had to say, today, that those had been the happiest five years of her life.

Turning her back on the restaurant and her memories, Maggie entered a small nondescript café on the *boulevard des Capucines* and, after finding a table and a coffee, settled herself in and pressed Grace's number on her cellphone. They had prearranged via texts the time for a brief call. Maggie couldn't believe how regimented and scheduled Grace's life had become now that both girls were in school. She seemed to have even less time than when they were home and underfoot. And she constantly talked about longing for summer when school was *out*. Maggie couldn't understand it at all.

"Hi, darling, right on schedule. I'm in a carpool waiting for Taylor's grade to emerge. Where are you?"

"I am sitting across from the *Café de la Paix*," Maggie said. "Eating a *macaron* and sipping an *espresso*."

"I officially hate you."

Maggie heard a honking in the background from Grace's end.

"These tennis moms are unbelievable," Grace muttered. "They drive their gargantuan SUVs so they can use them as battering rams to cut in front of you. But enough about my world. I see you are alive. Thanks for calling me after the dinner party."

"Sorry," Maggie said. "I forgot. No dramatics. I survived as you can see."

"Well? Did anything happen?"

"Oh, yeah, you know Jeremy? The one who I was sure killed Stan? He got killed that night."

Grace gasped. "At your dinner party?!"

"No, Grace, no," Maggie said patiently. "He was a no-show. He was murdered on the way to my apartment."

"Is that a coincidence?"

"Well, turns out I wasn't the only one who thought he did it. Only instead of throwing a lame dinner party to extract the confession from the guilty party, Bijou just hired a hit man and had him killed."

"She did not."

"She surely did. And told me everything."

"So now does she need to kill *you* to keep your silence?"

"No, I think she's done now."

"Unbelievable. I am shocked beyond shock."

Maggie heard another horn honking, this one much closer.

"Please, move that ancient Lexus before I run up over your big-ass back bumper," Grace called out sweetly.

"Jeeze, Grace. From this distance, car pool sounds kind of like *Call of Duty Black Ops IV*."

"You're not wrong," Grace said. "Except we're not allowed to use bayonets on school property. So does that wrap everything up nicely? Jeremy did it, Jeremy is iced?"

"I guess."

"You don't sound sure."

"I wanted a confession," Maggie said. "I wasn't all that sure it was him. I needed to hear him say so in his own words."

"Ahhhh. So how's Laurent these days?"

"Wow, I just got whiplash with that subject change, Grace."

"Which doesn't alter my question. How you two doing?"

"You know he's in St-Buvard and I'm in Paris, right?"

"I do. Is there a problem? Win and I can handle being apart for days at a time before thinking about filing for divorce."

"There may be a problem."

"Spill thy guts, darling."

"He seems to have taken a girlfriend while I've been up here."

Maggie heard Grace suck in a quick gulp of breath.

"I do not believe it," Grace said.

"Well, a woman answered his phone—"

"The cleaning lady, probably."

"We don't have a cleaning lady. And when I talked to Danielle she was all nervous and wanting to get off the phone with me when I asked about Laurent."

"She may not know the truth of the situation. It might look that way to her," Grace said, "but I know for a fact that it isn't."

"Really, Grace? For a fact?"

"Yes, darling, for a fact. Because I know your great big gorgeous hunk of a husband and I know he would never do that."

"I wish I knew it."

"I wish you did, too. You *should* know it."

"He won't answer or return my calls."

"Hmmm, I don't like that. He must be a little cranky."

"Cranky? Grace, he's fed up with me. He's had enough."

Maggie could hear the sounds of children laughing and screaming as if a dam of kindergartners had burst and were surrounding Grace's vehicle.

"Well, I have to say no one could blame him," Grace said. "And you know I adore you, darling, but you are a relentless pain in the ass. However, Laurent knew what was in store, trust me. And I can guarantee you he has not had enough. Having said that, it would be lovely if you could quit testing just how much the poor man can take."

"Oh, Grace, I'm such an idiot."

"I know, sweetie, but the good news is you don't have to continue on in this way."

"You don't think it's too late?" Maggie heard a car door slam and Taylor's high-pitched whine filled the car and wheedled its way across the Atlantic and into her ear.

"It's only too late, darling," Grace said, tiredly, "if you decide *not* to use some form of birth control. Otherwise, there's always a brighter day awaiting you. Taylor, shut up, sit down and put your goddamn seatbelt on! Gotta go, Maggie. Do me a favor, drink a *macchiato* for me, would you? God, I hate you."

TED GAVE her a kiss on the cheek and handed her the bottle of Pinot Noir.

"It's the one you said you liked so much last time," he said. "Wow. You look gorgeous tonight, my girl!" He gave her an overly dramatic once over and even took her hand to half-twirl her in order to see her from every angle.

"It's just my drinking wine and writer's group outfit," Maggie said laughing. "You should see me dressed for a work out."

"I have every intention of doing exactly that," Ted said. He clapped his hands together as if ready to dive right into the work. "But meanwhile, are you ready to have a crack editor rip through your prose and put you back on the right track, plot-wise?"

"Oh, is somebody else coming tonight?"

"You are a funny naughty little thing, Madame Dernier. Careful, I spank when provoked." He gave her his best raised eyebrow look and crooked grin that he happened to know for a fact was extremely effective with the ladies. Whether or not it was with Maggie was hard to tell since she reddened and retreated into the kitchen with the wine bottle.

"I'll get the cheese and crackers," she called over her shoulder. "Make yourself comfortable."

"As usual," he said, then turned to the living room where he immediately spotted Stan's laptop on the table. "Mind if I take a look at Stan's computer?" he said as he sat down at the table in front of it.

She didn't answer but appeared in the doorway of the kitchen, looking at him as if she were unsure what to say.

Good God almighty, Ted thought, *was she really not sure? How long was it going to take to get her to trust him?*

"Look, I'm cool with it if you'd rather not," he said, hoping his face didn't show his hurt.

"No, I'm sorry. Of course, look at it. I don't think the computer has any secrets to give up but if it does, I'm happy to share them with you."

"You sound really down tonight, Maggie. Want to go out instead? You know, hear some music? Be around people?"

Maggie shook her head and nodded at the laptop, giving approval. When she did Ted felt a rush of affection for her. *She's vulnerable, she's scared. What she needs right now is a friend, not one more person trying to get in her pants.* He scolded himself and then grinned ruefully. *If I can just be patient...*

He opened the laptop and typed in the password while

Maggie went into the kitchen. As soon as she disappeared, Ted reached into the leather mailbag he usually carried and drew out a carefully wrapped long-stemmed rose. It held its own little vial of water to stay fresh. He had toyed with the idea of putting it in a vase by her bedside but the more he thought of it—and he had thought of little else today—the more he liked the idea of laying it on her pillow. Like a promise of what might be.

Listening for her in the kitchen and pleased to hear she had started to hum, he got up and slipped into her bedroom. He took just a moment to imagine that *this* is where the magic might happen later tonight, and lay the rose on her pillow. *Even if it doesn't happen tonight,* he reasoned, *at least I'll be the last thing she thinks of when she climbs into bed*. Satisfied, he poked his head into the hall to make sure she was still in the kitchen and then tiptoed back to the living room.

After this, he vowed, *I will totally back off and be the ultimate guy pal, if that's what she wants. I'll just hang with her and not try to kiss those luscious lips or imagine the feel of that bottom in my hands... Stop it, Gilbert,* he growled to himself and reached over to wake up the laptop. *Yeah, this friends-only thing is gonna be a little tougher than I thought.*

MAGGIE BROUGHT out the bottle of wine and placed it on the tray with the two glasses and the plate of cheese, crackers and fruit. She had made a significant decision at the end of her long confusing day and she was looking forward to telling Ted. She would miss his input, his brotherly support and good natured humor. During this whole unpleasant experience over Stan's death, she knew he had tried to be a good friend to her in spite of hoping for more.

She peeked out into the living room where he sat staring at something on the laptop and gnawing a fingernail. It wasn't going to be possible to really stay friends, she thought as she watched him. As good looking and infatuated as he was, even someone as secure as Laurent would not stand for a continued friendship.

Laurent.

For better or worse, she had decided to take the train back to Arles first thing in the morning. There was no point in calling or texting Laurent to meet her. He had long since stopped all communications. She would call Danielle at the station and just wait, like a collection of forgotten luggage, until someone came and got her. And what would her reception be at Domaine St-Buvard? Maggie took a quick sip from her glass of Pinot Noir.

Whatever it was, it was. She deserved the worst, she would pray for a middle ground. If Laurent's girlfriend hadn't actually moved in, she might be able to worm her way back into Laurent's life—and their marriage. If she *had* moved in, well, Maggie would just have to take it a step at a time. While she could not blame Laurent if he had thrown up his hands in disgust with her, the larger part of her couldn't really believe that she couldn't make him hers again.

Somehow. Some way.

"You coming with that vino?" Ted called to her, breaking into her thoughts. "I can guarantee you're going to need it if you're going to read my latest chapter. We're talking rough, baby. But I know you'll be gentle."

Maggie smiled and picked up the tray. "Coming," she said. "And bringing the love juice to make both our manuscripts look better." The phone in the living room rang as she walked in and she set the tray down on the coffee table.

"That'll be the phone," Ted said, taking his glass of wine and turning back to the laptop screen.

"Yeah, no kidding," Maggie said, laughing. She picked up. "Hello?"

"Hi, Maggie, it's me," Diane said timidly. "Bet you're surprised to hear from me so soon?"

"Surprised but delighted," Maggie said, reaching for her own wineglass. "What's up?"

"Nothing really," Diane said. "I just wanted to know if tomorrow morning would be good for me to come by and look for some of the things of Stan's I was telling you about."

"Yeah, tomorrow's good," Maggie said. "I'm leaving pretty early, myself, so I might just leave you a key, if that's okay."

Ted turned to look at her and gave her a questioning look. She waved a hand at him. *Tell you in a sec.*

"I appreciate that, Maggie. I'm heading back to California tomorrow. But I wanted to say, since I know I didn't at lunch today, how glad I am that we've connected and how sorry I am that I didn't reach out sooner."

"Oh, Diane, I feel the same way!"

"It's just that my relationship with Stan was always so complicated and I guess I started to get a complex about his family, like they didn't want to know me, or something when, of course, how could they? They didn't even know I existed."

"Well, we know now, Diane. When you come tomorrow, let's make plans for all of us getting together, John, too, either in Atlanta or San Francisco."

Ted drank his wine and gave Maggie his full attention. *What's going on?* his facial expression read.

"I'd like that, Maggie. By the way, what did I interrupt you doing tonight?"

"I'm having a writer's critique session with Ted."

"Oh, is that what they're calling it now?"

Maggie grinned. Diane was actually teasing her. Maggie considered that a very good sign for the long term prospect of their relationship.

"We're just friends," Maggie said. He's decided to stay and work in Paris."

"Paris is a far cry from Juneau."

"It's Nome."

"What?"

"Ted's from Nome."

"Well, I don't know him hardly at all but I do know that he is from Juneau."

"That's not what he told me."

"Then he lied to you."

"Why in heaven's name would he lie to me about where he's from?"

Ted came and stood in front of her. He put his wine glass down. Maggie thought he had a strange look on his face but she rolled her eyes and pointed to the phone as if to say: *crazy lady.*

"All I know is that in his blog," Diane said, "Stan always referred to Ted as *Le Juneau Jambon*. You know, *the ham from Juneau*? I suppose Stan might've stretched the truth for the sake of the alliteration. That sounds like him so you're probably right."

As soon as Diane spoke the words, Maggie felt the room start to sway just the tiniest bit.

Jambon.

Maggie looked up from the floor and into Ted's eyes. Ted's flat, dead, cold eyes.

Diane was saying: "I mean, it was no secret that Stan thought Ted should retire from modeling. You've read his blog posts, right? Stan told me he had one coming up –well, it would've been this week—that was going to destroy Ted's career. Stan could be very harsh when he was in the mood."

An image of Stan's laptop desktop came to her with the folder *Published Posts*, which posed the obvious question that hadn't occurred to Maggie: *Where then, was the folder, Unpublished Posts?*

Not Jimbo, but *jambon*.

Le Juneau Jambon.

"Maggie? You still there?"

So that was why Ted always wanted so badly to meet with her in Stan's apartment. It wasn't to be with her, it was to get to her uncle's hard drive. And while he had no way of knowing what

Stan's last words to her were he had every reason to believe that eventually Maggie would find the unpublished posts and put it all together.

"Diane—"

Before she could say another word, Ted stepped forward and ripped the phone cord out of the wall.

"Bad wiring in these seventeenth century Paris apartments," he said throwing the phone down on the couch. "They're constantly going out on you."

16

"Anything you do," Maggie said, "will implicate you in my death. If you bind my hands, they'll know it wasn't suicide. If you grab me and try to throw me off the balcony, they'll see the bruises and know I fought for my life."

"Why would the police think of me in the first place?"

"I told a friend I suspected you."

"You're lying. You never suspected me."

"I did. From the beginning."

He actually laughed but Maggie saw his eyes dart to the front door as if he had heard a noise. He wasn't really sure if she were lying or not.

"If I turn up dead, she'll tell the police my suspicions."

"This only works if I believe you, Maggie," Ted said reasonably. "Which I don't. It honestly kills me that you would not let all this go."

"By *all this*, you mean Stan's murder."

"Do *not* take another step back into the kitchen, Maggie. Not another step. Bruises or not, I will stop you and I will not bother to mop up the mess later."

"I knew you were lying to me from the beginning," she said, stalling for time.

"I *wanted* you from the beginning," he said. "I honestly think I'm probably in love with you, even now. Bizarre, isn't it? Just because I killed Stan doesn't mean I stopped *feeling*."

Maggie's stomach heaved as he spoke. *He is confessing. I'm getting my damn confession!* She forced herself not to look at the voice-activated recorder left under the couch from last week's dinner party, its red *record* light glowing.

"You can't get away with this, Ted. Don't you see that?"

"Give me a break. You've seen the French cops. They don't care. You said yourself that they didn't even question you about Genevieve and *you* found the body."

Maggie's expression betrayed a sudden understanding and then a look of nausea flitted across her features. "You killed Genevieve?"

"She was at the station one of the times I was there being questioned. I couldn't have her confide that little gem to you when I hadn't mentioned it to you, now could I?"

"You were questioned by the cops?"

"Shocking, isn't it? Turns out the French cops aren't quite as useless as we thought, sweetheart. They checked out my alibi and it didn't hold up. Seems my date for the evening couldn't confirm I was with her during the time of the murder. She'd passed out too soon to remember."

"You came back to the party."

"As it happens, I did." He moved a step closer to her and held his hands out in front of him like she was a skittish filly he needed to calm before he could capture her. "I came back to get a little bit more of you, if you want to know. My heart was totally captured, *cherie*, literally since the moment I laid eyes on you."

"And you ran into Stan," she said. Her throat felt dry and raw as if she had been screaming. It occurred to her that screaming right now would probably escalate this little drama to its inevitable conclusion. But he might also be spotted fleeing the scene if she created a ruckus.

"And one thing led to another," he said, watching her eyes.

"But why?"

"Well, if you truly suspected me as you told your friend," he said with a smile, "then you must know the answer to that."

Maggie said nothing.

"I thought so. Well, there was a blog post that Stan had written that was going to end my career, if you must know. He was an evil, self-serving old bastard."

"The *Juneau Jambon*."

"Maybe you do know after all. In any event, he sent me a preview copy of the post the day before. To rub it in, to gloat, to taunt me with the impending doom of my income, my life. And all because I rejected him a few weeks earlier, if you know what I mean."

"That's a lie," she said.

"Well, we'll never know, will we?" He took another step toward her and glanced into the kitchen to telegraph to her that he knew what she was up to and he wasn't worried.

"Tell me," he said, his eyes wild and mad, "it was my name he whispered to you with his last breath, wasn't it?"

Maggie slowly shook her head. "No," she said. "If you want to know, he said *Tell Diane I love her*."

"I know he said my name! I know he did!"

"Nope. Not even close," she said, watching him disintegrate before her eyes.

"Liar!" he roared as he lunged at her with his arms outstretched. Maggie swiveled toward the kitchen, her own hands reaching wildly for the knife she knew was on the counter. Her fingers touched the handle when she felt a terrible pressure on her back and her breath knocked out of her in one harsh gasp. She fell to the floor of the kitchen, the knife clattering away from her and Ted's knee grinding into her hips from above.

He grabbed her hair and jerked her head off the floor until she thought her neck would break. He brought his face down to hers and whispered harshly into her ear. “Got any last words, bitch?” he snarled. “I promise to report them faithfully to your grieving husband who, by the way, I had the pleasure of speaking to not two days ago when you were in the bathroom and he called. I’m afraid I had to tell him that I was your lover and you were *not* in any condition to come to the phone. The French are so sensible about these things," he said. "He actually *thanked* me for telling him.”

Maggie could barely register his words through the veil of screaming pain shooting through her back and neck. She gave an incomprehensible gurgle in reply and he climbed off her.

“I’m afraid there will be quite a bit of bruising after all,” he said, panting as he yanked her off the floor in one movement. The relief of the removal of his weight was obliterated by the loud crack of her upper arm breaking in his hands. She groaned as he wrapped his fist around her long hair and used it to leverage her to her knees. She looked up into his face and saw only single-minded madness.

The pain in her arm vanished as quickly as it had gripped her and it occurred to her to be grateful for the shock she was almost certainly slipping into.

“On your feet now, Maggie,” he said in a normal tone of voice. “There you go, sweetheart. I can carry you but I promise you it’ll hurt if you make me do that. Just walk on your own steam to the balcony. You know how much you love Stan’s balcony? Didn’t we have our first date on that balcony?” He pulled back his hand and slapped her hard across the face. “Wakey-wakey, Maggie,” he said. “You want to be conscious for the way the story ends, don’t you?”

He pulled her by her broken arm to her feet and Maggie gasped with the fresh onslaught of pain. It was as if the rest of the apartment disappeared and all she could see looming before her was the magnificent presence of Notre Dame. As she took halting steps toward it and the balcony, Ted guiding and pulling her, she remembered how special the church had always been to her, how personal, even from childhood. A part of her realized she had been heading toward this point, toward this final communion with the church and what it meant to her since she was a little girl.

Ted reached the French doors, pulled them open and prodded her though them onto the balcony. Without bothering to close the doors, he grabbed Maggie by the back of her shoulders and then looped his arm under her knees and lifted her up and stood next to the balcony railing. He paused for just a moment, like a proud father might to show his toddler a better view of something amazing.

"If you see Stan," he said, his voice rasping with his exertion and his emotion, "tell him Ted says *rot in hell.*"

Maggie's vision was filled with the specter of the cathedral, filling up every bit of her sight, as complete and as glorious as an angel's chimera. She knew she was losing consciousness but when the moment finally came, it came as a searing bolt of pain that sprang from her shoulder and shot directly through her hips and her legs. And then the blue sky surrounding Notre Dame turned blessedly black.

Laurent heard the voice. Only one. He stood on the landing outside her door, his hand raised to knock, his expectation of the look on her face already in tiresome re-runs in his head. And then he heard the voice. Unlike his very American wife, Laurent was not accustomed to analyzing a situation for long. In his nefarious not-too-distant past, he had had to make dramatic decisions—often life and death decisions—in the time it takes to light a cigarette. Up to this moment, that ability had served him well. Today, he never got to the point where he thought that he might embarrass them both. He never considered the *what ifs.* It wasn't his way. When he heard the voice, he acted.

The door was unlocked, although he was prepared to break it down. It swung open to present a full-stage view of the drama unfolding within. A man held Maggie in his arms at the balcony railing. Laurent didn't stop to note if Maggie was alive or even if it *was* Maggie. In three long, silent strides, he was through the apartment and onto the balcony.

The man was so intent on hoisting Maggie over the railing that he didn't notice that Laurent was beside him until Laurent had grabbed his wife's shoulder and wrenched her from the man's grasp. When Maggie tumbled senselessly to the floor of the balcony, Laurent turned to the man and slammed his fist into his face. The punch propelled him backwards into the living room where he fell and cracked his head on the edge of the coffee table. He grabbed a candlestick off the table and hurled it at Laurent who easily dodged it as he advanced.

Don't kill him, Laurent said to himself as he grabbed the man and hauled him up to a standing position. *Try not to kill him.*

The man brought his arm up and down against Laurent's chest. He held a knife in the hand and Laurent felt the blade go into his flesh in a sudden electric shock. He flinched but never dropped his hands from the man. Without breaking his gaze on the man's fevered eyes, Laurent grabbed the man's knife hand and twisted it until he snapped the bones his wrist. The man screamed and dropped the knife but still Laurent didn't let go. He moved his hands from the man's shoulders to his neck.

Try not to kill him, he reminded himself.

Maggie and Laurent stood on the lock bridge of *Pont des Arts* gazing down at the green and choppy Seine below them. Maggie's mind was whirling with the events of the last few hours.

The police had taken Ted—ranting and wild-eyed, his hand dangling useless from his wrist—into custody. Maggie's recording of his confession, combined with the recent collapse of his alibi after a second police interview with the blonde model he was supposed to have been with, finally concluded the sad case of the murder of Stanley Newberry.

It had all happened so quickly—from the complete confusion that Maggie had faced not twelve hours earlier over who could possibly have benefited from Stan's death to the heartbreaking question of her continued status as Mrs. Laurent Dernier. Maggie now found herself befogged and numb trying to place the recent events in proper sequence.

And the emergency room painkillers hadn't helped.

Maggie's arm was in a cast and hung in a sling snugly to her chest. Laurent's knife wound had required ten stitches but it was a shallow cut and didn't seem to bother him at all. As she looked at him, she still found it hard to believe that he was with her, and that he had come to Paris. There were many questions to ask—not the least of them about the woman who answered his phone that night—but Maggie found she wasn't worried about Laurent's answers. Although she had no memory of his rescue of her from the balcony, just knowing that he had come for her in the end gave her the strength and resolution she needed to face the worst if it came.

"I suppose you think all this lock and key business is silly," she said, not looking at him, hoping her words would get him talking about where they stood as a couple.

Laurent was drinking from a tall Starbucks coffee cup, his eyes scanning both sides of the river as if looking for someone. Maggie still couldn't believe he was drinking a chain coffee but Laurent had merely shrugged and said: "If it is good coffee, why not?"

"No," he said slowly, "just about as far from what is true about love as there is."

Maggie was astonished. The very idea of Laurent making a proclamation about love, of all things, was unbelievable. She turned to give him her full attention.

"The idea that you can *lock in* love for two people," he continued, "and then toss the key in a river to make it binding is beyond silly." He looked at her and his expression was serious. "I think to love truly is to give the other the freedom to walk away." He waved a hand at the bridge of glittering metal locks. "Not affix locks and keys to the love like a prison." Maggie knew that Laurent had first-hand experience with the concept of being imprisoned.

"Is that why you were willing to let me go?"

"Regardless of what Jean-Luc says, I cannot force you to stay where you do not wish to be."

"I talked to that girl in St-Buvard," Maggie said suddenly, grateful for the drugs for helping her get the words out. "She answered your cellphone."

"*Qui*? Suzie? She never mentioned that." Laurent frowned. Either he was even cooler under pressure than he was famed for, Maggie thought, or he was not suffering from a guilty conscience.

"Did you sleep with her?"

He turned to look at her, and she could swear there was a hint of a smile tugging at his full lips.

"Would anyone have blamed me? My wife left me, you know."

"Don't tease me, Laurent. *No one* would have blamed you, least of all me. That's why I'm asking."

"Ach, Maggie," he said putting his hand to her cheek. "Your husband does not stray even when his wife abandons him. Even when pretty hitchhikers attempt to climb into his bed."

"I don't want to know the details.

"Your husband does not stray," he repeated softly, looking into her eyes. "*Je promis*."

Maggie took in a full lungful of air and eased it out gently. Somehow, she had made it through the quagmire without having to endure and scale the incomprehensibly high barrier of an affair between them. Thank God for Laurent. She turned back to the river to steady her breathing.

"But no key in the Seine for us," she said.

"While I am happy to do it if you wish it, I fear the weight of adding one more lock to this bridge may send the whole structure tumbling into the Seine."

Maggie laughed. "It's just symbolic, Laurent."

"If you want a symbol," he said, "why not give each other rings to symbolize a love with no beginning and no end? Oh, wait, we did that."

She made a face. She deserved this. This and much more.

He directed his attention back to the river. "Do you ever wonder how many of the owners of these locks have divorced or broken up?"

"A lot, I suppose," she said.

"This gesture of attaching locks to a public bridge is not a magic shield against failure, *cherie*. Instead of throwing a key in the river, why not just cross your fingers and hope very hard that your love lasts a lifetime?"

"I get it, Laurent. I do."

They were silent a moment. Maggie was surprised she wasn't cold. Laurent was serving as a large windbreak for her, protecting her against the worst of the frigid breezes that pummeled the little bridge.

"You still haven't said why you came to Paris," Maggie said. "Was it to bring me back?"

"No," Laurent said and Maggie felt her heart sink. "I only came to Paris to be with you," he said simply.

Maggie grasped at the hope that statement promised. "I can't imagine Jean-Luc was too impressed with your coming after me," she said.

"I do not take marriage advice from Jean-Luc." Laurent frowned and glanced at Maggie as if not understanding how she could even think it. "But as it happens, he urged me to retrieve you weeks ago. Forcibly, if necessary."

Maggie smiled at the thought of Laurent throwing her over his shoulder and whisking her back to St-Buvard to be with him there.

"It took me some time," he admitted, "to see that he was at least half right." Laurent looked down at Maggie and lifted her chin with his fingers so that she returned his gaze without wavering. "As long as you are unhappy, I cannot be happy. Domaine St-Buvard is a small price to pay if it can bring us back together."

"You would leave your vineyard?" Maggie was stunned and reached up for the hand that held her face.

"If it stands in the way of our being together," he said, "I would put a match to it myself."

"Laurent, I couldn't be happy knowing you gave up the thing you loved to be with me."

"*You* are the thing I love."

Maggie forced herself to look away to hide the tears she couldn't stop. After a moment, she cleared her throat and, fighting for mastery over her emotions, said, "You know, Laurent, I did find out one thing really important while I was here in Paris." She looked up into his face, his cheeks rosy from the wind, his eyes dark and probing hers. "I found out my home isn't in Atlanta after all, or anywhere else in the U.S. Turns out it's where ever you are."

Laurent smiled but said nothing. Maggie slipped her hand in his large, warm one and he pulled her close to him as they both looked out over the Seine.

"Take me home, Laurent," she whispered to him. "Take me back to *our* home."

EPILOGUE

"Maggie, you must come now! The soup is getting cold!"

"Just one more paragraph, Laurent! Can't you find something else to do for the time it takes to write one little paragraph?"

He filled the doorway. "Your paragraphs are not little. Or was that just one of your amusing metaphors?"

"Go check on a vine or water something out in the field. I'm almost done."

"It is dark out! I wouldn't be able to see my hand in front of my face."

"I just need to finish this. Five minutes. I'll be right down."

"*D'accord*. And then I will have you all to myself for the night, eh? Five minutes? *Bon*." He pointed a large finger at her and turned and left. Maggie sat facing the doorway with her laptop.

"Boy, *that's* a switch," Grace said, her image appearing on the Skype screen on Maggie's computer.

"I know, right?" Maggie laughed. "But I just want to finish my conversation with you." Stan's cat jumped up on Maggie's desk and began cleaning himself.

"That is the ugliest cat I have ever seen."

"Not surprisingly," Maggie said, petting the cat "the ugly ones are the ones who need a home most."

"I hope you're not trying your sappy wisdom out on me, sweetie," Grace said. "Because trust me, it works better in a novel. How is Petit-Four taking the new addition?"

Maggie glanced over at her poodle curled up on the bed. The dog's head rested on her feet but her eyes followed the cat as it moved. "She's secure in her place in the family," she said.

"Yeah, right. So tell me again, please. I *get* why Ted pushed Stan. Spur of the moment rage and all that. But then he killed Genevieve too? And was winding up to toss you over the balcony as well? Seems like he was really banking pretty hard on the incompetence of the Paris police."

"No, he was just starting to unravel by then," Maggie said. "He wasn't thinking clearly. Once he killed Stan, he really started to lose it bit by bit."

"Murder will do that to you," Grace said. "Or so I'm reliably told. I must say I'm a big believer in trying not to kill people who piss me off. What about Bijou? She still in jail?"

"No, she's out. But awaiting her trial so I'm not sure what will happen after that. I mean, the French are pretty understanding about crimes of passion but even *they* see a hit man as premeditated."

"And dear Denny romps away scott free?"

"He didn't do anything."

"Except break into your apartment, throw a lamp at you, steal your laptop and, if Bijou is to be believed, plan to murder you and throw your body in the river."

"He claims he knows nothing about any plan to kill me."

"Well, he would say that, wouldn't he?"

"The cops say he has no motive for wanting me dead."

"But we know he does, right?"

"I'm not sure, Grace." Maggie tried to pull the cat onto her lap but he hissed at her and jumped to the floor. "He had that whole Gumps embezzlement thing with Jeremy and Stan and Bijou. I mean, that was the reason he wanted into Stan's laptop so bad. But it was really only Jeremy who saw killing me as some kind of answer."

"Got any theories?"

"I think he was reacting to the fact that I was making it look like *he* was the culprit. He couldn't bear people thinking that *he* killed Stan. Even if circumstantial evidence cleared him in an actual court of law, public opinion in the fashion world would have tried and convicted him. That's my best guess. I think he really loved Stan."

"If you say so."

"The most important thing is that I've got closure," Maggie said. "The police have their killer, and I have a new cousin *and* a new friend in Diane."

"Not to mention a new cat."

"Yeah, not to mention that." Maggie turned away from the screen for a moment and yelled down the stairs. "Just five more minutes!" she called.

"I better let you go," Grace said. "I don't want to get on the wrong side of Laurent by keeping you. As far as that goes, how are things going with you two?"

"Good," Maggie said. "With me writing and all, life just feels a lot more balanced. Did I tell you my agent got me a two-book contract?"

"You did, but only the one time. I'm happy to hear about it as many times as you want to tell me."

"It's like you always said, Grace. I just needed something else in my life *besides* Laurent."

"Yes, well, you're going to have a *big* something else in your life in about four months and trust me, darling, you won't get a lick of work done then."

Maggie laughed and her hand dropped to her growing

middle beneath her long tunic "Oh, yes, I will," she said. "Laurent has promised he will be an enormous help when the baby comes."

"That's what they all say."

"I'm not listening to your negative vibes," Maggie said. "Laurent is different."

"Well, that's true," Grace said. "If anyone is good with both babies *and* their mamas, it's Laurent."

"I'm not sure how to take that."

"Take it and run, darling, as I must." Maggie could hear screeching in the background on Grace's end. "Give that big Frenchman a kiss for me. You told him I'm coming over for the birth?"

"I did. You better go, Grace. Sounds like someone's being murdered over there on your end."

"Oh, it's nothing we veteran mothers can't handle," Grace said and laughed. "I cannot wait for you to join the ranks."

"Me, too," Maggie said. "Goodnight, Gracie."

"'Nite, sweetie. You did good."

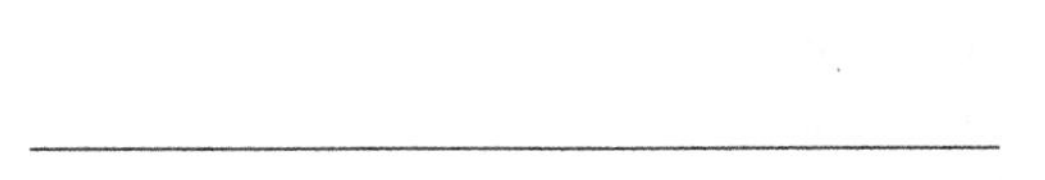

To find out what happens next, be sure and order *Murder in Aix*, the next book in the *Maggie Newberry Mysteries!*

WHAT'S NEXT

Interested in seeing what happens next to Maggie and Laurent? Check out *Murder in Aix, Book 5 of the Maggie Newberry Mysteries*!

Here is the beginning of *Murder in Aix*.

-1-

The moment Julia asked for the wine list, Maggie knew it was going to be *that* kind of lunch. Not that Maggie had anything against wine. Her husband was a vintner, for heaven's sake. They practically drank the stuff for breakfast. No, it was the fact that her friend felt the need for a bottle instead of just a glass or two. A bottle she knew wouldn't be shared because Maggie was eight months pregnant. *A bottle of wine at lunch in the middle of the work-week did not bode well.*

"You won't have any, Maggie?" Julia asked, still squinting at the wine list and not bothering to look at her. They'd gone through this a few million times before. Julia already knew the answer.

"Nope. Not today," Maggie said, smoothing a hand over the

fabric of the sundress that was stretched tightly across her stomach. "Hopefully, by this time next month."

The restaurant was situated just north of the main boulevard, *Cours Mirabeau*, in a tangle of streets known as *Vieil Aix*. This was the old section of Aix-en-Provence, and the part of France that Maggie found most charming. It had been worth the traffic and the lengthy walk past all the food markets to get to the little bistro. As usual, Julia had chosen well.

Julia ordered the wine and handed the list to the hovering waiter. Now that Maggie knew something was up—*and something was definitely up*—she watched her friend closely. When Julia called the day before to suggest lunch in Aix, she had sounded casual and unstressed. *Had she been drinking then, too?* While it was true they hadn't seen each other in a couple of weeks, they'd stayed connected by texts and by phone. Maggie felt she was very much up-to-date with Julia and her current project, an exhaustively comprehensive cookbook on culinary mushrooms.

Maggie had asked Julia to choose the restaurant since she was the one who lived in Aix and knew all the great ones. This one featured a wide, uncrowded terrace with an unobstructed view of *Place Jeanne d'Arc*. Maggie could see the tiny leaves from the ubiquitous plane trees littering the cobblestones of the terrace as prettily as if they'd been hand-placed. She sipped her *l'eau gaseuse* and tried to determine what was going on with her friend. "How're the 'shrooms coming?"

"It's transcendent, Maggie," Julia said, her eyes glassy with joy at the thought of her cookbook. "I am immersed totally and completely. I do not remember ever feeling this way about anything. Ever."

"We're still talking mushrooms?"

"I created this one dish and the aroma from the sautéed mushrooms—they were wild morels—was transformative. I literally left my body."

"No way."

"I kid you not. If only you would let me cook them for you," Julia said, nodding at the waiter as he poured her wine and retreated. "I didn't think people still had pregnancy food issues this far along. I thought that was first trimester stuff."

"Who knew? I won't even let Laurent burn toast in the house. I go into a hormone-induced rage."

"That is not believable," Julia said, sipping her wine. Maggie noticed she closed her eyes to savor it as it slid down her throat. "Laurent would *never* burn the toast."

"Well, I guess we're both being hyperbolic today. Laurent will *definitely* burn the toast the day *you* leave your body over a skillet full of fried mushrooms. Unless, of course, they're a different *kind* of mushroom."

"Oh, funny girl," Julia said, her English accent still sharply evident even after ten years in France. Her eyes crinkled as she smiled at Maggie. Her short blonde hair was a tousle of curls that belied her age. She was a good twenty years Maggie's senior but her youthful air and athletic build, coupled with a smile she was rarely without, had her often mistaken for her contemporary.

"You're really not sick of mushrooms yet?"

"I am not. And trust me, they are all I eat. My next door neighbor jokes with me that I put them on my morning cereal instead of berries."

"And you don't?"

"What can I say? I happen to think obsession is good for the soul."

"How very French of you."

"It is, isn't it? Oh! Did I tell you about the snake I stepped on yesterday?"

"Is this a metaphor?"

"I was doing my thing, foraging in the lower threshold of a vineyard just north of the city."

Maggie knew Julia spent at least half her day tramping about in the forests and meadows surrounding Aix looking for edible mushroom specimens. Julia was a big believer in foraging as the only true way to gather wild mushrooms, which she believed had the deepest flavor.

The server came with their meals and Julia stopped to produce a moment of praise at the presentation of the two large dishes of duck baked in a crust of salt and herbs on top of risotto with eggplant and tomatoes. Maggie, too, allowed a gasp of delight to escape as her plate was set in front of her. With the waiter mollified —Maggie had noticed he was becoming annoyed at the fact the two non-French women were spending more time talking and less time anticipating the main reason they were there—to eat—Julia leaned back into her story.

"I went straight to the base of this really ancient olive tree, covered in moss. Honestly, Maggie, you must come out with me sometime. The colors are so vivid and rich. Anyway, I must have stood there for a full ten minutes, staring deep into the depths of the moss until I saw it."

"The snake?"

"No, silly. Why would I step on the snake if I saw it first? No, I saw—almost completely hidden—the *trompette des morts.*"

"Oooh. *Death trumpets.* Yummy." Maggie spooned into her risotto.

"Well, the name may not be appealing," Julia admitted, "but the mushrooms themselves are to die for. Especially when sautéed with a large knob of butter and a simple seasoning of rosemary."

"You've got to try this, Julia. It is amazing," Maggie said as she enjoyed her first taste. "So when did you step on the snake?"

Julia shrugged and picked up her fork. "Oh, on the way out. At that point I wasn't looking down any more. My basket was full."

"Non poisonous, I assume?"

Julia looked up with a start. "What?"

"The snake. It wasn't poisonous?"

"Oh. No, I don't think so."

"Is everything okay, Julia?"

Julia sighed and reached for her wine. "Well, yes and no."

Maggie took a bite of her duck and waited. Julia would talk when she was ready.

"Jacques called," she said, shrugging.

Maggie frowned. "What did he want?"

"To meet."

"What did you tell him?"

"You really don't want me to see him, do you?"

"It's what *you* want that matters."

Julia sighed again and shrugged. "I told him okay."

Maggie knew Julia had been receiving the occasional note from Jacques asking if he could come by. It appeared he was getting impatient.

"Look, Maggie, I'm not getting back together with him if that's what you're afraid of. I just need some closure so I can move on."

Maggie gave her a skeptical look, but as Julia had probably figured, there was little she could say in response to that.

"He's been ill," Julia said. "I actually feel sorry for him. Things don't seem to be going well for him these days."

"When are you going to see him?"

"Tonight."

"*Tonight*? As in *after dark*? At *your* place? Tell me you're not meeting him alone at your place."

"I'm making him dinner."

Maggie shook her head.

"We have a few things to say to each other," Julia said. "*Private* things."

"He wants to get back together with you," Maggie said.

"Yes, but that will not happen."

"Are you sure?"

"So very sure, dearest. Not to worry on that score."

Maggie wedged her bulk behind the steering wheel of her Renault and took a moment to catch her breath. She hadn't been able to park very close to the restaurant, but the walk had been good for her. Still, her legs ached and there was a spasm in her back she couldn't seem to ease. She rolled down the window and let the cool breeze that had been whipping up the dried leaves and flower petals on the Cours Mirabeau caress her face. She placed a hand on her belly and smiled at the answering kick into the palm of her hand. Whoever was in there had *not* enjoyed the overdose of garlic at lunch.

"Settle down, *ma petite*," Maggie said. As she spoke, a cloud sifted across the sky and darkened the interior of the car a shade. Maggie frowned, her hand resting on the stick shift, and thought of Julia's excitement over her cookbook project. It was so like her to get so completely immersed in the recipe book. She was like that about everything—totally passionate to the point where she nearly lost all sense or perspective. Her relationship with Jacques Tatois was a good example of that, Maggie thought. Handsome in a wolfish sort of way, with penetrating blue eyes that seemed to see only one woman. Unfortunately for Julia, that hadn't necessarily meant one woman at a time.

She and Julia had connected a little under a year ago. Both ex-pats, they had found plenty to bond over when they met at a wine tasting hosted by Laurent's co-op in Avignon. Julia had attended on the arm of her then boyfriend, Jacques Tatois, an acquaintance of Laurent's from Paris. Julia and Maggie hit it off immediately. Grace Van Sant, Maggie's best friend, had recently moved back to the States, leaving Maggie feeling abandoned and lonely. Julia stepped neatly into the void and the two never looked back. In many ways, Maggie mused as she adjusted the car's rear view window and prepared to merge into traffic, Julia was actually closer in temperament and shared interests than Grace had been. Julia was creative, like Maggie. She was ruled by her passions and was spontaneous, like Maggie. And unlike Grace, she cared not a fig for fashion or status, appearances or money. Like Maggie.

Maggie drove carefully out of the city, mindful of the late afternoon traffic. She wasn't late getting back but she knew Laurent would be looking for her. As her pregnancy had advanced, he had become more and more attentive. She smiled at the thought.

Yes, meeting Julia last year had been the saving of Maggie in many ways. And while she still missed Grace—would *always* miss Grace—she had effectively replaced her friendship with someone who, just possibly, was a little more like her in the ways that mattered.

Which is why it was so frustrating to see her even considering opening herself back up to Jacques!

Maggie's cellphone chimed from inside her purse on the passenger's seat, alerting her of the receipt of a text message. Knowing she shouldn't but unable to help herself, she fished the phone out and glanced at the screen. It was from Grace: *Hoping the weather is warm this week, darling. I could use the change!*

Maggie dropped the phone back into her purse and, frowning, refocused her attention on the road.

Now what in the world did that mean?

Laurent pulled the *gratin* from the oven and set it on the zinc-topped table in the kitchen. He glanced at the hand-painted clock face next to the kitchen window and felt a small prick of worry. She's not late, he told himself. The light from the window was still enough to flood the kitchen without need for electric light. He wished she had allowed him to drive her to Aix—he could've gone to the *patisserie* and the *charcuterie* while she visited with Julia—but he understood she was feeling a little restrained lately.

It was harder to give her the space she wanted but he was determined to do it—*up to a point*.

The kitchen was simple and spare, with terra cotta–tiled floors and the large, zinc-topped table at its center. The sloping and spacious salon had a double set of ten-foot French doors that opened out onto a graveled courtyard. Their one hundred-year-old *mas* was a solidly constructed stone building made to withstand the powerful *Mistral*. The surrounding grounds included Laurent's vineyard—twenty-five hectares of local grape and lovingly pruned and tended vines—and another 15 hectares of sprawling lawns punctuated with olive, plum, fig, and cypress trees.

To Maggie's never-ending delight, lavender and rosemary bushes grew all over their property. On the slate terrace, she had set pots of lemon trees and bougainvillea once she finally gave up on her beloved azaleas and Georgia gardenias, which she planted every spring and watched die every fall. Laurent's herb garden was tucked neatly into a side corner of the terrace nearest the kitchen, an endless source of thyme, basil, lemon verbena, and several different kinds of rosemary. In the middle of the terrace, underneath a canopy of the tall plane trees, sat a large stone dining table.

Most summer evenings, while it was still pleasant—not too hot by day and yet not too cold in the evening—Laurent and Maggie ate outside, carrying the dishes and cutlery to the table in shallow wicker baskets. The last tomatoes of summer were served fresh-cut and drizzled with olive oil from the region, vinegar, and chopped fresh herbs from Laurent's *potager*.

When Maggie finally came home this afternoon, she had surprised him by bringing lamb chops from the *charcuterie* in Aix. He shelved the makings for the *pissaladier* he had planned and got the outdoor grill going instead. They settled down across from each other at the large stone outdoor table, steaming plates of grilled chops with rosemary, thyme and garlic redolent in the early evening air, Maggie found herself absolutely relaxed—even without the customary glass of *vin-du-Domaine St-Buvard*. Laurent served up a hefty spoonful of potato gratin with buttered gnocchi and Gruyere cheese on her plate. As usual, she had left all the kitchen work to him and gone straight upstairs to bathe and change clothes.

"You had a good lunch in town?" he asked.

"I did. But Julia is planning on seeing her ex-boyfriend, Jacques, tonight."

"Ahhh." Laurent served himself and then took a sip of his wine. It was one of theirs from the local co-op. "Where did you eat?"

Maggie stopped with her forkful to her mouth and grinned at him. "Because that is the most important part of my lunch," she said. "It was *Le Poivre*. Do you know it?"

Laurent shrugged, which could mean yes or no. Maggie was never sure which.

"Was it good?"

"Yes, it was wonderful. I had the duck. Mouthwatering. Not to worry, French national pride is safe from yet another innocuous luncheon by two unknowing foreigners."

"If you are unknowing, why would it matter?"

"Anyway, the other thing about the lunch, *besides* how the bistro managed to keep its one-star rating—"

"It was rated?"

"I'm teasing, Laurent. Not rated. Still really good. May I continue?"

He nodded and broke a piece off the baguette on the table and handed it to her.

"She is making dinner tonight for her ex-boyfriend, Jacques. You remember him, right?"

"*Le bâtard*," Laurent said on cue.

"Yes, that's right. The total *bâtard*. He wants to get back together with her."

Laurent looked up when Maggie stopped speaking, his expression blank.

"Well, don't you see? Julia is very vulnerable right now. She might well do it and that would be disastrous."

Laurent poured himself another glass of wine. "Surely a half glass could not hurt *le bébé*," he said. He reached for a small pitcher of water.

"Sure, okay," she said, holding out her glass. "Did I not ever tell you the story of how they broke up?"

"He hit her?"

"Okay, so I did tell you. Yes! He hit her during a drunken row."

"And for that she broke up with him?"

"Well, not that that isn't enough, but there was plenty of other stuff too. It was the icing on her cake, him slapping her."

"So a slap, not a hit?"

"You think there's a difference between slapping and hitting a woman?"

Laurent took a bite of his meal. "Of course."

Maggie frowned at him and took a sip from her wine glass. "Okay," she said. "One is bad. And the other is very, very bad."

"Are you worried, *chérie*?" Laurent asked, a smile tugging at the corner of his lips.

"Don't be silly."

"Because if ever I was tempted to beat *ma femme*, it would have been last year when you went to Paris and yet here you sit—intact and unharmed."

"Very amusing. In any case, I happen to know that Julia was beaten by her father."

"C'est terrible."

"Yeah, so Jacques taking a whack at her was all the worse for that."

"The chops are *parfait*, Maggie. *Superbe*."

"They are, aren't they? Well, you prepared them."

"But you thought to get them. And after an upsetting lunch, too."

"Well, I don't like to see Julia doing something I know she's going to regret."

"It is annoying when our friends must constantly ruin their lives when if they would just listen to what we tell them. No?"

"I see what you're doing, Laurent, and you're wrong. I am not interfering. I'm being a friend. I'm *helping*."

"Did she ask for your help?"

"The request was implied as soon as she told me Jacques was coming to dinner."

"And is she still having him to dinner?"

"Okay, fine. But as a friend, I reserve the right to tell my friends when they're about to make a horrible mistake."

"No wonder you have so many friends."

"I have just enough, thank you. And besides, it's an American thing. It doesn't translate over here and Julia isn't French so it works just fine for us."

"*Si tu le dit,*" he said with a teasing smile. *If you say so.*

After dinner, Laurent stacked the plates and the two sat in the oversize lounge chair on the terrace. Laurent draped a thick cotton throw across Maggie's lap. When he sat down next to her, she snuggled comfortably into his lap and was rewarded by the feel of his warm, strong arms enveloping her. It had been a long day, and she tired easily lately.

At one point Laurent laid a large hand on her belly, as if to feel the baby's movement.

"He just kicked!" Maggie said. "Did you feel that?"

"*Oui.*"

"Is our child going to speak both French and English?" she mused idly.

"Of course."

"That'll be nice." They were both silent for a moment, looking up at the night sky and watching the stars. "Does it ever scare you at all?" Maggie asked. "All the changes that are coming?"

"Non."

"Really? And you swear you've never done this before?"

"Not before you," he said.

"What if it makes us different? What if we disagree about major stuff in raising him? What if he looks nothing like you?"

Laurent laughed and kissed Maggie on the cheek. "I am secure," he said. "As long as he looks nothing like *Detective Inspecteur* Roger Bedard, I don't care."

Maggie turned to look at her husband in the semi-dark. "You don't really think that's possible, do you?"

"Not as long as what you told me is true, *non*."

A few years ago, Roger Bedard and Maggie had worked to solve a series of murders in Arles at a time when Maggie was struggling with her first year of marriage. Roger had made it very clear he would like nothing better than for Maggie to struggle right into his open arms.

"Change is good," Laurent said. "Without change, we stay the same and nothing grows." He patted her stomach.

"Yes, but we *just* figured out the happy marriage thing," Maggie said. "And it took us forever to do it. What if *this* change pushes us into a whole other realm of problems?"

"It probably will."

"Well, that's not good, Laurent!"

"Have faith, *chérie*. We will master all problems that come to us—even a demanding baby who wants to push *le papa* out of bed and keep *la maman* all for himself! Now *that* is a concern."

"You don't even know if it's a boy," Maggie said, turning back around and nestling closer to him, feeling and enjoying the heat from his body as an icy breeze wafted through the terrace.

"I know I will love you no matter what comes."

Maggie sighed with pleasure and relaxed deeper into his embrace. She could smell the scent of orange blossoms—gone many months ago—lofting down to her on the cold autumn breeze.

-2-

Jacques narrowed his eyes and watched the group pick their way across the parking lot toward the café. His eye was caught by a young woman who dropped her shoulder purse at her feet, followed by her cellphone, which skidded and bounced on the irregular stones. He could hear her moan of dismay and watched as her friends gathered around to help her pick up the pieces. The girl was wearing dark leggings with a form-fitting tunic pulled over the top. She had an athletic build and a fine, shapely bottom. Jacques licked his lips and found himself hoping she would look up—even in her crisis, even in the crowd—and see him. But the drama was quickly resolved and the group—and his new love—moved on and out of sight. He sighed, but felt happy for having enjoyed the little scene—even to have almost been a part of it. *If only she had looked up, even just for a second.* This was proof to him that he didn't need to sleep with a woman to enjoy her. If he never saw that girl again, he had enjoyed her immensely just sitting at his table at the café while he waited for his cousin to appear.

Where was that connard? Jacques flicked his eyes to the screen of his cellphone to confirm that the *trou du cul* was indeed late. *How can you be late for a rendez-vous at your own bar?* he thought, the pleasure of the girl quickly receding and replaced by the annoyance of being kept waiting. True, Florrie's people knew not to hand him a bill. And they were as attentive to him as they were to any of their paying-customers. That is to say, not very. But it didn't matter. *Florian's Café*, if you could call it that sat one street off the main highway. If you didn't know it was there, you would never find it. So far from Aix, there was no annoying stream of students or tourists that one was forced to endure. How Florrie made a living on the place, though, was a mystery.

Still. Free drinks or not, nobody likes to be kept waiting. Jacques caught the eye of the sole waiter and gave a nearly imperceptible nod. The man disappeared inside.

"*Allô, mon cousin*. You are waiting long?" Florrie appeared as if from thin air, rubbing his hands together but remaining standing in obvious anticipation of the embrace he expected from Jacques. Grumbling, Jacques lurched out of his chair and held his arms out to receive the hug and cheek kissing Florrie was clearly determined to bestow upon him.

"I am waiting only however long past the time you said you would be here," Jacques said, reseating himself at the table.

"Forgive me, cousin," Florrie said, heaving his heavy frame into the wicker chair at Jacques's table. "I had to take a call. Aunt Lily called to confirm that we would be by on Sunday for lunch. Now more than ever."

"Good God, the woman is relentless," Jacques said as he reached for his cigarette packet. The waiter appeared with a pitcher of water, and two more glasses of *pastis*. "Aren't we *always* there for Sunday lunch?"

"Well, one of us is, at least," Florrie said pointedly, pouring his drink and holding it up to watch the liquid instantly cloud into ribbons of milky yellow.

"Well, *one of us* may have to do for this Sunday as well. It appears that Julia and I are getting back together."

"Are you serious? That's wonderful, Jacques!" Florrie leaned over and squeezed his cousin's arm. Jacques had to admit the man looked genuinely pleased for him.

"When did this happen?" Florrie asked.

"Well, it hasn't exactly happened yet," Jacques said, lighting up his cigarette and blowing a large cloud of smoke into the air around his head. "I am seeing her tonight for dinner."

"She is cooking?"

"Yes, of course she is cooking. She loves to cook for me. You know that."

"I hope you like mushrooms. I hear that's all that's on the menu these days."

"Trust me, that is *not* all that's on the menu tonight." Jacques's eyes glinted with double meaning.

"Well, I'm glad for both of you. I always liked Julia. I was sorry to see you two break up. Just be careful, eh?"

"*Careful*? What the hell does that mean?"

"I just mean perhaps you should take it slow. She was very angry with you when you broke up. She said some things."

Jacques waved away Florrie's words as if they were no more than the choppy blue smoke floating between them. "We both said some things. People do when they are upset. *Ma belle* Julia is very passionate, eh? I would expect nothing less from her—in or out of bed."

"Just take it slow, Jacques," Florrie said.

Jacques put a hand to his midsection and winced. The pains were coming more and more frequently and he was nearly at the point of admitting he needed to see his doctor.

"Are you alright?" Florrie asked, worry stark in his dark brown eyes.

Jacques waved a hand dismissively at his cousin. "Yes, yes. Just a little gas. I'm fine."

"Well, you look like a groaning bag of shit if you want to know."

The woman who spoke the words stood behind Florrie, and because Jacques had his eyes closed as she approached he wasn't absolutely sure she hadn't just materialized amidst a cloud of black smoke and brimstone.

Florrie stood up immediately and faced her. She was petite, dark-haired and had obviously been very pretty at one time. That time was many years past, and now all that was left was the vestige of frustrated insistence and despair at not meriting the reaction from men she once took for granted.

"Annette," Florrie said. Jacques noticed his cousin neither greeted his ex-wife or offered her a chair. He just stood as if totally at a loss as to what to do. As Jacques's discomfiture receded, he found a prick of pleasure in his cousin's loyalty to him. Annette was formidable at any age and any stage. Even now, he could see heads turning to her from all over the café. And yet poor Florrie could only stand between the two ex-spouses, impotent and unsure.

Annette took a step closer to the café table and pointed a long polished finger at Jacques. At this range, he could see she had recently had some work done and he felt a moment's stirring for her—of sympathy, of understanding, of desire.

"You have failed yet again to pay the money that is owed to me, you bastard!"

Jacques took a long drag off his cigarette and motioned for Florrie to sit back down, but he didn't. "What money is that?"

"You know *what money*. The money necessary for your daughter to continue with her education. You know very well *what money*."

"I am not legally obligated to continue to pay that, as *you* know well, Annette. I have had this discussion with Michelle—"

"Well, *I* cannot pay it! I have no money!"

Jacques thought about suggesting she go to the same well that obviously paid for the expensive facelift she was parading about, but he didn't feel altogether well and was certainly not up for a public showdown on issues they had fought over endlessly already.

"Perhaps the poor child might find employment of some kind? I have a friend whose son did that—got a job. It was immensely appreciated by both parents, I'm told."

"You are despicable to let your only child wander the streets like a common panhandler to pay for her education."

"Well, that's certainly one way to do it, and I would applaud the child's initiative if that's what she chose to do."

"I hope you die of the gout," Annette snarled at him. "I hope your heart seizes up and strangles you in your bed—alone and desolate. I hope you die from all your sins at once."

"Thank you, Annette. Now please piss off. You're frightening the patrons."

"Your own daughter detests you!" Annette whirled around to face the more curious café diners. "She hates her own father and wishes he were dead."

"I'm sorry about this, Florrie," Jacques said as Annette pushed her way out of the café terrace and disappeared into the parking lot. Florrie vaguely shook his head as if to say *no problem,* but instead looked more like a man confused and undone by the situation. He sat down heavily and ran a hand across his face. Jacques thought about the changes to come—the money to come—and he smiled to himself. He drank down the last of his *pastis*, feeling the burn of the liquid as it edged its way down his throat. And he felt better.

Wash the death trumpets gingerly with a paper towel or other kitchen towel. Linen is good if you are wealthy enough to throw away a perfectly good linen towel cleaning the dirt off a mushroom.

Julia smiled to herself as she piled the newly cleaned mushrooms onto her chopping board. She would have to edit that entry later—or her editor would. Still, it amused her. She picked up one of the largest of the mushrooms and held it to her nose, inhaling deeply. Instantly, the moment that morning in the glade north of the city came back to her. Even the feel of the early morning air, a brisk breeze holding all the promise of winter, came into her mind and seemed to flit across her bare arms. She placed the mushroom down and picked up her chef's knife. She wasn't sure the time she spent each day foraging into the meadows and forest outside Aix weren't the best part of creating her mushroom book. She roughly chopped the mushrooms and set them aside before deseeding the green pepper she had purchased from the *Place Richelme* market that morning.

That was silly, of course. The search was just one more wonderful component to this her most amazing life project. Would she ever have imagined in her wildest dreams that one day she would become the recognized expert on culinary mushrooms? Was it possible to have imagined that even six months ago? Of course, she cooked. French or not, one could hardly escape *cooking* while living in France. But her impassioned industry, some might say driven fanaticism, to unlock the secrets of the simple mushroom—in all its glorious forms, in all its magical capacities—*that* had not manifested itself until after Jacques left her.

She nicked the tip of her finger with the sharp knife and dropped the utensil immediately in surprise. She couldn't remember the last time she had cut herself in the kitchen. She twisted a piece of paper towel around the stinging cut. The sensation, combined with the thought of Jacques, was enough to make her reach for a handful of the Death Trumpets once more and bring them to her nostrils. She inhaled deeply and felt her heartbeat slow, her pulse steady, the tension in her shoulders relax. It was appropriate, she decided as she dropped a large knob of butter into a hot skillet on her stove, that one achieved these life-altering fungi by groping—no, groveling—around on one's hands and knees—in the dirt and the muck no less. She watched the butter bubble and foam as it skidded its way around the perimeter of the pan, then she dropped in the Death Trumpets, the little bowl of crushed garlic and the diced pepper. She gave the handle of the pan a firm shake to redistribute the contents.

She could hear noises coming from the hall of her apartment building, and a quick glance at the kitchen clock confirmed it was time for the office workers to trudge up the stairs to their little sanctuaries within. What she had said to Maggie notwithstanding, she didn't know very many of her neighbors. They were happy to keep to themselves, as she was. She had chosen this apartment—deep in the heart of Old Town—during her first week in Aix. She was visiting a boyfriend who had moved here for business, and had long since moved on, and had fallen in love with the town. A small inheritance from her mother had allowed her to pack up her rented London flat and make the transition. She knew she left nobody behind in England. She often found herself wondering why that didn't bother her more.

She took the pan off the heat, setting it on a back burner, and walked to her front window, which overlooked the Rue Constantin. She opened the window to let the cold late afternoon air suffuse the little living room in her apartment. She spent so much time in the kitchen it often wasn't until she was nearly ready to suffocate from the heat and the smells of grilled, fried or baked mushrooms that she remembered to seek out a restoring breath of fresh air. She stood for a moment in the window, staring down into the street and watching the students, shoppers and workers, even a few tourists this late in the season, as they moved up and down the street below her.

And then she saw him. It was a wonder she hadn't seen him first. Unlike the constantly moving humanity, he stood silent and immobile, leaning against the single lamppost and smoking. And looking up at her window. Fighting the urge to retreat back inside, Julia forced herself to watch him as he watched her. It had been six months since she had last seen him. Six months since she had thrown him out, her face flushed and stinging from his neat backhand during their argument. Six months since she had closed the apartment door behind him and begun her life in Aix without him.

Six terrible months.

Six wonderful months.

She could see he was smiling now. It was that same old smile. The one that used to affect her so. The one that made her tummy flip-flop in anticipation of the moment he would take her into his arms and drill her with that all-possessing focus of his. The one that assured her she was the only one. No one else. Until, of course, there was.

Julia turned away from the sight of Jacques standing there and reminded herself that it wasn't just the slap, the lies and the other girl. *A girl!* No more than seventeen. How could she compete with that? Smooth skin, clear eyes, and eager heart. The child wore a midriff-baring top as easily and unselfconsciously as Julia did her flannel granny nightie.

No, it wasn't the lies and the infidelity. It was the undeniable, unassailable and relentlessly unavoidable evidence that Julia would never be young again—no matter how young she felt on the inside.

A man who took that away from you, she thought as she dropped her apron onto the couch and ran a hand through her short curly hair, *well, he should die a slow and horrid death.*

-3-

Sometimes Maggie swore she could smell the *Mistral*, that icy-cold wind that comes down the Rhône River Valley from the Alps to jolt the sun lovers of Provence back to their senses. As she sat with her laptop on the terrace of the beautiful stone *mas* she shared with Laurent, she found herself pulling her cotton cardigan tighter around her. Petit Four, her little hybrid poodle mix, was curled up next to her on the cushion of the bench where she sat. From here she could just see the form of her husband—always the tallest figure in any grouping—walking the perimeter of his vineyard with the men he had hired to bring in this year's harvest. She loved to watch Laurent, especially when he was unaware of her. At more than six foot four, she often thought his natural grace of movement belied his size. She watched him now as he moved easily between the carefully trussed vines, pointing out this one or that to his audience.

Maggie put a hand on her stomach and directed her attention back to her laptop screen. In the time it took to bury one uncle—hers, this time, not his—and make a baby, she and Laurent had somehow managed to pull off the impossible. They—particularly one malcontented American expatriate— had taken their marriage firmly by the horns and turned it all around. Her resentment of Laurent's focus on his vineyard evaporated when she realized how important his happiness, however it was derived, was to her. Then she realized how important *she* was to *his* happiness. That, and a two-book deal for a mystery series that came out of left field, had enabled Maggie to put Laurent's passion about his grapes into perspective—and to kick start her own passion.

Her editor had sent a series of changes on the first draft of her book. And while at first she almost had to sit down and put her head between her knees to keep from passing out, with time and the sturdy good sense from her straight-thinking husband, she soon accepted that strong revision was par for the course for most writers—even experienced ones. That, and soothing and encouraging phone conversations from both her agent and editor, soon had her breathing normally again. Even so, her editor had seen the need for a lot of changes to Maggie's first draft of a murder mystery set in Paris during Paris Fashion Week.

A *lot* of changes.

Maggie scrolled down the manuscript on her computer and found herself nodding more often than frowning at what the editor had pointed out. She knew her editor was just making sure the book was the best it could be. After all, it was Maggie's name on the jacket cover. She'd told Laurent, "Before I got this email from my editor, I thought I could write." As usual, Laurent was not in an indulgent mood and she had received a Gallic snort in response that could only be interpreted as *knock it off and get to work*. She smiled at the memory.

A motion glimpsed out of the corner of her eye made her look up in the direction of Laurent again and she was surprised to see him striding purposefully back toward the terrace where she sat. It was nowhere near lunchtime, and she was sure he meant to spend the morning in the vineyards. Before Laurent was halfway back to the house, Petit Four jumped down from the bench barking and ran to the double French doors that led back to the house.

Between Laurent and the dog, it was pretty clear someone was either at the front door or was rappelling down the walls into the upper bedrooms. Maggie got up and went into the house. *Now how had Laurent known someone was here*, she wondered. She had gotten used to his knack for hearing and seeing things that only bats and some carefully attuned dogs could hear, but she still marveled at the ability. As she reached the heavy front door to the *mas*, Maggie was already out of breath. Her pregnancy left her wilted and tired these days from the simplest exertions.

She pulled open the door and was stunned to find her best friend Grace Van Sant standing on Maggie's ancient slate threshold, a Louis Vuitton bag at her feet, a pair of Prada sunglasses on her nose, and her two-year-old towhead on her hip.

"Surprise, darling," Grace said, her voice trembling just a little. "We're here."

"I am surprised, is all, Grace," Maggie said after all the hugs and luggage had been dealt with, Grace comfortably scooted into the main lounge, a glass of Côte de Rhone in her hand, a small plate of crudités on the coffee table before her. "Delighted, but surprised. Why didn't you tell me you were coming? And where are Taylor and Windsor? Can you stay?"

From the minute her dearest of all friends had crossed into her home, bringing with her the ever-present whiff of Chanel No.

19 and a sense that her namesake, Grace Kelly, was trans channeling, Maggie knew something wasn't right. It wasn't just that Grace was here from Indianapolis without any advance notice at all. It wasn't the fact she had come alone, except for baby Zou-zou. It wasn't even the fact her excuses for the absence of her husband and other child were so vague. It was Grace, herself.

Grace Van Sant was rich and always had been. That kind of money for that length of time formed a person. It shaped the way they looked at the world, gave them a languor they could transfer to just about any situation they found themselves in.

Grace and Windsor had been living in Provence for three years before Laurent and Maggie arrived. Unlike Maggie, Grace had handled the language, the village, the food and the clothes as if she had been born to them. Everything was easy for Grace, Maggie had long believed. And she lived and moved like her name—smoothly, elegant, perfectly.

Which was why it was so disconcerting to see her now. The hand that held her sherry glass shook. She licked her lips repeatedly. She patted her hair as if not sure it was just right. And Grace was *always* just right. She constantly pulled out her cellphone to check the time. *Or was it to see who hadn't called?*

No, there was something definitely wrong and Maggie had a sinking feeling, a sinking, hard-to-believe feeling, she knew what it was.

"I told you I'd come for the birth," Grace said, smoothing out the nonexistent wrinkles in her Dolce & Gabbana slacks.

"That's not for a month or more," Maggie pointed out to her. "And I thought you'd let me know when and where so Laurent could come to the train station and pick you up."

"Yes, well, now I've saved him the bother."

"Is everything alright, Grace?"

"What? Don't be silly, darling! I come back to France for the first time in nearly two years and you think something's wrong? I'm not sure how to take that."

Maggie frowned, unconvinced, but Laurent entered the salon holding Zou-zou and deposited the baby into Maggie's arms.

"Lunch is ready soon, yes?" he said to them.

"Oh, that sounds divine, Laurent," Grace said, reaching out to take his hand as he moved to go back to the kitchen. "I can't tell you how glad I am to be here."

Laurent gave her arm an absentminded pat. "*Bien sûr*," he said over his shoulder. *Of course.*

Lunch was its usual Laurent-spectacular. It was mid September, but many days were already too cool for eating out-of-doors, and Laurent deemed this was one of them. He had Maggie set the long, oaken farm table he had inherited with the house while Grace put the baby down for her nap. When she returned, he handed her a glass of wine and motioned for her to take her seat at the table.

"One of yours?" she asked, sniffing the bouquet.

"*Non*," he said. "Much better. Well." He stopped and glanced at Maggie for a moment. "Perhaps not *much* better."

"Laurent's stuff is really good," Maggie said. "His last harvest was so, so good. Flinty and dry but a little sweet."

Grace took a healthy sip and sank down into her dining chair. "You're getting pretty good, yourself," she said to Maggie. "Learning the lingo after all this time?"

Laurent grunted and returned to the kitchen, but Maggie knew he was pleased with the interest she had taken in the vineyard and the effort she had made to learn what he did.

"Well, you know what they say," Maggie said seating herself. "*Petit à petit...*"

"*L'oiseau fait son nid.*" *Little by little, the bird builds its nest*. Grace nodded. "You guys look like you really figured it all out in the end."

"Don't jinx us, Grace. But, yeah. We're finally happy. What with the book and everything." She waved at her very large abdomen pressing into the side of the table.

"Yes, you definitely have your distractions. I can see. What about socially? Are you two just stay-at-homes or do you go out?"

"There are a few discos in Aix if you need some excitement," Maggie said dryly. "Or were you asking if I'd replaced you yet in the best friend department?"

"Can't slip much past you. I haven't found anyone in Indianapolis yet. It's a hard town to break into. I've put in my applications for best friend but so far nothing. I understand you and Danielle have gotten close?"

Danielle Alexandre was Maggie and Laurent's elderly neighbor. While it was true that after Grace left Maggie reached out to Danielle more than she had before, Grace knew well enough it could never be like what *they* had.

"I'm really too busy for palling around much lately," Maggie said. "It's a good thing you left, Grace. I would've had to dump you."

"Charming, dearest. And good to know."

Laurent entered with a large tureen of *bouillabaisse* and set it in front of the women.

"It's not fish, is it?" Maggie asked, peeking under the china lid of the tureen.

"Of course it is fish," Laurent replied, nonplused. "It is *bouillabaisse.*"

"You can't eat shellfish?" Grace asked, reaching for her napkin.

"She can eat anything," Laurent said firmly, giving Maggie a raise of his eyebrow. "It is just her little joke." He placed a large basket of garlic rounds on the table with a bowl of *rouille.*

"Oh, I have missed this," Grace said, and Maggie could swear her eyes watered when she spoke.

"Just fish soup, Grace," she said. "No biggie. Right, Laurent?"

But Laurent was off to the kitchen to fetch something else necessary to make the lunch perfect.

"Well, it's a biggie to *me,*" Grace said, spreading the *rouille* on a toast round. “I can’t remember the last time I had French food, let alone with friends.”

“Windsor working a lot?”

“You could say that. And Taylor is a full-time job. She’s worse now than ever. Plus, she hates me.”

“I’m sure that’s not true, Grace.”

Laurent returned with a large ladle and spooned the steaming and fragrant stew into three large stoneware bowls. As soon as they were served, Maggie’s cellphone rang.

“It could be my editor,” she said, looking at Laurent.

“You can call her back,” he said.

Maggie picked up her phone and looked at the screen. “It’s Julia,” she said and accepted the call before Laurent could speak. “Hey, Julia. What’s up?”

Laurent sighed heavily and flapped a linen napkin across his lap.

Grace nudged him with her foot under the table. “Who’s Julia?”

“*Une amie*,” he said. “They met last year. They have become close.” He frowned and looked at Maggie, who was off the phone. “*Qu’est-ce qui’il y a?*” he asked.

Maggie looked at him as if startled out of a daze.

“Maggie?” Grace said. “Is everything alright?”

“That was Julia.” She shook her head. “You’re not going to believe this.” She looked from Grace to Laurent. “Jacques is dead.”

-4-

Maggie sat in the large, sunny lounge in Julia’s apartment. She had bolted out the front door and into her Renault while Laurent and Grace walked down the long gravel drive trying to talk her into staying. In the end, Laurent insisted on driving her and ushered Grace back into the house to wait for them. He promised they would not be late. Now, he sat in one of the many cafés that lined the Cours and waited for Maggie to emerge from the apartment building.

"Was it suicide?" Maggie asked Julia gently. Julia was sitting straight-backed on her sofa, holding a glass of untouched wine in her hands.

"What?" Julia seemed to forcibly drag her attention back to Maggie from whatever private world she was seeing in her mind's eye. *Jacques as she had last seen him?* Maggie wondered. "No. No, I can't imagine. That wouldn't make sense. He wanted to reconcile, you know?"

Maggie nodded. "But," she said, "if you told him no, maybe he was so distraught that he..."

"No, Maggie. I mean, *yes*, I told him no but he didn't seem a bit distraught. If anything, he seemed...energized by my rejection. He was full-on for making me change my mind. He was up for the challenge. You know?"

Maggie didn't really, but she nodded. "When did he leave?"

"Right after dinner," Julia said, indicating the dining table with a jerk of her head. It was clear and tidy except for a glass bowl of nectarines. "He said he didn't feel well. I told you he was having problems?"

"Money problems?"

"Well, yes, that too, I think, but I'm talking about his health. He didn't feel good. I know he wanted to stay, but he left early. He looked terrible. Like he was in pain."

"How did you find out about...?"

"His bitch of a daughter called me," Julia said. Her mouth was pressed in a firm, tight line. "She called me screaming and... and..." Julia put her hands to her face and burst into tears. "She was horrible. Just horrible."

Maggie reached over and put her arms around her friend. "I am so, so sorry, Jules." She rubbed her back. Over Julia's shoulder, Maggie could see the large birdcage with the multi-colored lovebird in it. A friendly little thing normally, it seemed to be eyeing Maggie now in an indicting fashion, as if *she* were responsible for the unhappy sounds emanating from his mistress.

"I shouldn't blame her," Julia said, swallowing her sobs and trying to compose herself. "She found him, you see." She shook her head as if unable to clear the gruesome picture from her brain.

"At his apartment?"

"Yes. She was supposed to meet him there or something. I didn't get the whole story. And she found him on the floor. He must have...it must have happened last night. He was fully clothed. Oh, Maggie, I can't believe he's not in the world any more. I can't believe, it's impossible to believe, he'll never b-b-bother me again." Julia let her sobs break full force out of her and into her hands. Maggie held her and patted her back.

"I know, sweetie," she said. "I know."

The knock at the door made both of them jump. Annoyed at the thought it might be Laurent, impatient and coming to see what was taking so long, Maggie gave her friend a brief squeeze and jumped up to wrench open the door. When she did, she gave a gasp of bewilderment to find two uniformed police officers standing there flanking none other than Detective *Inspecteur* Roger Bedard—looking way too darkly handsome than any man had a right to.

"Roger!" she blurted out.

"I should have known," he said, shaking his head when he saw her. Then his eyes travelled down the front of her dress and his mouth fell open. "You're pregnant," he said, stupidly.

"And here I thought you weren't a good detective," Maggie retorted, her cheeks burning with embarrassment.

Quickly recovering himself, Bedard snapped out an order to his men and then pushed past Maggie into Julia's apartment.

"Hey, wait a minute," Maggie said. "You can't come in here without a warrant or something."

Roger moved to stand directly in front of Julia where she sat, stupefied, on the sofa. Without looking behind him, he held out a hand for the handcuffs he expected to fill it and spoke directly to Julia.

"Madame Patrick, I am placing you under arrest for the murder of Monsieur Jacques Tatois. Please stand up."

"Roger, no!" Maggie tried to reach where Roger and Julia were standing, but one of the uniformed police held out an arm to prevent her.

"Maggie, stay out of this," Roger said sternly. He spoke again to his men and the man who held his arm out against Maggie dropped it to his side, but he continued to block her from going any further.

"It's okay, Maggie," Julia called to her with a shaky voice. "It's a mistake and I'll get it sorted out." She turned to Roger. "Where?"

"Your consulate has been notified," he said. "You'll be held at the *Palais de Justice* here in Aix.

"I'm coming with you," Maggie said.

Roger and Julia both turned to her. "Maggie, no," they said, nearly in unison.

"I'll be fine, Maggie," Julia said as she turned away and allowed Roger to cuff her hands behind her back. "Have Laurent come pick me up in an hour."

Roger took Julia by the arm and shoved her past Maggie toward the door. Before exiting, he turned to Maggie. "I wouldn't bother."

Maggie could see the anger and hurt in his eyes, and something more. Shame. He knew he had no right to his feelings. In a moment he was out the door and gone, but not before Maggie thought she could hear Julia start to weep again.

~

"What do you mean *they're holding her overnight*?" Maggie waddled over to where Laurent stood in the living room of their home. He had just tossed down his cellphone and stood staring out the French doors into the distance, as if an answer might be out there that wasn't available anywhere else.

"Just that, *ma chère*," he said tiredly. "They will not release her tonight."

"But I told Julia you would come pick her up." Maggie looked helplessly at Laurent and then over at Grace, who was sitting quietly in an overstuffed armchair watching her.

"*Je sais*," he said, reaching an arm out to draw her close to him. *I know*. "But we must wait. They are not releasing her."

"Stop saying that!" Maggie put her arms around her husband. "Does this mean they have some kind of proof of her involvement? Is that possible?" Maggie looked up at Laurent as if expecting an answer and he shrugged.

Grace unwound her long legs from underneath her and stretched her back. She crossed her ankles. "I guess the ex-girlfriend or the ex-wife always tops the list of suspects. Makes sense."

"But he was alone when he died," Maggie said, pulling out of Laurent's arms and addressing Grace. "How can it be murder when he was all alone?" She looked at Laurent as if a new thought had just come to her. "Maybe the daughter did it. Julia said she was a bitch and didn't get along with her father. *And* she found the body. Isn't that like a classic rule of thumb? The person who finds the body is most likely the killer?"

"I have never heard of this rule," Laurent said, frowning. She saw him scanning the furniture in the living room for the glass of wine he had set down.

"Yes, I've heard of it," Grace said, nodding. "First the spouse and then the person who found the body. It's a classic formula."

"It's true, right?" Maggie said.

"Yeah, except for one thing," Grace said, picking up her own wineglass. "They arrested her for *murder*, not took her in for questioning, so they must know something."

"I can't believe this is happening," Maggie said. "I was going to introduce you two today."

"Oh, well."

"Maggie?" Laurent stepped back into the room and held up his car keys. I am going into the village, yes? You are alright here with Grace?"

Maggie nodded. "Fine, Laurent. If they call you—"

"I will go immediately. You are not to worry now, yes?"

"Okay." Maggie forced herself to smile at her husband. She knew he hated to see her stressed, especially this late in the pregnancy. When she heard the front door shut, she turned to Grace. "We need to do something."

Grace raised her eyebrows. "You mean like organize a jailbreak?"

Maggie sat down on the sofa and began pulling at the hem of her tunic. She stood up again in agitation. "I don't know what I mean," she admitted. "I just can't stand this, knowing that she's down there. Damn that Roger!"

"Roger Bedard?" Grace's eyebrows arched up. "*Your* Roger Bedard?"

"Oh, stop it, Grace. I haven't seen him in over a year."

"Did he know about..." Grace gestured to Maggie's very prominent baby bump.

"No reason why he should. We don't run in the same circles. I mean, I knew he was transferred to Aix only because Laurent heard it and passed it on to me."

"Darling Laurent. So civilized about the men in love with his wife. I suppose it's the French in him."

"Stop it, Grace. If you want to know, he's not at all civilized about it but he knows he never had anything to worry about—"

"Never? Careful about the history you attempt to rewrite,

darling," Grace said with a sly smile. "I was here at the time, remember?"

"Okay, *one* kiss. That's nothing to get derailed over."

"Does Laurent know about the one kiss?"

Maggie looked at her with exasperation. "Why are we talking about this? It's all water under the bridge. I'm practically ready to deliver Laurent's baby. There was clearly no harm done and all parties have retreated safely to their respective corners. And I would greatly appreciate it, Grace, if you forgot about the stupid kiss."

"Consider it forgotten," Grace said with a shrug. But her eyes met Maggie's and said otherwise.

As uncomfortable as this whole line of conversation made Maggie feel—especially with Roger showing up again in her life—she had to admit it was the first time since Grace had arrived that she had behaved in her old confident manner and Maggie hated to totally quash her teasing.

"He wasn't expecting to see me," Maggie said as she reseated herself. "And all this..." She gestured to her stomach. "God, Grace, he looked...hurt."

"Which isn't rational, right, sweetie?" Grace said, helpfully. "Whatever he felt for you or hoped to get from you was at least *mostly* all in his own mind, right?"

Maggie nodded. "Laurent and I have been getting along so well lately."

"I should hope so."

Maggie narrowed her eyes at her. "Not just because of the pregnancy, Grace. Ever since I got back from Paris and got involved with the book I'm writing, I've been able to see the things I was doing to sabotage my marriage."

"That's handy."

"Why are you being so glib?" Maggie's face flushed with annoyance. "How I was treating him *wasn't* easy to see and it *wasn't* easy to stop doing either. You act like I'm some kind of one-dimensional sitcom character. Did I not *tell* you how close Laurent and I came to tossing in the towel?"

"You did," Grace said, taking a sip from her wine, her eyes never leaving Maggie's.

"Then how can you be so flip? It was literally the scariest thing I've ever gone through."

"I'm sorry, Maggie. But like you said, you and Laurent had serious issues and I guess I'm just not buying into the whole *I solved it and everything's perfect now* scenario. Or do you honestly think having a baby will fix all that's wrong with your marriage?"

"What?!" Maggie sputtered.

"Look, I'm sorry, Maggie," Grace said hurriedly. "I just don't want you to think children will make a difference—except maybe to make everything worse. That's the truth of it and I'm sorry if you don't want to hear it."

Maggie took a long, steadying breath, trying to stay calm. She smoothed her tunic down over her tummy and forced herself to reach out for Grace's hand. "It isn't the baby that's changed things, Grace," she said firmly. "As I was trying to tell you, *I* changed the way I looked at living here in St-Buvard—in *France* —and *that* made everything else better."

"Well, that's great then," Grace said, her eyes filling with tears.

Maggie scooted over to her on the chair and Grace moved to accommodate her.

"Why are you here, Grace?" she asked quietly. "What's going on with you and Win?"

"Nothing good," Grace said, brightly, blinking back the tears. "Nothing good."

Laurent's nights out were rare and Maggie hated to begrudge him the few he did take. Besides his monthly co-op meetings in Aix where all the *vignerons* collaborated and exchanged notes, and his one night a week at *Le Canard*, the local pub in St-Buvard, he never went out after dark. Those rare times he did, normally he made her a dish of something that she either reheated or ate cold. Tonight he'd been distracted, and she found herself rummaging around in Laurent's other kingdom—the kitchen. Although Grace insisted she wasn't hungry and baby Zou-zou had already demonstrated she would eat anything in any condition at any time, Maggie still felt the need to rustle up something even if it was just cheese toast.

"I honestly don't bother at home," Grace said, shifting the chubby toddler on her lap.

"Well, that's because you have a cook, isn't it?" Maggie said from the interior of the refrigerator.

"Oh, I guess you're right. That could be the reason."

Maggie pulled out a plate of lamb slices, a tapenade and left-over potato gratin made with the gnocchi Laurent had served the night before. "I think I can do something with these." She put the dish of lamb on the counter and scooped out a piece of cold gnocchi and handed it to Zou-zou.

"Hungry, sweetie?" she asked the child, who popped the plump bit of potato and pasta into her mouth.

"She's going to be massive when she's a teenager," Grace said. "All she does is eat and those kinds of habits don't die easy."

"Oh, Grace, you exaggerate," Maggie said, laughing.

"You won't think so when she's ripping your refrigerator door off its hinges. I kid you not. The child is a bottomless pit."

"Laurent will love cooking for her," Maggie said. "He hates how I'm always watching my diet and swears he wouldn't care if I get fat."

"Laurent is about the only man I could honestly believe that about. He really loves you no matter what. How did you manage *that*?"

"I have no idea. Oh, look, he's got great tomatoes still, and this bread he brought home from Aix."

"He went shopping while you were with your friend?"

"You know Laurent. He wouldn't pass up their Wednesday Food Market if it was *me* they were arresting for murder."

"A bit of an exaggeration."

"Maybe, but only a bit. Anyway, it'll make a fine feast for us. We don't normally have good bread unless one of us has been in Aix or Avignon."

"The village still hasn't replaced the bakery?"

"Nope."

"Ah, well. Memories are long in this part of France."

"You can say that again. Here, take the wine. Just because I'm not drinking doesn't mean someone else shouldn't enjoy it. Oh, she likes the gnocchi, Grace! Didn't you, little bug? Is it weird she isn't talking yet?"

"Hush your mouth, Maggie Dernier," Grace said, putting the little girl on her feet and grabbing the bottle of wine. "The minute they start talking is the minute they start whining. I'm enjoying the peace while I can."

They settled back into the living room and Maggie spread their picnic out on the coffee table, which Zou-zou attacked with delight, grabbing up a fistful of tapenade and smearing it across her face in her attempt to get it into her mouth.

"Will that make her sick, do you think?" Maggie asked, reaching for a napkin for the child.

"I really don't know," Grace said. She broke off a piece of the bread and dipped it into the tapenade.

"Do you want to talk about it?"

"Not yet, if you don't mind."

"Okay. But that is why you're here, isn't it?"

"Is it?" Grace looked at her blankly, then away. "I suppose it is. Why else? To process it all. To say it out loud to my dearest friend and watch the expression on her face. You know, some cultures don't believe a thing is a fact until it's spoken. That's strange, don't you think? That you can keep something from being true just by not saying it?"

"I think people do it all the time."

Grace laughed but there was no mirth in the sound.

"Does Taylor know what's going on?"

Grace shrugged. "She's pretty solidly into her own little world. A normal kid couldn't help but know. But Taylor? I have no idea."

Maggie wanted to ask about Windsor. *Was he distraught? Was he fed up? Was he the guilty party?* She watched Grace as she pulled an anchovy out of Zou-zou's grubby little fist and replaced it with a carrot spear. She would talk when she was ready.

As if Grace could read Maggie's mind, she turned to her. "Tell me about your new best friend. How did you two meet?"

Maggie tucked a thin wedge of lamb into the heel of the crusty bread and spread a hefty dollop of tapenade over the top. "We met at a *fete* that Laurent's co-op put on. She was there with Jacques, the man who died, and we were the only two native English-speakers in the room."

"A natural recipe for instant friendship."

"Well, it kind of is, as you know," Maggie said pointedly. "She was English, not American, but we were both with Frenchmen and living in Provence and so we had a baseline of things in common. The more we talked...you know."

"The more you fell madly in love with each other."

"Well, Grace, we connected. Above and beyond the obvious things we have in common, we really enjoyed the time we spent together. I'm sorry you haven't made any friends in Indiana, but it's worse for me since, unlike you, I don't have a whole effing country of my own people to fall back on. It's pretty lonely over here and friendships mean more."

"Wow. Big speech, darling. And you're right. It's hard for me to complain about being friendless when I have drive-through banking and round doorknobs."

"Okay, Grace, I am not going to apologize for making friends. And if you were any kind of a *real* friend, you'd be glad I had someone to turn to after you left."

"Well, I'm sorry to be such a disappointment to you, Maggie," Grace said. "But even all the wonders of living back home again couldn't fill the hole left by the dissolution of our friendship."

"Now you're being dramatic. We Skype practically every day."

"Which is not the same as being together and solving mysteries like Lucy and Ethel the way we used to and getting into all kinds of trouble. In fact, I officially hate Skype."

Maggie laughed. "Grace, you're such a ninny. How can you possibly think there is a replacement for you in my life?"

"This Julia character certainly seems like she fits the bill."

"You are so unabashedly self-absorbed, it floors me. The poor woman is under arrest for murder!"

"You don't have to apologize for preferring one person over another, Maggie," Grace said, grabbing Zou-zou's hand before she reached the TV remote control.

"It's not a competition, Grace."

"You idiot, that's exactly what it is!"

Maggie stared at Grace with her mouth open. Zou-zou, whose hand Grace was still gripping, began to squirm away from her mother and make little grunting sounds.

Maggie shook her head. "I was in a bad way when you left, Grace."

"You're not going to blame—"

"Just listen to me. With all the other stuff going on, mostly Laurent and I doing a nosedive on the newlywed front, your leaving really kicked the stuffing out of me. I know it wasn't your fault, and that Windsor had a chance to make caboodles of money by selling his software company and then running it for the new owners in Indy. I get all that and I point no fingers. But it was really bad timing for me. And when I met Julia, it helped a lot. She was giving and funny and open and always accessible..."

"All the things I'm not."

"I *said* funny." Maggie smiled at her and Grace allowed a small one in response.

"She's not you, Grace. Never will be. But she's a dear friend and just as if something like this happened to you, I want to move earth and heaven to help her."

Grace looked up. "Aha!"

"What, aha?"

"I knew it! You want to clear her name."

Maggie looked around the room with exasperation. "We don't even know for sure that's necessary," she said evasively. "They'll probably release her in the morning."

"And if they don't?"

"Okay, yes, if they don't, I'm not going to sit here and do nothing."

"Well, then," Grace said reaching for her wineglass and holding up to toast Maggie, "I guess Lucy and Ethel are back in the saddle again after all."

5

The farmers' market in downtown Aix on the *Place Richelme* sits under the canopy of dozens of plane trees in full bloom that line the avenue. It has served as an outdoor food market since the middle ages. Laurent had left home before dawn so he would have the best pick of everything the market had to offer: peppers, glossy eggplants, tomatoes, strawberries that tasted like real strawberries, figs, apricots, peaches, plums, melons, and red currants like little glossy jewels in their tiny wooden baskets. The first stall he approached sold goat cheeses—hundreds of different varieties, little wheels of white that looked like carefully packaged gifts. He'd gotten home late last night, and still Maggie and Grace were not in bed. Although he worried about Maggie getting too tired, he was glad to see it. He didn't know what Grace's visit meant—except that it was more than just a visit—but he was glad to see her as a distraction to the current *désastre* with Maggie's friend, Julia.

Why do these terrible events always seem to follow Maggie? What were the odds that a murder would occur—if indeed that's what this was—the very day Maggie had lunch with the prime suspect? Laurent shook his head and paid the goat man for several packages of good cheese. He moved on to the salami and ham stall, but took a moment to look around to enjoy his surroundings. At this early hour not every stall was stocked and ready to go, but beyond the many fruits and vegetables there were still crate after crate of olives, chocolate, herbs and spices. The air of the market was redolent with the scent of *herbes des Provence* and lemons.

As Laurent approached a table full of *calissons*, the popular and ubiquitous iced cookie of ground almonds and preserved melons that Aix is famous for, and that his pregnant *femme* had a strong partiality for, he noticed someone in the crowd that he knew. It took him a moment to place him precisely, and when he did he couldn't help but wonder if it could really be coincidental that he was running into the cousin of the murder victim the very next day after the crime.

"Florian," Laurent called, shifting his bag of cheese to his other arm in anticipation of the handshake when the man noticed him.

However, when Florrie turned to see who'd called his name, Laurent thought he did the most amazing thing. Instead of acknowledging an acquaintance—for they were no more than that—and stretching out his hand in greeting, Florrie dropped his own bag, slapped both hands to his face and burst into tears. So stunned was Laurent by this reaction, he hurriedly moved to separate the man from the crowd by pulling him out of the flow of the quickly building sea of shoppers and tourists.

"Get control of yourself," Laurent said, giving Florrie's arm a firm shake. "Are you all right?"

Clearly, Florrie was *not* alright and Laurent cursed the fact that he'd seen him at all this morning.

"I am so sorry, Laurent," Florrie said, snuffling noisily into his hands and then his sleeve. "I don't know what came over me."

"Well, you have had a shock," Laurent said, eyeing him to make sure he wasn't going to start crying again. His eyes were red and deeply bloodshot, as if he'd been drinking heavily or crying, or both. He was a good-looking man and favored his dark-haired cousin in that way, with blue eyes and very straight white teeth. But there the resemblance ended. Jacques had always been razor sharp in his manner and inclined to cut. Florrie was the soft, affable one.

"I am so sorry to hear about Jacques," Laurent said, hoping it wouldn't start him off again. "It was a shock, I'm sure."

"I still cannot believe it," Florrie said, patting his pockets in search of a handkerchief of some kind. "I just saw him yesterday!"

"And he looked well?" Laurent wasn't sure why he asked that. He glanced back at the market. He had been hoping to get a good fish before they were all gone.

"Well, no, he didn't. Now that you mention it, he was complaining of not feeling well. Did you hear they arrested poor Julia? Well, of course you would, because of Maggie, *non*?"

Laurent nodded solemnly, forcing himself not to look at the line of people at the fish stall.

"It's ridiculous to believe *Julia* could hurt Jacques," Florrie said, finally extricating a badly soiled cloth from his pocket and mopping his wet face with it. "She must be so distraught. Have you talked with her?"

"Ah, no," Laurent said.

"Will they release her soon, do you think?"

"I am sure they will. Would you care to walk with me?" Laurent could see the fish he wanted from here, a very fat John Dory that would do nicely in the soup he wanted to make today. He began to edge Florrie in that direction.

"I begged him to take better care of himself," Florrie said as he trotted to keep up with Laurent's long stride. "He smoked. He drank too much. He ate the wrong things..."

Laurent got in line at the fish stall and relaxed enough to turn his attention fully to Florrie while he waited.

"Getting back together with Julia would have been the best thing he could have done," Florrie said earnestly. "I tell you, if it *was* murder, the police should be looking at his crazy daughter, Michelle. That girl is *demented*. I have seen her physically attack Jacques on more than one occasion."

"Do you know if she saw him that night?"

Florrie blinked at him as if having trouble understanding. Laurent felt sorry for him. Clearly he wasn't prepared to have his passionate theories derailed by facts or evidence.

"It's possible she did," Florrie said.

"I'm sure the police will check into her whereabouts during the time of his death," Laurent said, then turned to the fishmonger and pointed to the fish he wanted. When he turned back around with his prize all neatly packaged up, Florrie was gone.

Maggie tried to concentrate on the beauty of the broad avenue of the *Cours Mirabeau* with its row after row of ancient fountains and cafes beneath the majestic plane trees that lined the row. She had forgotten that Laurent was going into Aix this morning, which was supremely annoying since *she* was planning on going there, too, and they only had the one car. She hated taking a taxi in France—*it was literally risking your life the way those maniacs drove*—but her errand today couldn't wait. As she stared out the taxicab window, she tried to see if Laurent's Renault was parked somewhere visible, but didn't really expect to see it. While the traffic wasn't bad this time of day, it was not yet eleven, there was still a sizable crowd of tourists and shoppers clogging the grand avenue.

During the ride, Maggie allowed herself some time to decompress and reflect on her evening with Grace. It was clear Grace had left Windsor, but whether or not that was a formal leaving was yet to be determined since Grace wasn't talking. What *was* clear was how completely miserable Grace was.

How could this happen? Grace and Windsor were the perfect couple. And they had kids! Maggie could not imagine what could have occurred in their lives to cause something like this to happen.

With a supreme effort, Maggie put her friend's unhappiness out of her mind to concentrate on her morning. She intended to go to the jail in Aix to see Julia. Her phone calls to the number Roger had given her had been met with a very unhelpful recording. It was time for a little face-to-face, she thought grimly. But first, she would run by Julia's apartment and pick up a few clothes for her. If Julia were released this morning as everyone hoped, then it would just be a wasted half hour. But if this nightmare was going to go on any longer, Julia would want a fresh change of clothes.

She had the taxi stop outside Julia's apartment building and instructed the driver to wait for her. "*Dix minute*," she said firmly to the driver and then exited the cab and hurried up the stairs.

By the time she reached the landing on the second floor, she had to lean against the close walls and catch her breath. By the time she reached—much more slowly—the next landing, she had gone from hopefully wondering if all the noise she was hearing from the floor above her could be the result of construction of a lift being added to the 1890 apartment building to flat not caring. As she dragged herself to the final landing just before Julia's floor, the noise was clearly more of a destructive nature than constructive, with loud thuds and the sounds of breaking glass exploding in the narrow stairwell. Julia's apartment was one of two on her floor, but only hers had the sounds of a full-scale demolition coming out into the hallway through the wide open door.

Bewildered and tentative, Maggie edged her way to the door

opening. *Was Julia having scheduled work done? Was she being broken into?* In the brief space between crashes, Maggie could hear the sounds of her own labored gasps as she fought for breath after her climb. The silence startled her, and when she heard the sound of her own struggling breaths she began to feel afraid. Whoever was in there destroying Julia's apartment—for that was clearly what was happening—might not be very welcoming of an unexpected friend of Julia's on the threshold.

A loud crash ended the silence and Maggie used the moment to slip through the front door. Inside she saw a young woman of about twenty-five in the process of hammering to splinters with a very large axe the beautiful antique table that had been a birthday gift to Julia from her long-passed father. Maggie watched in horror as the girl brought the axe down on the table full force, the table's tiny hand-placed bits of mosaic shooting out in all directions like flints of wood from a chipper.

"Stop it!" Maggie screamed. "Stop it this minute!"

The girl whirled on Maggie, the axe gripped tightly in her hands, her eyes wild with hatred and anger. When Maggie saw her face, she knew the woman had to be related to Jacques. They shared the same dark hair and brown eyes, the same olive skin coloring. It was entirely possible that the girl was pretty, probably was, but it was impossible to believe it with her current expression of insane urgency. She took a step toward Maggie.

"I am an American," Maggie said without thinking. "Think twice before you dare to attack me. Remember...Saddam Hussein," she added stupidly.

The girl stared at her as if not understanding, although Maggie had spoken in clear, plain French. Slowly, Maggie could see the energy that the manic fit had given her begin to fade and the girl lowered the axe to her side, but she did not drop it.

"Who are you?" she asked. "Are you a friend of the English whore's?"

Maggie looked around the apartment, so much of it already

destroyed. The girl had obviously been here awhile. Julia's couch had been chopped into chunks of expensive fabric and batting. Her beautiful Royal Doulton tea set, the one she had brought with her from London, was in shards. Two paintings over the couch, neither expensive, were ripped and had gaping gashes in them. The birdcage was on its side and Maggie quickly went to see if the little bird still lived.

"I am cleaning up the bastard's love nest," Michelle said, finally dropping the axe to the floor. It hit with a thunk.

Maggie saw the bird huddling in a corner of the cage. She grabbed the handle of the cage and stood up with it. "I'm leaving now," she said, shocked to hear her voice sound strong and unwavering. "I intend to call the police as soon as I'm in my car. If I were you, I'd figure out what you're going to say to them."

Michelle straightened the hem of her tee shirt over her jeans and surveyed the damage in the apartment. "I will tell them that *you* did this!" she said defiantly. "It will be your word against mine."

Maggie walked to the door holding the birdcage. "Good plan," she said. "Then we'll just see who they believe." Before she could edge past the girl, Michelle turned and bolted out of the apartment, running down the stairs. Maggie listened to the sounds of her heels pounding the steps until they receded into silence as Michelle disappeared into the street.

Maggie looked at the poor little bird, still shivering in terror, and then at the ruined apartment. A feeling of incomprehensible sadness came over her as she closed the door behind her and began her own descent to the street below. Somehow she no longer felt very optimistic about Julia's chances for returning home any time soon.

To see what happens next, order *Murder in Aix.*

RECIPE FOR STEAK AU POIVRE

There are so many wonderful brasserie dishes in Paris and Laurent knows them all. His take on this classic is in its simplicity—which is always high on his list no matter if it's food or clothing or people.

You'll need:

Any four good fillets of steak. Tenderloin or rib eye are both good.

2 TB vegetable oil

3 TBs peppercorns, cracked

1/2 medium sized onion, chopped

¼ cup brandy

1 cup beef broth

¼ cup cream

As with any meat, bring it out of the fridge a good thirty minutes before you intend to cook it. Season it with salt and both sides. Heat the oil in a large, heavy pan.

Pat the steaks dry with paper towels and place them in the pan.

You want to sear the steaks so don't move them around. Leave them for at least three minutes, then flip each over to sear the other side. Turn the heat down to medium at this point until it's done the way you like it. When it is, remove to a baking sheet and sprinkle on crushed black pepper onto both sides, pressing into the meat.

Meanwhile, add the chopped onion to the pan and sauté for two minutes before adding the brandy. Deglaze as the sauce boils and then add the beef stock.

Boil the sauce down and add the cream. Boil it down again and then take it off the heat and add a little more pepper to the sauce. Pour the sauce over the steaks and serve immediately.

ABOUT THE AUTHOR

USA TODAY Bestselling Author Susan Kiernan-Lewis is the author of *The Maggie Newberry Mysteries,* the post-apocalyptic thriller series *The Irish End Games, The Mia Kazmaroff Mysteries, The Stranded in Provence Mysteries, The Claire Baskerville Mysteries,* and *The Savannah Time Travel Mysteries.*

Visit www.susankiernanlewis.com or follow Author Susan Kiernan-Lewis on Facebook.

Books by Susan Kiernan-Lewis

The Maggie Newberry Mysteries

Murder in the South of France

Murder à la Carte

Murder in Provence

Murder in Paris

Murder in Aix

Murder in Nice

Murder in the Latin Quarter

Murder in the Abbey

Murder in the Bistro

Murder in Cannes

Murder in Grenoble
Murder in the Vineyard
Murder in Arles
Murder in Marseille
Murder in St-Rémy
Murder à la Mode
Murder in Avignon
Murder in the Lavender
Murder in Mont St-Michel
Murder in the Village
Murder in St-Tropez
Murder in Grasse
Murder in Monaco
Murder in Montmartre
Murder in the Villa
A Provençal Christmas: A Short Story
A Thanksgiving in Provence
Laurent's Kitchen

The Claire Baskerville Mysteries

Déjà Dead

Death by Cliché

Dying to be French

Ménage à Murder

Killing it in Paris

Murder Flambé

Deadly Faux Pas

Toujours Dead

Murder in the Christmas Market

Deadly Adieu

Murdering Madeleine

Murder Carte Blanche

Death à la Drumstick

Murder Mon Amour

The Savannah Time Travel Mysteries

Killing Time in Georgia

Scarlett Must Die

The Stranded in Provence Mysteries

Parlez-Vous Murder?

Crime and Croissants

Accent on Murder

A Bad Éclair Day

Croak, Monsieur!

Death du Jour

Murder Très Gauche

Wined and Died

Murder, Voila!

A French Country Christmas

Fromage to Eternity

The Irish End Games

Free Falling
Going Gone
Heading Home
Blind Sided
Rising Tides
Cold Comfort
Never Never
Wit's End
Dead On
White Out
Black Out
End Game

The Mia Kazmaroff Mysteries

Reckless
Shameless
Breathless
Heartless
Clueless
Ruthless

Ella Out of Time

Swept Away
Carried Away
Stolen Away